RIDDLEY WALKER

BY THE SAME AUTHOR

NOVELS
The Lion of Boaz-Jachin and Jachin-Boaz
Kleinzeit
Turtle Diary
Pilgermann
The Medusa Frequency
Fremder
Mr Rinyo-Clacton's Offer
Angelica's Grotto
Amaryllis Night and Day
The Bat Tattoo
Her Name Was Lola

POETRY
The Pedalling Man
The Last of the Wallendas and Other Poems

COLLECTIONS
The Moment Under the Moment

FOR CHILDREN
The Mouse and His Child
The Frances Books
The Trokeville Way

RIDDLEY WALKER

Expanded Edition

Afterword, Notes and Glossary
by
Russell Hoban

With an Introduction by
Will Self

BLOOMSBURY

LONDON · BERLIN · NEW YORK

First published in 1980 by Jonathan Cape

This paperback edition published by Bloomsbury Publishing 2002

A CIP catalogue record for this book
is available from the British Library

Bloomsbury Publishing Plc, 36 Soho Square, London W1D 3QY

ISBN 978 0 7475 5904 7

10

Printed in Great Britain by Clays Ltd, St Ives plc

www.bloomsbury.com/russellhoban

FSC
Mixed Sources
Product group from well-managed
forests and other controlled sources
Cert no. SGS-COC-2061
www.fsc.org
© 1996 Forest Stewardship Council

The paper this book is printed on is certified independently in accordance with the rules of the FSC.
It is ancient-forest friendly. The printer holds chain of custody.

INTRODUCTION

This book breaks the alleged rules of literary composition. Of course, there aren't really any such rules, or if there are, they're there for deadheads who want to be taught naturalism by a berk in the Fens. But suchlike types say, 'Oh no, you can't set a book in the distant future' (or the near future for that matter), and, 'Oh no, you can't write a book in an entirely constructed dialect, complete with its own idiom'. I tell you it's lucky that these types are all gone and blown out the window while *Riddley Walker* is still alive and kicking. I don't think I could stand to be in a world with them while this book was dead.

One of the objections these tosspots have to books like this one is that it name-checks stuff from the time it was written in and dares to believe that it might endure, not just through ordinary suburban time, but even after a major Fall. So, in *Riddley Walker*, the residents of a post-nuclear holocaust Kent, where technology has regressed to the level of the Iron Age, smoke hash and roll it in rizlas. But I don't think this is an anachronism, because hash-ingesting seems to me to be an obviously Iron Age sort of a thing to do. I'm not even talking about getting stoned, I mean the way the stuff gunges up your fingernails and its elemental feel, as if it were the earth itself.

Anyway, that's the only thing or product that's mentioned by its right name in *Riddley Walker*. If you're going to extract others you have to read the text with full attention. I've done that and I couldn't. The presence of hash makes sense also because of its role in the world described by the book. It's the travelling show men and their local interpreters who get paid in 'cuts' of hash, and this seems appropriate. Hash is a reverie-producing substance and these men are in the business of promoting a government through collective access to narratives of dreams and dreams of narrative, the fragments of a collective consciousness that has been shattered like a glass bowl dropped on a tile floor. Leastways – that's what I think.

More serious objections will focus on the nuclear holocaust angle. Surely that was a post-World War Two thing, and all gone now with the end of the Cold War? Every generation gets the end-of-the-world anxiety it deserves; it used to be transcendental, then it became elemental, and now it's environmental. It's one of the inherent problems of futuristic fiction that it's more likely to become dated than writing about the present, and certainly historical fiction. (Although with the benefit of hindsight we can definitely discern how one era's depiction of another is a portrait of itself.) I think that's why so many contemporary writers only set their novels in the past: they imagine that in the torque that lies between now and then lies a profound force, that can power their work into posterity. They feel that, because they're so uncertain about what's happening to the world under their very eyes, they best retreat to an adamant Arcadia of real – and fictional – values.

But *Riddley Walker* isn't out of date at all. On the contrary, it reads as fresh and vivid today as it has since it was first published twenty-two years ago. My hunch is that given the book's particular (and near-unique) attributes, this extent of survival indicates that it will stride on further into the future and become that most unfashionable of things, a classic.

The post-nuclear holocaust setting of the book is not essential to *Riddley Walker*'s meaning or effects, because this is not a book about the past masquerading as one about the future. On the contrary, this is a book about the delusion of progress, a book about the confused collective dream that humanity terms 'history', a book about what consciousness might be. It is a grand book, a demanding book, a destabilising book. Even though the furniture of the postlapsarian world described in its pages comes from our technological era of television broadcasts, air travel and nuclear energy, *Riddley Walker* could be set in the ashes of any civilisation, that of the Romans or the Sumerians, the Mayans or the Harappans. Indeed, it's all too easy to envisage a film or a theatrical production of *Riddley Walker* taking place at the feet of the megalithic statues of Easter Island. All that's central to the book can be summed up by our hero's lament as he stands beneath the 'girt shyning weals' of Fork Stoan: 'O what we ben! And what we come to . . . How cud any 1 not want to get that shyning Power back from time back way back? How cud any 1 not want to be like them what had boats in the air and picters on the wind? How cud any 1 not want to see them shyning weals terning?'

It's Hoban's great insight to have understood that the opposite of hubris is shame (or rather, shame is its aftermath, its hangover, its swollen head in the grey dawn of cultural capitulation). By seeding the Judeo-Christian shame myth with the hubris of Promethean humanitarianism, Hoban has engendered a timeless portrayal of the human condition. We are doomed ever to feel shameful about our detachment from nature, consciousness depends on dualism, and yet the destruction of that consciousness (both symbolised and potentially actualised by nuclear fission) will result only in still more shame.

It is this shame that emotionally animates *Riddley Walker*, that provides – as it were – the book's special affects. Riddley himself is both a seer in the waiting and a man of action. He does things – and then he writes them up. For the post-apocalyptic world of Inland, crawling its way back to self-consciousness (both individual and collective), he is the first writer. Steeped in shame and driven to recover the knowledge of a past he has only the most scant idea of, he sets off on a nightmarish series of treks across an indistinct and terrifying landscape.

Riddley's awareness of a race of superheroes who lived before is at once specific to his situation, and general (in so far as we can comprehend it) to the mental topography of many people at this stage in their evolution. Riddley may walk the grassed-over thoroughfares of late twentieth-century Kent, but he is also traversing mythological paths, which in their straights and turns contain the encoding of existence itself. Riddley is an Australian Aboriginal youth on walkabout, he is a Homeric hero on a quest, or any other individual human being who seeks through a picaresque to discover the nature of his world.

A word about Riddleyspeak. I don't want to anticipate Hoban's own note on this in his afterword – but I can't avoid it. *Riddley Walker* just is difficult to read – there's no point in denying it. By forcing the reader to slow down, Hoban does his text no favours, while bestowing upon it the greatest of respect. We don't want slow, we don't want considered, we don't even want profound. The cod-naturalism that infects so many texts is not an arbitrary convention, it's the very essence of what modern identity is. The idea that what I say to you will be immediately and lucidly comprehended is one of the most prosaic delusions of this most neurotic age. Everyone wants to be *understood* as if the world were in a position to provide *unconditional love*. This is balls. Riddley write-cum-speaks to us from the cusp of literate culture, and, in the very phonetic crudeness (from our angle) of his orthography, lies the vigour of his coming-into-being. Riddley wrestles sense out of the inchoate written language, and in so doing demands that we do the same. Hoban tells us that the novel took him five years to write and that by the end of it he'd become a bad speller. I guarantee that one reading – however long it takes you – will leave you unable to shake Riddleyspeak, and with it Riddleyvision. Yet once you are able to read *Riddley Walker* fluently, you have gone beyond the world that Riddley himself experiences. The sensation of groping in the dark that you'll have while deciphering this text is exactly what it is all about. True fictional praxis.

Hoban is of the generation that witnessed the dropping of atomic bombs on Hiroshima and Nagasaki. Like his near-ish contemporaries, Anthony Burgess, J.G. Ballard and William S. Burroughs, he sought to create a text that conveys a sense of the re-evaluation of all values implied by this doomsday weapon. Burroughs gave embodiment to fictional worlds that were connected up out of the disjointed dreamscapes of aberrant experience, while Burgess trafficked in dystopia – a most dangerous drug. As for Ballard, his terminal moraines and vermilion sands and timeless fugues are closest in spirit to the world of *Riddley Walker*, but they are aeons away in terms of its sense of time. Ballard's work renders surreal the connection between the individual and the collective, between psyche and culture, but he remains in thrall to the particular course of the twentieth century. In *Riddley Walker,* Hoban's mind-forged linkages between the remote past and the remote future join with his sense of a language eroded into being, to create a text that is frightening and uncanny.

At the very end of the original *Planet of the Apes* movie, the astronaut played by Charlton Heston escapes from the ape-dominated society and rides off along the deserted shoreline. He hasn't got too far when he encounters the Statue of Liberty buried up to its neck in the sand, and realises (as do the film's audience) that what he thought was an alien planet is in fact our own earth in the distant future. In my view this shocking image, coming as it did at the end of that most Promethean of decades, the 1960s, was a kind of tocsin, alerting humanity to the folly of its quest for immortality and the stars. *Riddley Walker* presents the reader with the opportunity to experience this uncanniness for page after page. Feel free to marvel.

Will Self, London 2002

Acknowledgments

On March 14th, 1974 I visited Canterbury Cathedral for the first time and saw Dr E. W. Tristram's reconstruction of the fifteenth-century wall painting, *The Legend of Saint Eustace*. This book was begun on May 14th, 1974 and completed on November 5th, 1979.

Thanks are due to Dennis, Pamela, and Clare Saunders of Canterbury; to Percy Press, Percy Press junior, Fred Tickner, and Bob Wade of the British Puppet and Model Theatre Guild; to Stuart McRae and Paul Burnham of Wye College (the map is based on one sketched for me by Paul Burnham); and to Hans Kruuk of the Institute of Terrestrial Ecology in Banchory.

For much encouragement and many useful talks I am indebted to Leon Redler, Jonathan Lewis, Richard Holt, John Gordon, and my wife, Gundula. I thank my sons Jake and Ben for being good company during many working hours. I am particularly grateful to Leon Garfield, who put aside his own work to read new drafts whenever I asked him to; his responses invariably put me in better touch with what I was doing and his comments were always of practical value.

And to Tom Maschler, my publisher, who's game for anything and always generates a sympathetic electricity that helps the work along, my thanks.

R. H.

To Wieland

Jesus has said:
Blessed is the lion that
the man will devour, and the lion
will become man. And loathsome is the
man that the lion will devour,
and the lion will become man.

Gospel of Thomas, Logion 7
Translated by George Ogg

The quotation is from *New Testament Apocrypha* by E. Hennecke, edited by
W. Schneemelcher, S.C.M. Press Ltd, 1963. English translation copyright
© Lutterworth Press, 1963.

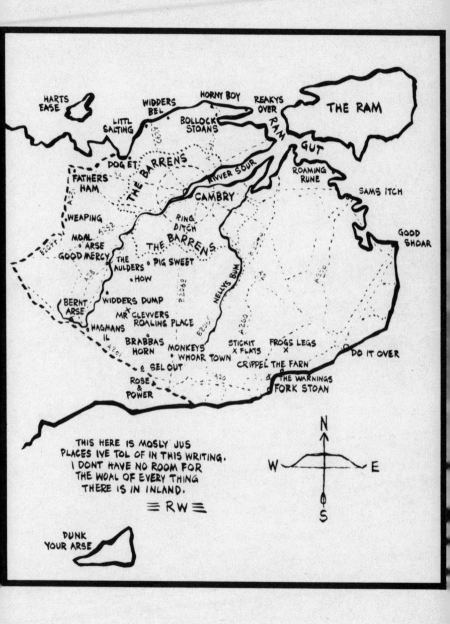

THIS HERE IS MOSLY JUS
PLACES IVE TOL OF IN THIS WRITING.
I DONT HAVE NO ROOM FOR
THE WOAL OF EVERY THING
THERE IS IN INLAND.

≡ RW ≡

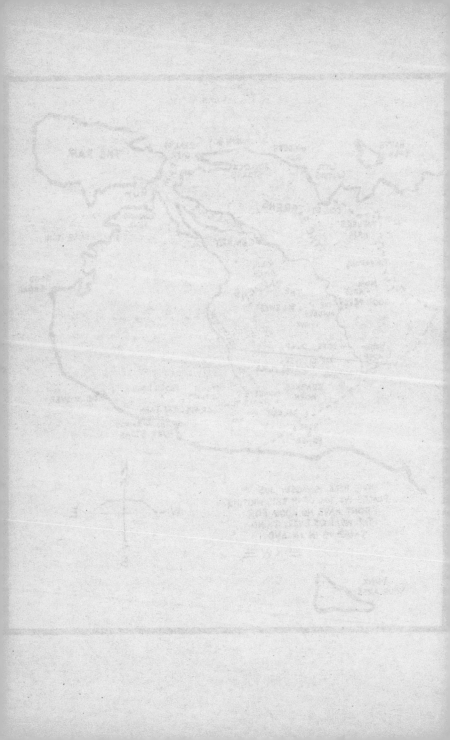

Riddley
Walker

1

On my naming day when I come 12 I gone front spear and kilt a wyld boar he parbly ben the las wyld pig on the Bundel Downs any how there hadnt ben none for a long time befor him nor I aint looking to see none agen. He dint make the groun shake nor nothing like that when he come on to my spear he wernt all that big plus he lookit poorly. He done the reqwyrt he ternt and stood and clattert his teef and made his rush and there we wer then. Him on 1 end of the spear kicking his life out and me on the other end watching him dy. I said, 'Your tern now my tern later.' The other spears gone in then and he wer dead and the steam coming up off him in the rain and we all yelt, 'Offert!'

The woal thing fealt jus that littl bit stupid. Us running that boar thru that las littl scrump of woodling with the forms all roun. Cows mooing sheap baaing cocks crowing and us foraging our las boar in a thin grey girzel on the day I come a man.

The Bernt Arse pack ben follering jus out of bow shot. When the shout gone up ther ears all prickt up. Ther leader he wer a big black and red spottit dog he come forit a littl like he ben going to make a speach or some thing til 1 or 2 bloaks uppit bow then he slumpt back agen and kep his farness follering us back. I took noatis of that leader tho. He wernt close a nuff for me to see his eyes but I thot his eye ben on me.

Coming back with the boar on a poal we come a long by the rivver it wer hevvyer woodit in there. Thru the girzel you cud see blue smoak hanging in be twean the black trees and the stumps pink and red where they ben loppt off. Aulder trees

1

in there and chard coal berners in amongst them working ther harts. You cud see 1 of them in there with his red jumper what they all ways wear. Making chard coal for the iron reddy at Widders Dump. Every 1 made the Bad Luck go a way syn when we past him. Theres a story callit *Hart of the Wood* this is it:

Hart of the Wood

There is the Hart of the Wud in the *Eusa Story**[*]** that wer a stag every 1 knows that. There is the hart of the wood meaning the veryes deap of it thats a nother thing. There is the hart of the wood where they bern the chard coal thats a nother thing agen innit. Thats a nother thing. Berning the chard coal in the hart of the wood. Thats what they call the stack of wood you see. The stack of wood in the shape they do it for chard coal berning. Why do they call it the hart tho? Thats what this here story tels of.

Every 1 knows about Bad Time and what come after. Bad Time 1st and bad times after. Not many come thru it a live.

There come a man and a woman and a chyld out of a berning town they sheltert in the woodlings and foraging the bes they cud. Starveling wer what they wer doing. Dint have no weapons nor dint know how to make a snare nor nothing. Snow on the groun and a grey sky overing and the black trees rubbing ther branches in the wind. Crows calling 1 to a nother waiting for the 3 of them to drop. The man the woman and the chyld digging thru the snow they wer eating maws and dead leaves which they vomitit them up agen. Freazing col they wer nor dint have nothing to make a fire with to get warm. Starveling they wer and near come to the end of ther strenth.

The chyld said, 'O Im so col Im afeart Im going to dy. If only we had a littl fire to get warm at.'

---

* Iwl write down the *Eusa Story* when I come to it.

2

The man dint have no way of making a fire he dint have no flint and steal nor nothing. Wood all roun them only there wernt no way he knowit of getting warm from it.

The 3 of them ready for Aunty they wer ready to total and done when there come thru the woodlings a *clevver* looking bloak and singing a littl song to his self:

My roadings ben so hungry
Ive groan so very thin
Ive got a littl cook pot
But nothing to put in

The man and the woman said to the clevver looking bloak, 'Do you know how to make fire?'

The clevver looking bloak said, 'O yes if I know any thing I know that right a nuff. Fires my middl name you myt say.'

The man and the woman said, 'Wud you make a littl fire then weare freazing of the col.'

The clevver looking bloak said, 'That for you and what for me?'

The man and the woman said, 'What do we have for whatfers?' They lookit 1 to the other and boath at the chyld.

The clevver looking bloak said, 'Iwl tel you what Iwl do Iwl share you my fire and my cook pot if youwl share me what to put in the pot.' He wer looking at the chyld.

The man and the woman thot: 2 out of 3 a live is bettern 3 dead. They said, 'Done.'

They kilt the chyld and drunk its blood and cut up the meat for cooking.

The clevver looking bloak said, 'Iwl show you how to make fire plus Iwl give you flint and steal and makings nor you dont have to share me nothing of the meat only the hart.'

Which he made the fire then and give them flint and steal and makings then he cookt the hart of the chyld and et it.

The clevver looking bloak said, 'Clevverness is gone now but littl by littl itwl come back. The iron wil come back agen 1 day and when the iron comes back they wil bern chard coal in the hart of the wood. And when they bern the chard coal ther stack wil be the shape of the hart of the chyld.' Off he gone then singing:

Seed of the littl
Seed of the wyld
Seed of the berning is
Hart of the chyld

The man and the woman then eating ther chyld it wer black nite all roun them they made ther fire bigger and bigger trying to keap the black from moving in on them. They fel a sleap by ther fire and the fire biggering on it et them up they bernt to death. They ben the old 1s or you myt say the *auld* 1s and be come chard coal. Thats why theywl tel you the aulder tree is bes for charring coal. Some times youwl hear of a aulder kincher he carrys off childer.

Out goes the candl
Out goes the lite
Out goes my story
And so Good Nite

Coming pas that aulder wood that girzly morning I fealt my stummick go col. Like the aulder kincher ben putting eye on me. No 1 never had nothing much to do with the chard coal berners only the dyers on the forms. 1ce a year the chard coal berners they come in to the forms for ther new red clof but in be twean they kep to the woodlings.

It wer Ful of the Moon that nite. The rain littlt off the sky cleart and the moon come out. We put the boars head on the poal up on top of the gate house. His tusks glimmert and you cud see a dryd up trickl from the corners of his eyes like 1 las tear from each. Old Lorna Elswint our tel woman up there

4

getting the tel of the head. Littl kids down be low playing
Fools Circel 9wys. Singing:

> Horny Boy rung Widders Bel
> Stoal his Fathers Ham as wel
> Bernt his Arse and Forkt a Stoan
> Done It Over broak a boan
> Out of Good Shoar vackt his wayt
> Scratcht Sams Itch for No. 8
> Gone to senter nex to see
> Cambry coming 3 times 3
> > Sharna pax and get the poal
> > When the Ardship of Cambry comes out of the hoal

Littl 2way Digman being the Ardship going roun the circel til
it come chopping time. He bustit out after the 3rd chop. I use
to be good at that I all ways rathert be the Ardship nor 1 of
the circel I liket the busting out part.

I gone up to the platform I took Lorna a nice tender line of
the boar. She wer sitting up there in her doss bag she ben
smoaking she wer hy. I give her the meat and I said, 'Lorna
wil you tel for me?'

She said, 'Riddley Riddley theres mor to life nor asking
and telling. Whynt you be the Big Boar and Iwl be the Moon
Sow.'

> When the Moon Sow
> When the Moon Sow comes to season
> Ay! She wants a big 1
> Wants the Big Boar hevvy on her
> Ay yee! Big Boar what makes the groun shake
> Wyld of the Woodling with the wite tusk
> Ay yee! That wyld big 1 for the Moon Sow

She sung that in my ear then we freshent the Luck up there
on top of the gate house. She wer the oldes in our crowd but
her voyce wernt old. It made the res of her seam yung for a
littl. It wer a col nite but we wer warm in that doss bag.
Lissening to the dogs howling aftrwds and the wind wuther-

ing and wearying and nattering in the oak leaves. Looking at the moon all col and wite and oansome. Lorna said to me, 'You know Riddley theres some thing in us it dont have no name.'

I said, 'What thing is that?'

She said, 'Its some kynd of thing it aint us but yet its in us. Its looking out thru our eye hoals. May be you dont take no noatis of it only some times. Say you get woak up suddn in the middl of the nite. I minim youre a sleap and the nex youre on your feet with a spear in your han. Wel it wernt you put that spear in your han it wer that other thing whats looking out thru your eye hoals. It aint you nor it dont even know your name. Its in us lorn and loan and sheltering how it can.'

I said, 'If its in every 1 of us theres moren 1 of it theres got to be a manying theres got to be a millying and mor.'

Lorna said, 'Wel there is a millying and mor.'

I said, 'Wel if theres such a manying of it whys it lorn then whys it loan?'

She said, 'Becaws the manying and the millying its all 1 thing it dont have nothing to gether with. You look at lykens on a stoan its all them tiny manyings of it and may be each part of it myt think its sepert only we can see its all 1 thing. Thats how it is with what we are its all 1 girt big thing and divvyt up amongst the many. Its all 1 girt thing bigger nor the worl and lorn and loan and oansome. Tremmering it is and feart. It puts us on like we put on our cloes. Some times we dont fit. Some times it cant fynd the arm hoals and it tears us a part. I dont think I took all that much noatis of it when I ben yung. Now Im old I noatis it mor. It dont realy like to put me on no mor. Every morning I can feal how its tiret of me and readying to throw me a way. Iwl tel you some thing Riddley and keap this in memberment. What ever it is we dont come naturel to it.'

I said, 'Lorna I dont know what you mean.'

She said, 'We aint a naturel part of it. We dint begin when it begun we dint begin *where* it begun. It ben here befor us nor I dont know what we are to it. May be weare jus only sickness and a feaver to it or boyls on the arse of it I dont know. Now lissen what Im going to tel you Riddley. It thinks us but it dont think *like* us. It dont think the way we think. Plus like I said befor its afeart.'

I said, 'Whats it afeart of?'

She said, 'Its afeart of being beartht.'

I said, 'How can that be? You said it ben here befor us. If it ben here all this time it musve ben beartht some time.'

She said, 'No it aint ben beartht it never does get beartht its all ways in the woom of things its all ways on the road.'

I said, 'All this what you jus ben telling be that a tel for me?'

She larft then she said, 'Riddley there aint nothing what *aint* a tel for you. The wind in the nite the dus on the road even the leases stoan you kick a long in front of you. Even the shadder of that leases stoan roaling on or stanning stil its all telling.'

Wel I cant say for cern no mor if I had any of them things in my mynd befor she tol me but ever since then it seams like they all ways ben there. Seams like I ben all ways thinking on that thing in us what thinks us but it dont think like us. Our woal life is a idear we dint think of nor we dont know what it is. What a way to live.

Thats why I finely come to writing all this down. Thinking on what the idear of us myt be. Thinking on that thing whats in us lorn and loan and oansome.

2

Walker is my name and I am the same. Riddley Walker. Walking my riddels where ever theyve took me and walking them now on this paper the same.

I dont think it makes no diffrents where you start the telling of a thing. You never know where it begun realy. No moren you know where you begun your oan self. You myt know the place and day and time of day when you ben beartht. You myt even know the place and day and time when you ben got. That dont mean nothing tho. You stil dont know where you begun.

Ive all ready wrote down about my naming day. It wernt no moren 3 days after that my dad got kilt in the digging at Widders Dump and I wer the loan of my name.

Dad and me we jus come off forage rota and back on jobbing that day. The hoal we ben working we ben on it 24 days. Which Ive never liket 12 its a judgd men number innit and this ben 2 of them. Wed pernear cleart out down to the chalk and hevvy mucking it ben. Nothing lef in the hoal only sortit thru muck and the smel of it and some girt big rottin iron thing some kynd of machine it wer you cudnt tel what it wer.

Til then any thing big we all ways bustit up in the hoal. Winch a girt big buster rock up on the crane and drop it down on what ever we wer busting. Finish up with han hammers then theywd drag the peaces to the reddy for the melting. This time tho the 1stman tol us word come down they dint want this thing bustit up we wer to get it out in tack. So we ben sturgling with the girt big thing nor the woal 20 of us cudnt shif it we`cudnt even lif it jus that littl bit to get the sling unner neath of it. Up to our knees in muck we wer. Even with the drain wed dug the hoal wer mucky from the rains. And col. It wer only jus the 2nd mooning of the year and winter long in going.

We got hevvy poals and leavering it up jus a nuff to get a roap roun 1 end of it we had in mynd to shif that girt thing jus a littl with the crane so we cud get it parper slung then winch it out of there. It wer a 16 man treadl crane with 2 weals 4 men inside 4 men outside each weal. Userly I wuntve ben on the crane we all ways put our hevvyes on them weals. All we had tho wer 20 in all and we neadit some mussl on the leaver poals so I wer up there on the lef han weal with our hardes hevvy Fister Crunchman we wer the front 2 on that weal. Durster Potter and Jobber Easting behynt us. Straiter Empy our Big Man he wer down in the hoal with Dad and 2 others. Us on the out side of the weals looking tords the hoal and them on the in side looking a way from it.

We took up the slack then Straiter Empy give the syn and Chalker Marchman the Widders Dump 1stman chanting us on:

Gone ter morrer here to day
Pick it up and walk a way
Dont you know greaf and woe
Pick it up its time to go
    Greaf and woe dont you know
    Pick it up its time to go

Roun we gone with the roap winching in and the A frame taking the strain. Straiter Empy and Skyway Moaters leavering the girt thing wylst we wincht and Dad and Leaster Digman working the sling unner.

London Town is drownt this day
Hear me say walk a way
Sling your bundel tern and go
Parments in the mud you know
    Greaf and woe dont you know
    Pick it up its time to go

Weals creaking stoppers knocking 32 legs going. The roap

gone iron hard and the girt big thing coming up out of the muck all black and rottin unner the grey sky. A crow going over and it had the right of us.

Dad and me looking up at the crow. I knowit that crow wer going to say some thing unner that grey sky. I knowit that crow wer going to tel.

The crow yelt, 'Fall! Fall! Fall!' I dont know if I wer falling befor he said that or not. The treadls wer wet and slippy but I had a good grip on the railing any how I thot I did. But there I wer with my feet gone out from unner me and nothing in my han. Falling I wer I knockt Durster Potter and Jobber Easting luce and they grabbit me they dint have nothing else to hol on to. Fister Crunchman cawt my arm only the railing he had holt of with his other han come a way in his han and off he gone with the res of us. I cud see in my mynd how funny it musve lookit I wer near larfing with it only I seen that weal going backards and I heard some thing tear luce it wer the stoppers 2 on each weal all 4 gone whanging off. Boath weals screachit and the 4 bloaks on the out side of the other weal shot off tords the hoal like stoans out of a sling. Wel it wer the load took charge and SPLOOSH! Down it come that girt big thing it made a jynt splosh and black muck going up slow and hy in to the air. That girt old black machine fel back in to the muck with my dad unner neath of it. It all happent so fas the crow wer stil in site he larft then. 'Haw! Haw! Haw!' and off he flappit.

We pickt our selfs up then all but 1 of us. The roap wer stil fas to the girt big thing. We all got on that roap then we dint use the weal winch only the A frame and the pullys. Chalker Marchman chanting us on the strait pul:

> Heard it and the news of 10
> Sling your bundel haul agen
> Haul agen and hump your load
> Every bodys on the road

We shiffit the thing and got Dad out from unner. Parbly it kilt him soons it come down on him he dint have no time to drown in the muck. He wer all smasht up you cudnt tel whose face it ben it mytve ben any bodys.

I begun to clym all over that thing then. That girt big black thing. I wer looking to see if it had a name stampt in or raisd up in the iron of it like them things do some times. It had a shel of old muck stoan hard unner the new muck tho nor I cudnt fynd no name.

Every 1 wer saying, 'What is it Riddley whatre you doing?'

I said, 'My dad ben kilt by some thing I dont even know the name of aint that a larf.' I begun larfing then I cudnt stop.

They let me have my larfing out but I wer stil wanting some thing some kynd of las word some kynd of onwith. If I wernt going to get it from Dad at leas I wantit some thing for onwith even if it wernt nothing only the name of that girt black thing what smasht him flat so you cudnt even tel whose face it ben. I said that to Fister Crunchman.

He said, 'You look at your dads face Riddley thats what Widders Dump done to him theres your onwith.'

I said, 'It wernt Widders Dump done it to him it wer me I los my footing and I pult you with me. It wer me made the woal of us lose our perchis.'

Fister said, 'That load wer too much for that weal. It wernt us falling kilt your dad it wer the stoppers coming luce and the weal took charge.'

Straiter Empy said, 'Fisters right it wer too much of a load for that weal.'

Chalker Marchman said to Straiter, 'It wer you lot put it on the weal. All I tol you wer to get that thing out of the hoal. You cudve draggit cudnt you I never give you the do it for the weal. Any how that weal wudve ben all right if youd had a nuff hevvyness on it and kep your hevvyness where it ben meant to be.'

Straiter said, 'Widders Dumpwl give comping station for Brooder Walker tho youwl do that much wont you.'

Chalker Marchman said, 'O yes wewl sen Reckman Bessup with it hewl road back to fents with you.'

We borrert a drag to take Dad hoam. Going back to fents

then all of us. They give us ful days meat at Widders Dump and Reckman Bessup he wer ther connexion man he brung the comping station. What we callit dead mans iron and he carrit on his back.

We wer going out thru the gate when there gone up behynt us the death wail loud and strong it musve ben 40 peopl at leas. All them voyces going up black and sharp and falling a way in a groan: AIYEEEEE.

I said to Reckman Bessup, 'That cant be for my dad he wernt nothing to them.'

He said, 'Its a babby dead beartht. That babby come in to the worl dead same time as your dad gone with Aunty.'

I said, 'Is there a connexion?'

He said, 'Not 1 as Iwl make.'

Going back slow then there come dogs follering on our track we hadnt seen none that day til then. Shapit black is how I think of them tho mos of them are patchy colourt. Its the hy leggitness of them. Ther thick necks and littl heads and littl ears. It wer the Bernt Arse pack with ther black and red spottit leader. All of them head down and slumping on behynt us jus out of bow shot. I wer looking at the leader and waiting for some thing I cud feal it in my froat. He dint have his head down he had it up and looking tords us.

There begun to be some rowling and yipping and yapping from the other dogs then crowding the leader and him terning. Grooling and smarling he wer but the others crowdit on him then the leader he come running tords us. The other dogs dint foller they hung back and he come oansome.

All of us stoppt then and looking at the dog. Not 1 of us put arrer to string we all knowit wernt that kynd of thing. I steppt out a littl way from the others and they all movit a way from me it wer like some thing you do in a dream. Straiter Empy said, 'Riddley hes offering and hes favering you.'

I stood there and holding ready with my spear. Nothing like it never happent befor but it wer like it all ways ben there happening. The dog getting bigger bigger unner the grey sky and me waiting with the spear. It dint seam like the running brung him on tho he wer moving fas. It wer mor like he ben running for ever in 1 place not moving on jus getting bigger bigger til he wer big a nuff to be in front of me with his face all rinkelt back from his teef. Jus in that fraction of a minim the dogs face and the boars face from my naming day they flickert to gether with my dads face all smasht. I helt the spear and he run on to it. Lying there and kicking with his yeller eyes on me and I finisht him with my knife.

Straiter Empy said, 'Look how his teefs woar down and hes all girzelt. A old leader come to his time and crowdit out come back to us to dy. Ive heard of it but I never seen it befor. Its Luck to you Riddley.'

We laid the dog acrost Dads legs. Reckman Bessup said to me, 'This dogs offert his self to your dad. Made his Plomercy and now theywl boath look at the nite to gether.'

I said to Reckman Bessup, 'Heres my dad dead and this dog and that babby at Widders Dump all on the same day. Be there a connexion?'

He said, 'Whynt you stop asking me that. What I connect is shows I aint no tel woman nor I dont know nothing about blips nor syns.'

I said, 'Thats as may be but youre stanning here and seen what happent plus you ben at Widders Dump this morning.'

He thot on it a littl then. A sour man but cudnt help getting a littl interstit. He said, 'I wunt try no tel but you can tel your oan self. Every 1 knows if you get blipful things to gether you take the farthes out 1 for the nindicater. Whats the farthes out 1 of the 3 youve namit?'

I said, 'The dog.'

He said, 'Whats a dog? Its some thing you cant get close to. They keap ther farness nor you cant trap them nyther theyre too clevver. Plus theyre a danger theywl eat you if they catch you oansome and they go mad at Ful of the Moon. So here youve got a far thing come close and a danger thing as cudnt be trappt offers its self. How old myt you be?'

I said, 'I jus come 12 at Ful of the Moon.'

He said, 'Heres a old woar out leader took by a boy what

13

aint a boy no mor hes come 12 and a man. You hearing any tel?'

I said, 'The far come close took by the littl come big.'

He said, 'You said it I dint. I dont say no farther you bes tel your oan self on from there. No use asking other peopl they dont know no moren you do. Now your dads gone youwl be connexion man at How Fents peopl wil be asking you in stead of you asking them. You bes start putting things to gether for your self you aint a kid no mor.'

When we movit on the dogs they slumpt off back to Bernt Arse Dead Town it wer like they only come out that day for that 1 thing. Smoak coming up in Bernt Arse from the out poast there wer all ways hevvys there on rota from the Ram. Every day we gone the same way to and from and every day we seen that smoak nor I never give it no thot. This day tho every thing begun to look diffrent. Like I never seen it befor. You know that kynd of playsy kids have some times. Its a funny face paintit on a flat peace of wood and theres 2 hoals to roal the eyes in to. Clay ball eyes and you slant the face 1 way and the other til they roal in to the hoals. Wel this day it seamt like the worl begun to roal. The worl begun to seam like 1 big crazy eye and roaling. I wer afeart it myt roal right off the face and dispear.

Looking at that smoak coming up in the dead town and my mynd stil running on the dogs. There ben the dead towns all them years. Ram out poasts in 1 part of them and dogs hoalt up in other parts. And all them years you heard storys of dog peopl. Peopl with dogs heads and dogs with peopls heads. Some said come Ful of the Moon they all run to gether in the Black Pack. Dogs and dog peopl to gether. The Ram dint allow no 1 in the dead towns but when I ben littl we use to sly in when ever we got the chance and kids a nuff for crowd. Trying if we cud see dog peopl. Fork Stoan it ben befor we livet near Bernt Arse. We never seen nothing only the hevvys and they all ways seen us off qwick. We heard things tho some times. Singing or howling or crying, or larfing you cudnt qwite say what it wer or what it wernt.

My dad use to say all that about the dog peopl wer jus so much cow shit. He said hewd give odds it wer plittical and no dogs heads to it at all. Wel this aint the place to say no mor about it Iwl tel that part when I come to it. Ive only wrote this down here becaws my mynd ben running on it that day and if itd run farther I mytve knowit mor. There aint that many sir prizes in life if you take noatis of every thing. Every time wil have its happenings out and every place the same. What ever eats mus shit.

We got back to fents and then the death wail gone for Brooder Walker. We done comping station then. Reckman Bessup he said, '1 of yours is dead with us. I have it on me wil you take it off me?'

I said, 'Yes Iwl take it off.' I took the iron off his back then. That wer the onlyes iron I ever seen out of all them years jobbing at Widders Dump. 5 10wts of iron for Brooder Walker.

My dad he wer 33 when he dyd. My mum she dyd of the coffing sickness when I wer 5. This what Ive ben writing down here it happent when I ben with How Fents. On the Bundel Downs near the Rivver Sour about 4 faggers Norf and Eas of Bernt Arse Dead Town and about 15 faggers Souf and Wes of Cambry.

3

This is stil that same day Im writing down here. The day my dad got kilt. We put the dogs head on the poal on top of the gate house. Lorna Elswint up there with it. Littl Kids zanting down be low. Playing Black Pack and singing:

> Ful of the Moon Ful of the Moon
> Ful of the Moon nor dont look back
> Folleree Folleroo on your track
> Oo hoo hoo Yoop yaroo
> Folleree Folleroo follering you
> If they catch you in the darga
> Arga warga

Lorna she lookit over the side she said to the kids, 'There aint no Ful Moon this nite there aint no Black Pack running. Its 2 days pas the Ful.'

Littl Nimbel Potter he said, '3rd of the Ful and stil shewl pul. My dad he seen Riddley Walker kil that dog and my dad he said that dog wil fetch.'

Lorna said, 'Fetch what?'

Nimbel said, 'Fetch some 1 over to the dog peopl.' He laid his head over on 1 side to show his neck and he showit his teef like he wer a dog and going to bite.

Lorna said, 'Nimbel you ever seen any dog peopl?'

Nimbel said, 'O yes Ive seen them times a nuff.'

Lorna said, 'Whatd they look like then?'

Nimbel said, 'They throw a wite shadder dont they. Every body knows that.' He ternt his self roun then and gone back to playing with the others. Singing:

16

Gennl men wil do it front to back
When they do it with the ladys of the Ful Moon pack
All the ladys do it back to front
When they drop ther nickers and they show ther
Moony in the holler moony on the hil
If you wont do it then your sister wil

I gone up on the gate house and looking at the head. The
day gone colder. The muddling from the rains froze hard and
the calling of the crows col on the air. Looking at that old
leaders woar down teef.

Lorna said to me, 'You heard the story of why the dog wont
show its eyes?'

I said, 'No I never.'

She said, 'Thats what happens with peopl on the way down
from what they ben. The storys go.' She tol me the story
then. This is it wrote down the same:

Why the Dog Wont Show Its Eyes

Time back way way back befor peopl got clevver they had
the 1st knowing. They los it when they got the clevverness
and now the clevverness is gone as wel.

Every thing has a shape and so does the nite only you
cant see the shape of nite nor you cant think it. If you put
your self right you can know it. Not with knowing in your
head but with the 1st knowing. Where the number creaper
grows on the dead stoans and the groun is sour for 3 days
digging the nite stil knows the shape of its self tho we dont.
Some times the nite is the shape of a ear only it aint a ear
we know the shape of. Lissening back for all the souns
whatre gone from us. The hummering of the dead towns
and the voyces befor the towns ben there. Befor the iron
ben and fire ben only littl. Lissening for whats coming as
wel.

Time back way way back 1 time it wer Ful of the Moon
and a man and woman sqwatting by ther littl fire.
Sqwatting by ther littl fire and afeart of the nite. The dog

wer in the nite and looking tords the fire. It wernt howling it wer jus looking at the fire. The man and woman seen the fire shyning in the dogs eyes. The man throwit meat to the dog and the dog come in to them by the fire. Brung its eyes in out of the nite then they all lookit at the nite to gether. The man and the woman seen the nite in the dogs eyes and thats when they got the 1st knowing of it. They knowit the nite the same as the dog knowit.

You know what they got 1st knowing of. She has diffrent ways she shows her self. Shes that same 1 shows her moon self or she jus shows her old old nite and no moon. Shes that same 1 every thing and all of us come out of. Shes what she is. Shes a woman when shes Nite and shes a woman when shes Death. The nite bearths the day. Every day has the shape of the nite what it come out of. The man as knows that shape can go in to the nite in the nite and the nite in the day time. The woman as knows that shape can be the nite and take the day in her and bearth the new day.

Wel they got that 1st knowing they got it looking in the dogs eyes in the Ful of the Moon. When the man and woman got that 1st knowing from the dog they made a contrack with the dog in the Ful of the Moon. They roadit on to gether with the dog and foraging to gether. Dint have no mor fear in the nite they put ther self right day and nite that wer the good time. Then they begun to think on it a littl. They said, 'If the 1st knowing is this good what myt the 2nd knowing and the 3rd be and so on?'

They cawt a goat and lookit in its eye. You know what eye the goat has its the clevver eye. The man and woman looking in that clevver eye and they thot: Why shud we be foraging the woal time? They cawt other goats they made a fents and pent them up. They gethert weat and barly they had bread and beer then they wernt moving on the lan no mor they startit in to form it. Stoppit in 1 place then with sheds and stock and growings. They wernt outside in the nite no mor they wer inside looking out. The nite jus lookit dark to them they dint see nothing else to it no mor. They los out of memberment the shapes of nite and worrit for ther parpety they myt get snuck and raidit. They made the dog keap look out for ther parpety.

Every morning they were counting every thing to see if any thing ben took off in the nite. How many goats how many cows how many measurs weat and barly. Cudnt stop ther counting which wer clevverness and making mor the same. They said, 'Them as counts counts moren them as dont count.'

Counting counting they wer all the time. They had iron then and big fire they had towns of parpety. They had machines et numbers up. They fed them numbers and they fractiont out the Power of things. They had the Nos. of the rain bow and the Power of the air all workit out with counting which is how they got boats in the air and picters on the wind. Counting clevverness is what it wer.

When they had all them things and marvelsome they cudnt sleap realy they dint have no res. They wer stressing ther self and straining all the time with counting. They said, 'What good is nite its only dark time it aint no good for nothing only them as want to sly and sneak and take our parpety a way.' They los out of memberment who nite wer. They jus wantit day time all the time and they wer going to do it with the Master Chaynjis.

They had the Nos. of the sun and moon all fraction out and fed to the machines. They said, 'Wewl put all the Nos. in to 1 Big 1 and that wil be the No. of the Master Chaynjis.' They bilt the Power Ring thats where you see the Ring Ditch now. They put in the 1 Big 1 and woosht it roun there come a flash of lite then bigger nor the woal worl and it ternt the nite to day. Then every thing gone black. Nothing only nite for years on end. Playgs kilt peopl off and naminals nor there wernt nothing growit in the groun. Man and woman starveling in the blackness looking for the dog to eat it and the dog out looking to eat them the same. Finely there come day agen then nite and day regler but never like it ben befor. Day beartht crookit out of crookit nite and sickness in them boath.

Now man and woman go afeart by nite afeart by day. The dog all lorn and wishful it keaps howling for the nites whatre gone for ever. It wont show its eyes no mor it wont show the man and woman no 1st knowing. Come Ful of the Moon the sadness gets too much the dog goes mad. It follers on the man and womans track and arga warga if it catches them.

The fires col
My storys tol

I said to Lorna, 'I thot it ben Eusa made the 1 Big 1.'

Lorna said, 'I never said he dint.'

I said, 'Wel you jus tol in this story it ben that man and woman done it plus they bilt the Power Ring and all.'

She said, 'You hear diffrent things in all them way back storys but it dont make no diffrents. Mosly they aint strait storys any how. What they are is diffrent ways of telling what happent.'

I said, 'Ben there a strait story past down amongst the tel women?'

She said, 'There bint no tel women time back way back. Nor there aint never ben no strait story I ever heard. Bint no writing for 100s and 100s of years til it begun agen nor you wunt never get a strait story past down by mouf over that long. Onlyes writing I know of is the *Eusa Story* which that aint nothing strait but at leas its stayd the same. All them other storys tol by mouf they ben put to and took from and changit so much thru the years theyre all bits and blips and all mixt up.'

I said, 'That about the 1st knowing in the story. How they got it looking in the dogs eyes. Be that blip or jus a way of saying or what?'

She said, 'Why you asking?'

I said, 'Wel that old dog I kilt I lookit in its eyes dint I. Nor I never got no 1st knowing out of it did I.'

She said, 'May be you got it only you dont know it yet.'

I said, 'Have you got it?'

She said, 'Every bodys got it its in every 1 of us only we cant get to it til it comes to us 1 way or a nother.'

I said, 'Its come to you aint it.'

She said, 'Yes its come to me nor there aint no use asking what it is becaws its what there aint no words for.'

Wel any way thats the story of why the dog wont show its eyes.

Back then in this time I ben writing of I never knowit any 1 ben dog kilt only a kid it wer Follery Digman he got dog et years back. It wer Ful of the Moon and he staggelt behynt a trade crowd coming back. Some times other times of mooning it lookit to me like the dogs ben near ready to come frendy only it never happent. Nor I never heard of no 1 tame a pup. Heard of some 1 got 1 1ce I dont know how they done it. They never tamit tho. Soons it got big a nuff it dug unner the fents and gone.

Theres dogs in the *Eusa Story*. Folleree & Folleroo. Theyre mor blip dogs nor real 1s tho.

4

We done the berning that nite on the bye bye hump. The moon wer cloudit over and a hy wind blowing. I put the 1st torch to the stack then Straiter Empy for the crowd then Reckman Bessup for Widders Dump then Lorna Elswint for las. Arnge flames upping in the dark and liting all the faces roun. Catching that time of that nite stoppt on all them faces. You cud smel the berning sharp on the air mixt with the meat smel from the divvy roof. Dogs begun to howl it wer coming and going on the wind. The fire blowing in the wind and the sparks whup off in to the dark and gone. Dark and gone. Befor the wording we sung *Sarvering Gallack Seas*:

> Pas the sarvering gallack seas and flaming nebyul eye
> Power us beyont the farthes reaches of the sky
> Thine the han what shapit the black
> Guyd us there and guyd us back

Straiter Empy said, 'Thine hans for Brooder Walker.'

We all thinet hans then roun the fire and Straiter Empy wordit 1st. He said, 'Brooder Walker. A good man and done good connexions. Done his bes for this crowd like his father done befor him. Like his son wil after him. Out of the dark he come and in to the dark he gone. In to the 1st knowing and the Master Chaynjis.'

Reckman Bessup wordit nex. He said, 'Brooder Walker. He wer a connexion man the same as me. I never seen him doing no connexions tho Ive only seen him jobbing on the form and this day Ive crowdit back to fents with him with dead mans iron on me. He connectit shows for you. Connectit with a shovvel or a leaver poal for us. Put his han to what ever he done and took a good grip on it.'

It gone right roun the circel then every 1 saying a word or 2 even if it wernt nothing only 'Bye bye Brooder.' I had las wording only I dint say nothing I kep my words for him inside me. Then we unthinet. The fire berning hot and hy and Lorna Elswint up front for the tel. Face all sharp and rinkelt in the fire lite and the shadders moving on it.

She wer looking at the fire then looking up in to the dark. She said, 'Bond fires thats what they use to call them. Big fires they use to bern on hy groun to lite them others back to fetch us. Boats in the air o yes. Them air boats as never come back. Becaws them as got a way to the space stations they jus done ther dying out there in stead of down here. Now here we stan and singing that song to bern our dead. No 1 coming back to get us out of this. Onlyes way wewl get out of it is to dy out of it.' She dint say nothing for a littl jus stanning there and looking up in to the dark. Dogs howling in the sylents and the wind moaning.

Lorna lookit roun at every body slow. She had a way of doing it youwd hear the crowd like groan a littl unner ther breaf for craving what shewd say. She said, '3 things and blipful all of them. 1 is Brooder Walker kilt in the digging. 2 is the babby dead beartht at the form. 3 is the old dog offering and took by Brooder Walkers son. You bes be careful thinking on it tho becaws if you start out with Brooder Walker dead youwl easy fynd false foller and get mixt up with your fealings.

'Bes go slow and scanful then. Bes dont start with Brooder Walker dead. Les jus tern it roun and look at it the other way. Put it in a diffrent foller and look at it backards starting with 3 in stead of 1. 3 is the dog. Think on that dog and what wer he? Old he wer and teef woar down. See him on your track and coming at you. Coming from behynt and you tern roun and look and there hes coming to you oansome getting bigger bigger. Offering. Thats what youwl say. Hes offering. Say agen what is he? Old and woar out. Wheres he coming from?

23

Coming from behynt you. Mynd you he aint coming from in front of you. No that old and woar outs coming at you from behynt. What dyou do? Hol your spear and let him run on to it same as Riddley Walker done.'

Every body looking at me like they wisht theyd had the chance. I fealt like I mus be some 1 special right a nuff.

Lorna said, 'Very good and wel done you. All that old and woar out what ben follering on behynt its gone now. Cleart a way. Now weare ready for the new so let it come. Hooray here comes a babby you cant ask bettern that for new. Its a form babby mynd you that. Mark you that and noat you wel. Heres that babby which its No. 2 counting backards and its the same frontwards its the middl 1 of the 3. O dear o dear o dear that babbys dead beartht. Why in the worl did that littl new life come in dead?

'Where ben that new life coming in to? Widders Dump. You know what they ben doing there. It aint jus only forming they ben doing there with stock and growings they ben digging they ben croaking iron. They ben digging up that old time Bad Time black time. Now weare at the las weve come to No. 1 and Brooder Walker. Widders Dump and thats where Aunty come for him. Stoan boans and iron tits and teef be twean her legs. Brooder Walker dug her up and she come down on top of him o yes.

'Our connexion man and what ben he connectit to? You heard it out of this formers mouf the 1 as brung the dead mans iron. Brooder Walker ben connectit to a shovel and a leaver poal and digging up Bad Time. Ben that a right connexion or a wrong 1?' She lookit roun and waiting for a anser to that. Peopl looking 1 to a nother and some to Reckman Bessup and some to me nor they wunt say nothing.

Lorna said, 'O yes youwl want to think on that you dont want your mouf to walk you where your feet dont want to go. Wel never mynd. Youve seen what come of that connexion. Now its broak weve got to make a new 1.'

Peopl looking at me then. Brooder Walkers son and going to be the new connexion man.

Lorna said, 'Every thing in its time weve stil got things to deal with this nite. Les jus tern them 3 things roun agen and have 1 las look. 1 the old connexion broak and finisht. 2 the form brings in a babby dead. 3 is the nindicater and its a dead dog. Its the old and woar out run its self on to a yung spear out of our crowd. Myt there be mor to it as wel? O yes I dessay there myt. Whats in that old woar out dog? You know whats in that dog its 1st knowing. 1st knowing and the old ways from back befor the clevverness. Thats all new to us tho innit. Becaws weve never had it yet. So that dog is dubbl blipful. Its the old going out plus its the new coming in and that new is old old 1st knowing. Took by 1 of ours.

Theres my tel
Keap you wel

Every body looking at me agen. I cud stil hear them words in my ears: 'Took by 1 of ours.' Lorna looking at me as wel. That wer when I begun to feal like the dog wernt no where near the end of it. I begun to feal like peopl wer looking to me for some thing mor.

We gone back to the divvy roof then. I skint the dog and we roastit then every 1 et some of it. 'Telling for us and walking with us,' Lorna said. When I had that old leader on his back to make the long cut down the middl his front legs wer like out stretcht arms it took me strange to see that.

Aftrwds I skint the head as wel. I had in mynd to sew the head and body skin to gether and make a hood. I wer going to take the teef out of the skul and dril hoals in them and put them all roun the face hoal of the hood. I never did get to do any of that tho.

5

After that tel that nite every 1 begun to look at me diffrent.
Winking and like dodging ther heads or giving me the thums
up syn. Even Straiter Empy. I said to Lorna, 'Im begining to
feal like youve put some thing on me only I dont know what it
is.'

She said, 'Ive put some thing on you have I. Be that Truth?
Aint there some thing without me putting it on you? Some
thing coming to you? Like a far thing come close?'

Wel she had me there I cudnt say no becaws I did have that
in my mynd. The far come close took by the littl come big.
Dint realy know what that far come close myt be I wer
waiting for it to show its self.

Nex morning after the berning the Bernt Arse Pack follert
us the woal way from How Fents to Widders Dump. New
leader he wer all black and when ever I lookit back he had his
head up and looking at me with his ears prickt up. Driffing
closer like he wer looking for a staytmen from me only he
dint know if I knowit so he stayd out of bow shot.

When we got to the digging there wer the girt big thing
what kilt Dad it wer stil in the hoal where we lef it. Chalker
Marchman the 1stman of the digging he wer talking to a littl
nothing looking witey bloak dint look no moren 10 years old.
It wernt the shortness of him I aint a tall man my self but this
1 he lookit like his dad pult out too soon when they ben
making him. Witey hair and pinky eyes nor you cudnt see his
eye brows they wer that lite. Dint even have the beginnings
of a beard.

When we come up to them Chalker Marchman poynting to
the girt big thing he said to Straiter Empy, 'You can put a

26

crew to busting this wewl melt it down like all ways.'

Straiter lookit to me and I lookit to him and we boath lookit at that girt big thing what ben the death of my dad becaws they wantit it out of the hoal in tack.

Straiter said, 'Bus it up?'

The littl witey bloak said, 'Thats right. This aint Eusas head it aint no good to us.' He said it like you do when the other bloak dont know what youre talking about becaws hes out of it. Pressurs littl barset I thot. I dint have no idear what he meant by 'Eusas head'.

When the littl witey bloak talkit Straiter dint look at him he lookit to Chalker Marchman. Chalker said, 'Bes get on with it. This heres Belnot Phist from the Mincery.'

So we got on with it. Chalker tol us Belnot Phist wernt 10 he wer 16 so at leas he wernt a kid. That dint make it no easyer taking do its from him tho. You cud see he knowit too and it thrilt him. All the time busting up that big thing I wer thinking how my dad dyd so that littl nothing bloak cud look at it and say he dint want it becaws it wernt Eusas head. We droppt the buster on it then we finisht up with han hammers. It were ful of stoany muck and rottin iron weals and gears it wer mor earf and stoan nor iron I never did fynd out what it wer. Jus 1 mor thing to make us feal stupid. Hammering and breaving in old rottin iron and thinking on Belnot Phist and Eusas head.

Belnot Phist wer stopping on at Widders Dump. That same day he put a crew to cutting timber for a new projeck of his. It wer going to be some kynd of a working. Where they gone for the timber it ben a special place of myn. Where the old track sydls the hy groun sholder. It wer woodit with oak there. Hy groun on 1 side of the track and on the other it sloaps off sharp tords Widders Dump. The track runs pas that holler they call Mr Clevvers Roaling Place it wer the track we all ways took going to and from the form. It wer the shape of the groun I liket and the feal of it. That fealing you get on hy groun over looking the low. Some times sydling that sholder youwd see crows be low you cruising. Looking down from there at Widders Dump it seamt so low and littl it lookit easy ternt a way from. Back then I never 1ce ben on that hy groun sholder oansome. Never ben any where at all oansome. Never in my woal life put foot outside a fents without at leas 5 mor for dog safe. I ben saving up that hy groun in my mynd tho. Thinking may be some time there myt come a time Iwd chance it oansome. I dint want no woodlings cleart there I jus wantit that place lef the way it ben. I tol my self never mynd but I myndit.

That day who ternt up at Widders Dump it wer the Big 2 down from the Ram. Abel Goodparley & Erny Orfing the Pry Mincer & the Wes Mincer they all ready ben Shorsday Week with the sess men which they revver newit the fraction for the Ram and done a show. They wernt dew agen til Rising but here they wer. 1 of ther sir prize visits they done that every now and then. We wer busting iron in the hoal and here they come a riving. Goodparley & Orfing the Big 2 when they pult in some where they dint tern up like outpaths and lorn in the worl. They roadit with 50 hevvys and 6 road crowd from the las place plus they had pigeons 1 to be let go every place they lef safe. Them 6 exter road crowd you myswel call them hossages the Big 2 dint realy trus no 1 too far nyther fents nor form. My dad use to tel me his dad tol him the Goodparley & Orfing they had in his day (Roadman Goodparley & Fronter Orfing it ben) they never roadit with no Ram hevvys they jus only had 6 road crowd for dog safe from the las fents like any 1 wud. That Goodparley & Orfing back then they use to say, 'It dont make no odds what happens to us therewl all ways be a nother Goodparley & Orfing.' These 2 tho they wernt taking no chances they wer doing ther bes to keap it the same Goodparley & Orfing.

Being the Big 2 they only done ther 4 shows a year regler plus special 1s now and then but they liket to look like ful time Eusa show men they kep ther faces shavit and all. Orfing the littl 1 he carrit the fit up and Goodparley the big 1 he carrit the weapons the same as regler Eusa show partners done even tho they cudve had the hevvys carry the fit up and the weapons and them as wel. Goodparley had a big face with littl eyes like lookouts looking over the top of a fents and he wer all ways smyling with his big sqware teef. Orfing had a face like a limpit.

Befor we lef Widders Dump that day there come word to us as Goodparley & Orfing wud be over to How Fents after meat. To put the scar on me and they wer going to do a show as wel. Befor I get to that I bes write out the *Eusa Story* the same as it ben wrote out 1st and past on down to us. Its all ways wrote down in the old spel. Every body knows bits and peaces of it but the connexion men and the Eusa show men they all have the woal thing wrote down the same and they have to know all of it by hart. You wunt have seen the woal thing wrote out without you ben a Eusa show man or connexion man or in the Mincery. No 1 else is allowit to have it wrote down the same which that dont make no odds becaws no 1 else knows how to read.

It wants to start a new peace of paper with a number to its self. So like the former said when he foun a ewe in his doss bag:

'Please tern over.'

29

6

The Eusa Story

1. Wen Mr Clevver wuz Big Man uv Inland thay had evere thing clevver. Thay had boats in the ayr & picters on the win & evere thing lyk that. Eusa wuz a noing man vere qwik he cud tern his han tu enne thing. He wuz werkin for Mr Clevver wen thayr cum enemes aul roun & maykin Warr. Eusa sed tu Mr Clevver, Now wewl nead masheans uv Warr. Wewl nead boats that go on the water & boats that go in the ayr as wel & wewl nead Berstin Fyr.

2. Mr Clevver sed tu Eusa, Thayr ar tu menne agenst us this tym we mus du betteren that. We keap fytin aul thees Warrs wy doan we jus du 1 Big 1. Eusa sed, Wayr du I fyn that No.? Wayr du I fyn that 1 Big 1? Mr Clevver sed, Yu mus fyn the Littl Shynin Man the Addom he runs in the wud.

3. Eusa sed, Thayr int aul that much wud roun hear its mosly iyrn its mosly stoan. Mr Clevver sed, Yu mus fyn the wud in the hart uv the stoan & yu wil fyn it by the dansing in the stoan & thay partickler traks.

4. Eusa wuz a noing man he noet how tu bigger the smaul & he noet how tu smauler the big. He noet the doar uv the stoan & thay partickler traks. He smaulert his self down tu it he gon in tu particklers uv it. He tuk 2 grayt dogs with him thear nayms wer Folleree & Folleroo. Eusa ternt them luce he put them tu the stoan & castin for partickler traks & tu the dansing.

5. Foun the syn uv dansing on partickler traks thay dogs &

follert harkin 1 tu the uther hot & clikkin & countin thay gygers & thay menne cools uv stoan. Smauler & smauler thay groan with Eusa in tu the hart uv the stoan hart uv the dans. Evere thing blippin & bleapin & movin in the shiftin uv thay Nos. Sum tyms bytin sum tyms bit.

6. Cum tu the wud in the hart uv the stoan. The stoan sky gone dark the stoan win gon stil. Thay dogs gon crinje then & wimpert. Eusa sed tu thay dogs, Garn the trak & fyn.

7. Thay dogs stud up on thear hyn legs & taukin lyk men. Folleree sed, Lukin for the 1 yu wil aul ways fyn thay 2. Folleroo sed, Thay 2 is 2ce as bad as the 1. Eusa sed, I woan be tol by amminals. He beat thay dogs & on thay gon.

8. In the dark wud Eusa seen a trak uv lyt he follert it. He cum tu the Hart uv the Wud it wuz the Stag uv the Wud it wuz the 12 Poynt Stag stud tu fays him & stampin its feat. On the stags hed stud the Littl Shynin Man the Addom in be twean thay horns with arms owt strecht & each han holdin tu a horn.

9. Eusa sed tu the Littl Man, Yu mus be the Addom then. The Littl Man sed, I mus be wut I mus be. Eusa wuz angre then he wuz in rayj becaus he had a shutin weppn but the Littl Man wun even cover his self. He stud nekkit with his arms owt strecht be twean thay horns.

10. Eusa tuk his weppn in his han he sed tu the stag, Wy doan yu run? Yu no wut I am goin tu du. The stag sed, Eusa yu ar talkin tu the Hart uv the Wud. Nuthing wil run frum yu enne mor but tym tu cum & yu wil run frum evere thing.

11. Eusa shutin the Stag with his weppn & down it cum. Eusa grabbit the Littl Man by his 2 owt strecht arms & holdin him lyk twichin for water with a hayzel.

12. Eusa sed tu the Littl Man the Addom, I nead tu no the No. uv the 1 Big 1 & yu mus tel me it. The Littl Man the Addom he sed, Yu du no it Eusa its in yu the saym as its in

31

me. Eusa sed, I doan no it yu mus tel it tu me. The Littl Man sed, Eusa yu no wut that 1 Big 1 is its the No. uv thay Master Chaynjis I doan hav no werd tu tel it. Eusa sed, If yu woan tel in 1 may be yul tel in 2. Eusa wuz pulin on the Littl Mans owt strecht arms. The Littl Man sed, Eusa yu ar pulin me a part. Eusa sed, Tel.

13. Eusa wuz angre he wuz in rayj & he kep pulin on the Littl Man the Addoms owt strecht arms. The Littl Man the Addom he begun tu cum a part he cryd, I wan tu go I wan tu stay. Eusa sed, Tel mor. The Addom sed, I wan tu dark I wan tu lyt I wan tu day I wan tu nyt. Eusa sed, Tel mor. The Addom sed, I wan tu woman I wan tu man. Eusa sed, Tel mor. The Addom sed, I wan tu plus I wan tu minus I wan tu big I wan tu littl I wan tu au! I wan tu nuthing.

14. Eusa sed, Stop ryt thayr thats the No. I wan. I wan that aul or nuthing No. The Littl Man the Addom he cudn stop tho. He wuz ded. Pult in 2 lyk he wuz a chikken. Eusa screamt he felt lyk his oan bele ben pult in 2 & evere thing rushin owt uv him.

15. Owt uv thay 2 peaces uv the Littl Shynin Man the Addom thayr cum shyningnes in wayvs in spredin circels. Wivverin & wayverin & humin with a hy soun. Lytin up the dark wud. Eusa seen the Littl 1 goin roun & roun insyd the Big 1 & the Big 1 humin roun insyd the Littl 1. He seen thay Master Chaynjis uv the 1 Big 1. Qwik then he riten down thay Nos. uv them.

16. Thay dogs howlt & a win cum up. Thay ded leavs wirlt & rattelin lyk ded birds flyin. Thay grayt dogs stud on thear hyn legs & talkin lyk men agen. Thay sed, Eusa aul thay menne leavs as rattelt thats how menne peapl yu wil kil. Then thay dogs begun tu tel uv tym tu cum. Thay sed, The lan wil dy & thay peapl wil eat 1 a nuther. The water wil be poysen & the peapl wil drink blud.

17. Eusa kilt boath dogs he shot them ded. The shynin &

the lyt gone owt the wud gon darker nor the darkes nyt. Eusa cudn see nuthing he stumelt owt uv the wud & tu the stoan & owt agen nor never lukt behyn him.

18. Eusa had thay Nos. uv thay Master Chaynjis. He run them thru the Power Ring he mayd the 1 Big 1. Eusa put the 1 Big 1 in barms then him & Mr Clevver droppit so much barms thay kilt as menne uv thear oan as thay kilt enemes. Thay wun the Warr but the lan wuz poyzen frum it the ayr & water as wel. Peapl din jus dy in the Warr thay kep dyin after it wuz over. Mr Clevver din cayr it wuz aul the saym tu him poyzen wuz meat & drink tu him he wuz that hard. Eusa with his wyf & 2 littl suns gon lukin for a nuther plays tu liv.

19. Evere thing wuz blak & rottin. Ded peapl & pigs eatin them & thay pigs dyd. Dog paks after peapl & peapl after dogs tu eat them the saym. Smoak goin up frum bernin evere wayr. Eusa with his famile gon tu the cappn uv a boat & Eusa giv him munne tu tayk them a way. The cappn sed, Munne is no gud enne mor. Eusa thot he lookit lyk the Littl Shynin Man he wuzn shur tho. Thayr wer hevve men on the boat thay tuk Eusas wyf thay thru Eusa & his 2 littl boys off. Eusa stanin on the shor wachin that boat pul a way with his wyf & nuthing he cud du.

20. Bad Tym it wuz then. Peapl din no if they wud be alyv 1 day tu the nex. Din even no if thayd be alyv 1 min tu the nex. Sum stuk tu gether sum din. Sum tyms thay dru lots. Sum got et so uthers cud liv. Cudn be shur uv nuthing din no wut wuz sayf tu eat or drink & tryin tu keap wyd uv uther forajers & dogs it wuz nuthing onle Luck if enne 1 stayd alyv.

21. Eusa & his boys on thear oan thay wernt with enne 1 els. Eusa wun go near no uthers he wuz afeard if enne 1 myt no him. Eusa dursn sleap much thay boys wer tu littl tu stan gard long. Mosly Eusa jus closd his iys a littl at a tym nevver long. He din lyk tu sleap much enne how he wuz

afeard he myt pul his self in 2 lyk he dun the Littl Shynin Man. Plus menne tyms he seen 2 grayt dogs on thear trak he din wan tu get snuck by them.

22. 1 day Eusa wuz holt up in a barmt owt plays by the rivvr. He wuz so tyrd he tol his 2 littl boys tu keap luk owt & he closd his iys. Eusa herd a sylens then lyk his ears closd up. He opend his iys he thot he wuz dreamin. He seen the Littl Shynin Man in 2 peaces. The Right syd uv him had the nek & hed the Left syd uv him had his cok & bauls. Each $\frac{1}{2}$ wuzn hopin on its 1 leg it wuz waukin lyk it wuz tu gether with the uther $\frac{1}{2}$. Thay 2 peaces uv the Littl Shynin Man wer waukin be twean thay 2 grayt dogs wich wer Folleree & Folleroo the saym.

23. The taukin $\frac{1}{2}$ uv the Littl Man sed tu Eusas 2 littl boys, Ar yu hungre? Thay sed, Yes. He sed, Cum with me then I wil giv yu sumthing. Off thay gon 1 with Folleree & 1 with Folleroo. 1 hedin tords the rivvr 1 a way frum it & each with $\frac{1}{2}$ uv the Littl Shynin Man.

24. Eusa sed, This is a dream. He opent up his iys but thay ben open aul redde. Eusa cudn wayk up no moren he aul redde wuz. Eusa cault thay dogs by naym he wisselt them bak but thay wun com. He cault the Littl Man but nyther $\frac{1}{2}$ wud tern roun. He cault his 2 boys thay kep goin as wel thay wun luk bak.

25. Eusa run after them as wer hedin tords the rivvr. Thay gon in tu the water & swimin acros & Eusa after them. Eusa tryd tu swim but his arms gon hevve & no strenth in his legs. He had tu tern bak then evere thing gon blak for him.

26. Eusa wuz lyn on the groun by the rivvr. Thayr apeerd tu him then the Littl Shynin Man he wuz in 1 peace. Eusa sed, Wy arn you in 2 peaces? The Littl Man sed, Eusa I am in 2 peaces. It is onle the idear uv me that cum tu gether. Yu ar lukin at the idear uv me and I am it. Eusa sed, Wut

is the idear uv yu? The Littl Man sed, It is wut it is. I aint the noing uv it Im jus onle the showing uv it.

27. The Littl Man sed, Eusa wut is the idear uv yu? Eusa cudn say enne thing. The Littl Man sed, Yu doan hav tu say wut it is. Jus say *if* it is. Eusa stil cudn say enne thing.

28. Eusa sed, Nevver myn that wayr ar my 2 littl boys? The Littl Man sed, Eusa thay gon 2 diffren ways a way frum yu. Eusa sed, Yu tuk them a way. The Littl Man sed, Wel Eusa it mayks a chaynj dunnit. Eusa sed, Wut dyu mean?

29. The Littl Man sed, Eusa yu wantit thay Master Chaynjis & this is 1 uv them. In the wud in the hart uv the stoan yu pult me in 2 yu opent me lyk a chikken. Yu let thay Nos. uv thay Master Chaynjis owt. Now yu mus go thru them aul.

30. Eusa sed, I no I dun wut I dun & I wish I hadn but Im thru with aul that now I jus wan tu liv qwyet. The Littl Man sed, Eusa yu ain thru with aul that yur onle jus beginin. Yuv got aul thay Master Chaynjis in frun uv yu. Yuv got them aul tu go thru.

31. Eusa sed, Is this a dream? The Littl Man sed, No. Eusa sed, Wuz the uther a dream then? Wen I had a wyf & childer? The Littl Man sed, No Eusa that wuzn no dream nor this ain no dream. Its aul 1 thing nor yu cant wayk up owt uv it. Eusa sed, I can dy owt uv it tho cant I. The Littl Man sed, Eusa yu dy owt uv this plays & yul jus fyn me in a nuther plays. Yul fyn me in the wud yul fyn me on the water lyk yu foun me in the stoan. Yu luk enne wayr & Iwl be thayr.

32. Eusa sed, Wuz it yu the cappn uv the boat that tuk a way my wyf? The Littl Man sed, Probly it wuz. Eusa sed, Wy cant yu leav me aloan? The Littl Man sed, Eusa wear 2 ½s uv 1 thing yu & me. I cant leav yu aloan no moren yu cud leav me aloan. I nevver cum lukin for yu did I Eusa. It wuz

yu cum lukin for me that tym wen yu kilt the Hart uv the Wud in the hart uv the stoan & yu foun me. Yu let thay Chaynjis owt & now yuv got to go on thru them.

33. Eusa sed, How menne Chaynjis ar thayr? The Littl Man sed, Yu mus no aul abowt that I seen yu rite thay Nos. down in the hart uv the wud. Eusa sed, That riting is long gon & aul thay Nos. hav gon owt uv my myn I doan remember nuthing uv them. Woan yu pleas tel me how menne Chaynjis thayr ar? The Littl Man sed, As menne as reqwyrd. Eusa sed, Reqwyrd by wut? The Littl Man sed, Reqwyrd by the idear uv yu. Eusa sed, Wut is the idear uv me? The Littl Man sed, That we doan no til yuv gon thru aul yur Chaynjis.

7

This what Im writing down now its the nite after my dads berning. The nite I took the scar.

It ben pissing down rain since befor we lef Widders Dump. I all ways liket the rain. Liket on the back track coming up to hy groun in the dark. Seeing our nite fires thru the rain and smelling the meat smel from the divvy roof.

After meat I gone up on the hy walk and looking out for Goodparley & Orfing. Lissening to the rain dumming down on my hard clof hood and thinking how itwd soun on dog skin. Persoon I heard the horn blow 'Eusa show' then the poynt hevvys come out of the rainy dark in to the lite of the gate house torches. 1 of them lookit up at me and said, 'Trubba not. Eusa show.' I never knowit Goodparley & Orfing say ther oan Trubba not they all ways sent a hevvy in front of them. I said, 'No Trubba' then I opent and in they come hevvys 1st. Goodparley & Orfing dint come thru the gate til ther oan men wer in the gate house. They wunt walk unner a gate house other whys.

Soons they come in the littl kids all come sploshing thru the puddls in the torch lite singing:

No rumpa no dum
No zantigen Eusa cum

All of them running to touch the fit up and fealing for the figgers in it. Goodparley smyling with his big sqware teef like he lovit childer and Orfing shoving them out of the way. The hevvys gone to the divvy roof all but 2 as come to my shelter with Goodparley & Orfing for the wotcher. 1st 1 hevvy gone in then the Big 2 then the other hevvy then me.

When Dad ben a live I all ways ben there when he done the wotcher. This time doing it my self and with the Big 2 not jus regler Eusa show men it took me strange. Dads things all roun the shelter. His weapons and his anrack hanging on ther pegs. His paper and ink and pens on the locker. His doss bag. Even his smel stil there. His smoak and his sweat but no Dad. The black and red spottit dog skin peggit on the wall with the 4 legs out stretcht and the candl flame shimmying in the wind.

Orfing unslung the fit up and leant it agenst the wall. Goodparley put down his weapons and we all sat down. 1 hevvy sqwatting by the door and the other stanning gard outside.

Goodparley said, 'Wotcher?'

I said, '2 cuts hash and 50 rizlas each. Our meat your meat 2ce. Eat here sleap here eat for the out path and safe crowd to the nex fents.' Not that the Big 2 ever meatit nor slep at our fents but thats what you said.

Goodparley said, 'Done.'

I give the hash and the rizlas then we all roalt up and smoakit. Smelling the rain and lissening to it dumming on the thatch. Outside the littl kids wer stil zanting in the puddls they wer singing:

> No rumpa no dum
> No zantigen Eusa cum

Goodparley said, 'Its too bad about your dad Riddley.'

I said, 'Yes it is.'

He said, 'Wel thats behynt us now innit. Now youre going to be the new connexion man and making new connexions.'

I said, 'No it aint jus behynt us its all roun us. Over and unner as wel.' That wer the hash talking.

He said, 'Wel yes every thing is innit. Now youwl be taking the scar tho and looking a head.'

I said, 'Yes theres a lot to look a head to. Like croaking iron at Widders Dump. We do the croaking and they get the iron.'

He said, 'Riddley theres other things to do as wel.'

I said, 'Yes and they all smel of cow shit dont they.'

He said, 'Riddley theres a time for every thing and the time for moving crowds is past innit. You take a crowd of 30 or 40 out foraging naminals and moving 1 place to a nother theyre using up mor groun nor 100 may be 150 living on the lan and forming it with stock and growings. You jus cant have all of Inland for your forage groun no mor.'

I said, 'Looks like we cant have none of it. Them forms ben largening in our forage groun and sqweazing us out littl by littl whynt you jus finish the job and be done with it. If our times pas whynt you just wipe us out all to gether?'

The hevvy by the door lookit over to Goodparley like asking with his eyes shud he stomp me. Orfing said to me, 'You bes not work your jaw too hard your head myt come luce all on a suddn.'

Goodparley said to Orfing, 'Hes all right Erny he jus gets easy stoand.' Then he said to me, 'I dont mynd taking a littl time with some 1 if I think theyve got the mynd for it. Riddley youre going to be taking the scar you mus know your Eusa. Dyou have *Eusa 31* in memberment?'

I said it off the same:

31. Eusa sed, Is this a dream? The Littl Man sed, No. Eusa sed, Wuz the uther a dream then? Wen I had a wyf & childer? The Littl Man sed, No Eusa that wuzn no dream nor this ain no dream. Its aul 1 thing nor you cant wayk up owt uv it. Eusa sed, I can dy owt uv it tho cant I. The Littl Man sed, Eusa yu dy owt uv this plays & yul jus fyn me in a nuther plays. Yul fyn me in the wud yul fyn me on the water lyk yu foun me in the stoan. Yu luk enne wayr & Iwl be thayr.

Goodparley said, 'Wel said Riddley. Now tel me this. If Eusa cant wake up out of it then whats he got to do?'

I said, 'Wake up in to it.'

He said, 'Thats it. And if Eusa cant dy out of it then whats he got to do?'

I said, 'Live in to it.'

He said, 'Very good. And wheres he going to fynd that Littl Shyning Man?'

I said, 'In the wood or on the water or in the stoan.'

He said, 'O yes thats what it says in *Eusa 31* youve learnt it off all right. Wel what about it then? Youve seen stoans and wood and water. Have you seen that Littl Shyning Man?'

I said, 'How dyou mean that?'

He said, 'I mean it like I say it. With your eyes. Have you seen that Littl Shyning Man in the wood or on the water or in the stoan?'

I said, 'No.'

He said, 'Ben looking for him have you?'

I said, 'No.'

He said, 'Why not? Wunt you be interstit to see him? See if hes in 1 peace or 2 or what ever?'

I said, 'I dont know how youre asking that.'

He said, 'Im asking strait.'

I said, 'The Littl Shyning Man aint nothing Iwd look for. Not with my eyes any how.'

Goodparley said, 'You dont think hes nothing real do you. You dont think hes nothing only a idear.'

I said, 'Do you?'

He said, 'Riddley what if I tol you Im looking for that Littl Shyning Man. Looking for him to put him to gether. Wud you call that good or bad?'

I said, 'Good.'

Goodparley said to Orfing, 'You see what I mean Erny? Every body wants it put to gether. You ask any 1 theywl say the same thing its the naturel way to feal.'

Orfing said, 'He aint talking on the same Littl Shyning Man as you and wel you know it.'

Goodparley said, 'Theres jus only the 1 Littl Shyning Man and wel *you* know it Erny. It dont matter what you think youre talking on he is what he is. His self he never claimt he wer the knowing of it he jus only said he wer the showing of it.'

'Which is blip,' said Orfing. 'Like Ive all ways said.'

'Which is blip and moren that its realness and all,' said Goodparley.

Orfing said, 'Hes realness right a nuff but he wont never be your kynd of realness Abel. He aint nothing you can dig up like old iron he wernt never meant to be that.'

Goodparley said, 'Now weare coming to the curse roads of it Erny now weare getting down to terpitation. Youre the man for that are you. Youre the man for what it all means.'

Orfing said, 'Yes Im the man for what it all means any body is as looks at whats there nor dont look at what aint there. What the Littl Shyning Man is hes jus what ever cant never be put to gether. There aint no moren that to it nor you cant make it be mor. Any thing as *can* be put to gether aint the Littl Shyning Man its some thing else.' The hash musve had him perwel lucent up I never heard him say that much befor.

Goodparley said, 'Erny youre such a downer youre going to down your self right in to the groun 1 day. You can say what you like Im saying wewl get it put to gether weve got it all in front of us and going to make it happen. Youre looking sideways but Im looking frontways and going to get every body moving that way form and fents boath. I dint come Big 2 to stan in the mud and sing for boats in the air. Weare going to do things here weare going to get things moving.'

It soundit to me like the 2 of them wer each 1 talking to his self not to the other I dint realy want to get mixt in with it. I jus kep shut.

Goodparley looking over to me then he said, 'Riddley dyou think Im stupid?'

I said, 'Why wud I think that?'

He said, 'I dont know. Becaws Ive got littl eyes and I smyl too much. Becaws youre yung. Wel never mynd. You mus be getting perwel tiret of us 2 sitting here and moufing Mincery binses back and forth you mus be boart to death with it. Persoon you wont even want to be no connexion man you wont want no part of all that foolishness.'

I said, 'O yes I wil Im on for it.'

He said, 'You want that scar do you. Want to be connexion man and foller on your dad.'

I said, 'I myt as wel keap it going down the line.'

He said, 'Why keap it going? You think its some thing good?'

I said, 'I dont know I never thot on that part of it. Its what my dad done and Iwl do it and all.'

He said, 'Yes why not. Riddley wud you tel me if you thot I *wer* stupid?'

I said, 'If you askit me.'

He said, 'Yes I beleave you wud. Wel all right les put that scar on you and get you startit doing your connexions.'

We gone to the divvy roof then for the scar take. Torches berning and the woal crowd there. Befor we done it Goodparley & Orfing fittit up for the show what theywd be doing right after. The show Iwd be watching with a new scar on my belly and thinking on my 1st connexion.

Lorna Elswint up front with us for letting the blood and cutting in the scar. Goodparley and me stript off down to our trowsers and stood facing each other with all the crowd looking on. I had to stan on some fire wood so my belly wud be hy a nuff. Orfing stanning nex to me to tel me what to say.

I said to Goodparley, 'Wheres Eusa?'

He said, 'In my belly. Fear belly and brave belly. Hot and col. Emty and ful.'

I said, 'Wheres his mark?'

He said, 'On me from a nother on him from a nother. You asking for that mark?'

I said, 'Im asking for that mark.'

He said, 'How wil they know it when its on you?'

I said, 'Its on me to make it knowt.'

Lorna Elswint took her neadl and let some blood out of Goodparleys right arm and smeart it on his scar.

Goodparley said, 'My belly to your belly and your belly to Eusa.' He shovit his hairy belly agenst me so hard the fire wood I wer stood on gone slyding and I had to grab him not to fall down.

He said, 'Take that for a blip.'

I steppt back with his E pirntit in his blood on the right side of me. 3 stroaks for Eusa:

Which ever way you pirnt it on its never backards.

Lorna took the knife and cut it in me. Then she prest the clay in to it and she tyd the wrappings roun. Then I cudnt see them 3 stroaks I cud feal them tho. Tharbing a littl and I thot of them like 3 moufs on me and waiting to say some thing. Waiting to say my 1st connexion after I seen the Eusa show.

8

Goodparley & Orfing had a red and black stripet fit up it ben stanning there ready to go and littl kids creeping in and out of it wylst we ben doing the scar take. Orfing cleart the kids out he tol them ther heads wud tern to wood if they dint come out of it qwick. He all ways said the same thing trying to be joaky. The kids knowit he parbly wudve knockit ther heads to gether if there hadnt ben no other groan ups looking on thats why they liket giving him bother.

Goodparley give me the nod and I stood up for the show talk. Same as my dad in his time and his dad befor him.

I said, 'Weare going aint we.'

The crowd said, 'Yes weare going.'

I said, 'Down that road with Eusa.'

They said, 'Time and reqwyrt.'

I said, 'Where them Chaynjis take us.'

They said, 'He done his time wewl do our time.'

I said, 'Hes doing it for us.'

They said, 'Weare doing it for him.'

I said, 'Keap it going. Chances this time.'

They said, 'Chances nex time.'

I said, 'New chance every time.'

They said, 'New chance every time.'

I sat down then. Goodparley inside the fit up. Orfing stanning by for the patter. Looking at the fit up. Nothing to see only the red back clof with black smoak and arnge flames paintit on it and the emty space where Eusa wud come up.

Orfing gone close to the fit up and talking to the lower part where Eusa wer inside readying to show nor you cudnt see him yet. He said, 'Trubba not.'

Eusas voyce from down inside said, 'No Trubba.'

Orfing said, 'Wel if there aint no Trubba whynt you come up where we can see you?'

Eusas voyce (which it wer all ways a low and sorrerful kynd of voyce even them times when you myt think Eusa myt be jollyer nor other times) said, 'It dont make no diffrents if I come up or not you cant see me any how.'

Orfing said, 'Why cant we see you?'

Eusas voyce said, 'Becaws the main part of me aint where you can see it.'

Orfing said, 'Eusa no body wants to see the main part of you we jus want you to come up and do a show.'

Eusas voyce said, 'Thats a larf innit. How can I do a show if I cant show the main part of me?'

Orfing said, 'Eusa what is that main part you keap talking on?'

Eusas voyce said, 'Its that same part what I do my bes work with innit.'

Orfing said, 'Wel Eusa its the same with all us bloaks we all do our bes work with that same part dont we.'

Eusas voyce said, 'You dont or you wunt be talking so stupid. Its my head Im talking about thats my main part.'

Orfing said, 'Eusa be you saying its your head we cant see?'

Eusas voyce said, 'Thats what I ben saying.'

Orfing said, 'Why not? Why cant we see your head?'

Eusas voyce said, 'Becaws its burrit in the groun thats why.'

Orfing said, 'Eusa this aint no time to stick your head in the groun weve got work to do weve got a show to do.'

Eusas voyce said, 'Orfing you aint very qwick are you I cud get better patter peeing agenst a wall. I aint stuck my acturel head in the groun nor I aint talking on the head Im talking with.'

Orfing said, 'What head be you talking on then Eusa?'

Eusas voyce said, 'When I say my head its jus a way of saying. Only its over your head innit. May be your heads the 1 whats burrit in the groun.'

45

Orfing said, 'Eusa wunt it make life easyer all roun if you jus come up and done your show?'

Eusas voyce said, 'Thats your Trubba Orfing you keap looking for a easy life you wont move nothing frontways that way.'

Eusa come up then slow and scanful like all ways terning his woodin head this way and that and his paintit eyes taking us all in. Many and manys the time Id lookit back at them staring blue eyes. Since back befor I cud member it even. Only this time it seamt like it wer the 1st time I wer seeing him and I wer afeart of him. The way he kep terning his head it made me think of that thing with no name looking out thru our eye hoals.

Orfing said, 'Wel Eusa if youre ready to show then I can sit down now.'

Eusa said, 'Yes Im ready to show and Iwl tel you this aint no made up show this time its all trufax from the Mincery and ben wrote down the same.'

Orfing said, 'Trufax is it. This heres going to be the parper stablisht men story is it.'

Eusa said, 'Thats what its going to be right a nuff.'

Orfing said, 'May be I bes stan up then.'

Eusa said, 'You bes sit down Orfing dont give me no inner fearents.'

Orfing sat down then.

Eusa lookit roun on all of us agen. He said, 'This here what youre going to see it happent time back way back when I workit for Mr Clevver.'

Orfing said, 'O that ben ever so far back. Long time long time 1000s and 1000s ever so many. You wunt do nothing like that now you wunt bring on no Bad Time agen wud you.'

Eusa said, 'You can res your mouf now Erny we dont nead no mor patter Im showing now.'

Orfing said, 'Yes you are youre showing right a nuff. Wel carry on Eusa I wont say no mor.'

Eusa said, 'Right you are and let that be the las of it.'

Orfing dont say nothing mor.

Eusa says to us, 'This is time back way back like I said.' He goes down and he comes up with paper and pen and ink and a measuring stick and a triangl. Hes writing writing hes numbering hes drawing lines all over that paper. Hes thinking hard hes mummering to his self then hes scratching his head and hes thinking some mor. He groans a littl then he says, 'All these here numbers and that its all too much to keap in 1 head and programming my self. What I nead is a nother head and bigger so it can do some of this hevvy head work for me.'

Eusa does down agen and hes clanging and banging hes huffing and puffing and hammering it souns like hes bellering up a reddying fire and hes beating some thing on a hanvil.

Persoon Eusa comes up agen this time hes got like a iron hat on his head. 2 long wires coming out of the top of the hat and littl pegs on the ends of the wires. Plus theres a cranking handl on the side of the iron hat. Eusas trying to shif some kynd of a box its biggern he is. He gets the box heavit up on to the show board. He says, 'Hoo! Thats a hevvy 1.' Theres a cranking handl on the side of the box as the 1 on Eusas hat. 2 littl hoals and a slot in the top of the box and a nother slot in 1 end of it.

Eusa says, '2 heads are bettern 1.' He takes them 2 wires coming out of his hat and he pegs them in to the hoals in the box. He says, 'Now Iwl jus input a few littl things in to my No. 2 head.' Hes terning that crank on his iron hat. Rrrrrrrrrrrr.

Eusa says, 'Now les see if it works.' He takes a peace of paper and he says out loud what hes writing on it: 'Whats my name?' He puts the peace of paper in the slot in the top of the box he says, 'Now les see if you can anser that.'

Eusa terns the crank on the side of the box and a peace of paper comes out of the slot in the end of the box. Theres writing on the paper. Eusa reads it out: *'My name is Eusa.'*

Eusa says, 'Thats the ticket.' Hes terning the crank on his iron hat some mor then. Hes inputting all kynds of knowing out of his head in to the box.

Mr Clevver comes up and hes watching Eusa and lissening to him. Eusas mummeling all kynds of numbers and formlers it souns like hes inputting all the knowing there ever ben in the woal worl out of his head in to that box. Hes saying the Nos. of the rain bow and the fire qwanter hes saying the smallering Nos. and the biggering Nos. plus it souns like hes saying some thing about the 1 Big 1. Mr Clevver hes leaning closer and closer hes lissening lissening.

Mr Clevver he says to Eusa, 'Thats a guvner lot of knowing youre inputting in to that box parbly theres knowing a nuff in there for any kynd of thing.'

Eusa says, 'Thats about it. I dont think theres many things you cudnt do with that knowing. You cud do any thing at all you cud make boats in the air or you cud blow the worl a part.'

Mr Clevver says, 'Scatter my datter that cernly is inter-sting. Eusa tel me some thing tho. Whyd you input all that knowing out of your head in to that box? Whynt you keap it in your head wunt it be safer there?'

Eusa says, 'Wel you see I cant jus keap this knowing in my head Ive got things to do with it Ive got to work it a roun. Ive got to work the E qwations and the low cations Ive got to comb the nations of it. Which I cant do all that oansome in my head thats why I nead this box its going to do the hevvy head work for my new projeck.'

Mr Clevver says, 'What is that new projeck of yours then Eusa?'

Eusa says, 'Good Time.'

Mr Clevver says, 'Eusa did I hear you say Good Time with a guvner G and a guvner T?'

Eusa says, 'Thats what I said and thats how I said it. Good Time which I mean every thing good and every body happy and teckernogical progers moving every thing frontways farther and farther all the time. You name it wewl do it. Pas the sarvering gallack seas and all that.'

Mr Clevver says, 'Youve got all that in that box have you?'

Eusa says, 'You myt say Ive got the nuts and balls of it in that box which is my No. 2 head but Ive got the master progam in my regler head which is the 1 on my sholders.'

Mr Clevver says, 'Wel Eusa youre a parper wunner you are. Im realy looking forit to having that Good Time seakert yes I am.'

Eusa says, 'O no Mr Clevver this aint no seakert nor it aint jus for you its Good Time for every body.'

Mr Clevver says, 'You mus be joaking Eusa who dyou think youre working for.' With that he takes holt of the cranking handl on Eusas iron hat which the hat is stil on Eusas head and the wires peggit in to the box. Rrrrrrrrrr. Mr Clevvers cranking that handl 10 times fastern Eusa ever done.

When Mr Clevver finely leaves off cranking you can see Eusas perwel woar out. Mr Clevver he says, 'Wel Eusa old son les see how much you know now. Can you tel me the Nos. of the rain bow and the fire qwanter?'

Eusa he says, 'I never heard of nothing like that Guvner.'

Mr Clevver he says, 'Wel never mynd them how about 2 plus 2 what wud that come to?'

Eusa says, 'I wunt know Guv I realy cudnt say.'

Mr Clevver says, 'Very good Eusa my boy now jus 1 mor thing. Whats your name?'

Eusa says, 'I dont know.'

Mr Clevver says, 'Thats it then Ive emtit you out right a nuff. Now Ive got the head with the knowing and youve got the head with the nothing.' He unconnects Eusas wires then he picks up the box. Says, 'Bye bye Eusa all bes' and off he goes. Eusa stanning there in his iron hat with his wires hanging down he dont have nothing to say.

Down comes the Littl Shyning Man hes hanging there in the air hes in 2 peaces. He says, 'Wel Eusa it looks like youve los your head dont it.'

Eusa says, 'I dont know what Ive los I aint very qwick.'

The Littl Shyning Man says, 'Wel Eusa you bes qwicken up fas then becaws there gone Good Time and here comes Trubba.'

Eusa says, 'It looks like you seen Trubba all ready you aint even in 1 peace.'

The Littl Man says, 'Eusa dont you know who done this to me dont you know who toar me in 2? Dont you know who opent me like a chikken time back way back in the wood in the hart of the stoan?'

Eusa says, 'How cud I know that?'

The Littl Man says, 'Becaws youre the 1 as done it.'

Eusa says, 'I dint know that Ive los it clean out of memberment.'

The Littl Man says, 'Eusa lissen to me now that dont matter. You and me weare 2 ½s of 1 thing it dont matter if you tear me a part or I tear you a part. But the 1 as tears the other a part has got to put some thing to gether nor you aint done that. Thats why Im in 2 peaces now and 2 peaces is what Iwl be in til you get your head back. Dyou know why?'

Eusa says, 'No I dont.'

The Littl Man says, 'Becaws you wont put nothing to gether til then thats why. You wont put no Good Time to gether now. Becaws Mr Clevvers going to do a Bad Time with that head of yours nor there wont be no Good Time til you get it back. Bye bye Eusa qwicken up as fas as you can the worl dont wait for no 1.'

The Littl Shyning Man goes up and Eusa goes down and it looks like thats the end of the show. Orfing jumps up then he goes over to the fit up and talking to the lower part of it like he done befor the show. He says, 'Oy! Eusa! Hang on a minim.'

Eusas voyce says:

> Eusas ben and showd
> Eusas on the road

Orfing says, 'Eusa youre getting in front of your self you aint ready to road yet you aint done with this here show.'

Eusa shoots up then he says, 'Erny youre the 1 whats getting in front of your self and going to fall over your self and all if you dont go careful. Youre getting in your oan way is what youre doing Erny.' Eusas face cant change its all ways the same but when youre watching him move a roun and lissening to what hes saying and the torch fires shimmying and all hewl look pernear any way hes talking. This time he looks like hes getting his serkits jus that little bit over loadit.

The show board is near a head hyer nor Orfing so Eusa is wel up of him. Orfing backs off a littl so he can look Eusa in the eye. He says, 'Getting in *your* way is what you mean innit Eusa?'

Eusa says, 'I dont think youwd want to do that Erny. You know youwd end up with a face ful of foot pirnts and a hart ful of sorrer.'

Orfing says, 'Eusa Ive had the boath of them this long time now and waitful for a bettering.'

Eusa says, 'Erny you aint going to stan there and weary me you aint going to boar me to death you aint going to come the hevvy staytmen are you? You dint call me back for that did you? Whatd you call me back for?'

Orfing says, 'You know why I callt you back Eusa.'

Eusa says, 'If I did I wunt be asking wud I.'

Orfing says, 'Eusa you know what the *Eusa Story* says. Every body knows it even them as cant read. It wer you as opent up the Littl Shyning Man and let the Nos. of the Master Chaynjis out.'

Eusa says, 'Yes I done that right a nuff I never said I dint.'

Orfing says, 'Plus you put the 1 Big 1 in barms dint you. It says in *Eusa 18*: "Eusa put the 1 Big 1 in barms then him & Mr Clevver droppit so much barms thay kilt as menne uv thear oan as thay kilt enemes." Yet now in this here show youre telling us it bint like that. Youre telling us you dint do none of them Bad Time things youre putting it all on Mr Clevver. Youre saying he took your knowing and he done it all. All this long time we ben beleaving it like you tol it in the *Eusa Story* and now you come on telling it woaly diffrent. What in the worl makes you think weare going to beleave a new story now?'

Eusa says, 'This aint nothing new dint I tel you this is trufax and wrote down the same at the Mincery.'

Orfing says, 'If its trufax then why you ben telling it diffrent all these years? Whyd you pick now to change your story?'

Eusa says, 'Erny youre a parper holfas aint you. You get your teef clampt down on some thing nor you wont let go you jus hol fas.'

Orfing says, 'Im jus only saying what any 1 myt say enn I. The shows are diffrent all the time thats how its meant to be. Which a show is some thing youre doing right now in this here time weare living in and youre doing the Chaynjis with Eusa. New things happening and new chances every time. Thats how its meant to be and thats how we all ways do it. But that story ben wrote time back way back nor you cant change it no 1 never ever changit the story befor this. That storys got to stay the same what ever it is and nothing changit.'

Eusa says, 'Erny whats the diffrents any how?'

Orfing says, 'What dyou mean by that?'

Eusa says, 'Whats the diffrents if I done the acturel Bad Time things my self or if I dint?'

Orfing says, 'Wel if you dint do it then it aint on you is it.'

Eusa says, 'And if it aint on me then what?'

Orfing says, 'Then youre free aint you. Nothing on you and the worl in front of you. Do what ever you like.'

Eusa says, 'There you are and said it out of your oan mouf. Which wud you rather? Have the worl in front of you and free or have some thing hevvy on your back for ever?'

Orfing says, 'Eusa it dont matter what youwd rather youve got to go by how things are. Youve got to go by whats Truth and what aint.'

Eusa says, 'Cut my froat and gard my witness if I aint telling Truth. I never made no barms nor never droppit none.'

Orfing says, 'Here we come roun agen its a fools circel. If you dint make no barms nor drop no barms then whyd you say you did when you wrote down that story? Dont cut your froat now or some 1 I know wil have a bloody finger.'

Eusa says, 'Whyd I say I did?'

Orfing says, 'Thats what I said. Whyd you say you did?'

Eusa says, 'Erny you know how it is when you blame your self.'

Orfing says, 'No I dont. How is it?'

Eusa says, 'Wel youwl oversay wont you. Youwl say wersen you realy done. What ever it myt be. Say youve lef a knife

52

where a babby gets holt of it and cuts its self. Heres the babby all bloody and youwl say, "O dear o dear o dear I done that dint I. Its on me all this blood."'

Orfing says, 'Wel it is innit. I mean if you hadnt opent up the Little Shyning Man the Addom and let out the Nos. of the Master Chaynjis of the 1 Big 1 then if you hadnt put that knowing in that box . . .'

Eusa says, 'If I hadnt some 1 else wudve done. Whyd the Hart of the Wud stan why dint it run? Whynt the Littl Shyning Man hop it whynt he vack his wayt out of there dubbl qwick 1st time he ever seen me? Iwl tel you why its part of ther game thats why. The Hart of the Wud and the Littl Shyning Man the Addom they cant live without you get the knowing of them nor you cant get the knowing of them til you kil the 1 and open up the other. Then its on you innit. Hevvy on your back for ever. Thats my las word this nite.

> Hump my load
> Down the road
> Its Eusa roading out

That wer my 1st Eusa show being connexion man. Showt by Abel Goodparley & Erny Orfing the Big 2 the Pry Mincer & the Wes Mincer on the nite I took the scar.

9

After the show they snuft the torches then every body got in littl clumps in the divvy roof hummering and mummering and getting pist. Goodparley & Orfing when theyd fittit down they drunk a littl with Straiter Empy and Flora Miltan Empys wife and his nexters and all the seanyer members which now I were 1 of them. Goodparley dint say nothing to me he dint even look at me it wer like hed los me out of memberment and tirely. Orfing dint say nothing nyther only at leas he lookit at me like he knowit I wer a live. After a littl I jus wantit my oan sylents not thers I got up and going out of the divvy roof. Goodparley finely lookit my way then like he cud acturely see me. He begun nodding his head and he said to me, 'Thats ther game you know. They cant live without you kil the 1 and open up the other. Youve got to do it its the onlyes way to keap them going.'

I noddit my head and all. Dint say nothing. Orfing put his han on my sholder and give me a littl shake frendy. I put up my hood and gone out in to the rain. Out to the fents and up on the hy walk.

Lissening to the nite and the rain. I leant my back agenst the fents and looking to the divvy roof. There hadnt ben no Trubba for a long time but we stil hadnt put no sides on it. Sit there nite after nite getting pist with 1 eye on the dark not to get snuck. Lissening to the rain dumming on my hood and looking at the candls and the nite fires in the roof and the crowd all sat there with the rainy dark all roun them. You know some times you get a fealing you dont want to put no words to.

Durster Potter that wer Nimbel Potters dad come a long the hy walk he wer on look out. He said, 'I wunt want to be out this nite.' Rain streaming down him and you cudve rung about a buckit of water out of his beard.

I said, 'You *are* out tho. You cant get no wettern you are.'

He said, 'I mean on the out side of the fents.'

I wer thinking how some fents poals and a gate make all the diffrents.

The Big 2 dint drink long jus only for the pearents of it then they roadit out. Ther hevvys come up in the gate house and on the hy walk same as when they come in.

Goodparley lookit up and seen me in the lite of the gate fires and he done some mor nodding. Orfing lookit up and raisit his han. I dint hear him say nothing but I seen his mouf move. I thot he wer saying, 'Good Luck.' Off they gone then in to the rain.

I had off nex day no digging to do only in my head for Nex Nite and my connexion. I had a nuff and moren a nuff to connect with all I had to do wer sort it out my head wer perwel humming and spinning with it.

Come the nite and stil raining. Dumming on the divvy roof and the wind blowing and spattering in every time it veert and the torch fires shimmying and smoking. Peopl shushing the kids and waiting for Straiter Empy and me to do the askings.

Straiter said, 'Eusas come to us agen. Weve lookit and weve lissent.'

I said, 'Ive lookit and Ive lissent as wel.'

He said, 'How is it with you? On or off?'

I said, 'On.'

He said, 'Is there a connexion?'

I said, 'Theres all ways a connexion.'

He said, 'Is there a reveal for this crowd?'

I said, 'Theres all ways a reveal if itwl come.'

He said, 'Is it come?'

I said, 'Yes its come. Eusas forage is our meat. Eusas pain is our gain if we look and if we lissen.'

He said, 'Tel us.' Then he sat down.

Every body looking at me waiting to hear what kynd of connexion Brooder Walkers boy wer going to do. On my belly

I cud feal them 3 stroaks pulling. Torch fires shimmying and the rain spattering in and the shadders shaking over us inside the roof. Faces all ternt to me out of bodys what lookit like wet bundels throwt down on benches and steaming in the warm. Our crowd pong rising which it wer mud and wet it wer meat smoak and sweat long soakt in to the levver and the wool and the hard clof. Suddn it comes to you: What can any body tel any body?

I said, 'All right here I am your new connexion man which Im the son of your old connexion man Brooder Walker him as ben kilt in the digging at Widders Dump for a peace of old rottin iron. Here goes my 1st connexion then.'

Befor I write down that 1st connexion I bes say a word or 2 about connexions and I myt as wel tel Truth. When my dad ben a live I all ways thot I cud do better connexions nor him when my chance come. How he done it he wud mummel slow and qwyet and start and stop with long sylents be twean and mosly his connexions wernt nothing very as citing. Every body liket them tho. They all ways gone strait to the hart of the matter plus they wer jus that littl bit else nor mos peopl wuntve thot of it qwite the same way.

Like the time back when I ben 7 or 8 when Littl Salting Fents got largent in by Dog Et Form. That ben up on Top Shoar and we ben down by Fork Stoan then in Crippel the Farn Fents. Every body heard of it tho and talking on it. Dog Et tol some cow shit story of a Outland raid from over water they said thats how Littl Salting got ther Big Man kilt plus 8 mor dead and the res of the crowd sparsit out to who ever wud take them in. In that woal story Dog Et tol there bint a word of Truth only how many dead. Every body knowit Dog Et said, 'Les largen in to gether' and Littl Salting said 'No' which then it wer arga warga for them.

Wel the Pry Mincer and the Wes Mincer done 1 of ther specials dint they. Coarse they done. My dad tol me that show over when he ben lerning me. I myt as wel tel it here then when I write down the connexion for it thatwl show his styl.

That show ben done by the same Goodparley & Orfing as done the show Ive all ready wrote down. I dont have only the las part of the patter.

Orfing says, 'Eusa when you coming up?'

Eusa says rather his voyce says, 'I dont know. Longs I stay down no 1 cant put me down.'

Orfing says, 'Eusa you dont soun very salty.'

Eusas voyce says, 'May be thats why every body ben trying to salt me.'

1st figger up aint Eusa its a bloak with a pan of salt. Hes singing a littl song to his self:

'I am the man
With salt in his pan
Every body knows I am a salty man'

Hes singing like that going backards and forit with his salt pan.

Mr Clevver comes up then. Hes stanning there watching the salting bloak and hes hummering to his self a littl. The salting bloak stops and hes looking at Mr Clevver.

Mr Clevver says, 'Salty bloak are you.'

The salting bloak says, 'I reckon Im as salty as the nex 1.'

Mr Clevver says, 'Parbly you are mos of the time. This heres a nice littl peace of shoar.'

The salting bloak says, 'O yes its a good a nuff peace of shoar.'

Mr Clevver says, 'You bes in joy it wylst you can. Have good pleasur and good measur wylst youve got it.'

The salting bloak says, 'What dyou mean? This here peace of shoar its ben myn and it all ways wil be.'

Mr Clevver says, 'You myt know whats ben but you dont know what wil be. You bes keap your eye on Eusa.'

The salting bloak says, 'What for?'

Mr Clevver says, 'Becaws hes got his eye on your peace of shoar.'

The salting bloak says, 'Wel he better take his eye off it then. Any 1 trys to move in on me wil fynd his self in Trubba. This heres my groun and Iwl stan my groun.'

Mr Clevver says, 'And Iwl stan right behynt you. Here comes Eusa now.' Mr Clevver goes down then.

Up comes Eusa leading a cow. The salting bloak is looking at him hard. Eusa looking out to 1 side all scanful.

The salting bloak says, 'Oy! Whatre you looking out for then?'

Eusa says, 'Looking out for raiders. Im worrit over this shoar.'

The salting bloak says, 'Dont you worry over this shoar. Its my groun and Im right here on it and wide a wake.'

Eusa says, 'Yes I know only Im worrit any how. Heres you oansome on the shoar with no hevvy fentses and heres me jus inlan of you. Any body gets pas you is going to be headit my way aint they. Whynt you and me largen in to gether wewl be 2ce as strong then.'

The salting bloak says, '2ce as strong but ½ as oansome. Iwl keap this shoar my self. All bes and theres the out path.'

Eusas off then and the Littl Shyning Man comes down hes in 2 peaces. He says, 'Onlyes way Iwl get put to gether is when peopl pul to gether.'

The salting bloak says, 'Whynt you pul your self to gether no 1 wil do it for you in this worl.'

The Littl Shyning Man says, 'I cant pul my self to gether.'

The salting bloak says, 'Wel I can. So Iwl stan my groun oansome.'

The Littl Shyning Man goes up out of site then Mr Clevver comes up agen. Hes jus stanning there agenst the back clof behynt the salting bloak and looking on. The salting bloak says, 'I aint worrit Iwl be snuck from the sea side its the Eusa side Im worrit about.' Hes keaping a sharp look out tords where Eusa gone off.

Wylst the salting bloak is looking that way here comes a hevvy bloak in a boat hes coming from the other side. Hes got a club in his hans and hes coming sly. He jumps out of his boat and knocks the salting bloak on the head. Down goes the salting bloak. Off goes the hevvy bloak where Eusa gone and back he comes with Eusas cow. In to the boat with the cow and the salt and a way he goes. Mr Clevver looking on the woal time he dont do nothing he dont lif a han hes jus stanning there.

The salting bloak comes up agen hes holding his head and no 1 in site only Mr Clevver. Salting bloak says to Mr Clevver, 'Why dint you help me?'

Mr Clevver says, 'I said Iwd stan behynt you and I done that.' Hes larfing then he goes off.

Eusa comes up agen hes holding his head as wel. Eusa and the salting bloak holding ther heads and looking at each other.

Eusa says to the salting bloak, 'Whats the matter with your head?'

Salting bloak says, 'It aint as hard as the club what basht me thats whats the matter with it. What about you?'

Eusa says, 'I ben basht the same plus my cow ben took off.'

Salting bloak says, 'My salt ben took as wel.'

Eusa says, 'I thot you ben on your groun and wide a wake. How come you ben snuck?'

Salting bloak says, 'I ben looking inlan and got raidit from the sea.'

Eusa says, 'I ben looking to the sea but he come roun behynt and raidit me from inlan. You cant be looking every way at 1ce when youre oansome.'

Salting bloak says, 'May be we bes largen in to gether itwl be the safes thing for boath of us.'

Eusa says, 'Iwl yes with that.'

Then Eusa and the salting bloak get fents poals and theyre largening in to gether and thats the end of the show.

Reason Ive wrote down this woal show is so I cud put in my dads reveal at the end of it. Like Ive said he tol me that show over when he ben lerning me. He ben prowd of his reveal for that 1 moren mos he done becaws for 1ce the crowd movit on his words.

Goodparley & Orfing when they done that show Ive jus wrote down they fittit down and off they gone like all ways. Nex day come and Nex Nite in its tern and our woal crowd with Littl Salting on its mynd and craving for how Dad wud connect that cow shit show. Dad he dint keap them waiting all nite for his reveal he let them get back to ther drinking early. When he gone up front for his connexion he scratcht his head and coft a littl and lookit a roun and like $\frac{1}{2}$ smylt then he jus said, 'Wel you know there it is. A littl salting and no saver.'

He dint say no moren that. The crowd $\frac{1}{2}$ of them larft out and $\frac{1}{2}$ of them syd deap. Nex day our Big Man which it ben Jack 1stfynd then not Straiter Empy he callit the crowd to gether to talk summit. Nex thing we done we pult out of Crippel the Farn and come up to How Fents which ben stanning emty. Reason we done it wer Hoggem Form they wer right nex to us at Crippel the Farn they had the same look in ther eye as Dog Et had befor they swallert Littl Salting.

Getting back now to my 1st connexion I dint want no 1 to think I wer trying to be a nother Brooder Walker nor I dint want to come on with nothing flash. I had in mynd to take it slow and make it solid. Put 1 thot to a nother like ring poals in poal hoals and holders to ring poals and rafters to holders and the reveal on top of it all like thatch. So you cud all ways go back from the reveal and get a good look at how the woal thing ben bilt and that wer going to be the Riddley Walker styl.

There ben a nuff and moren a nuff to connect with I dint jus only have the front patter and the show I had all that what Goodparley & Orfing said at the wotcher plus all that exter patter after the show. I ben wunnering if may be Orfing ben butting heads with the Ram with some of that patter. Wunnering if he ben doing it for me to use some way. Any how I wernt going to wayst it.

My dad use to tel me, 'Dont look for your reveal til its ben.' He all ways put his self parper ready for Nex Nite but he claimt he never acturely knowit what he wer going to say til he heard the words coming out of his mouf. Wel I wunt chance that on my 1st connexion I wantit to know where I wer going so I cud make sure I got there. So I had my reveal ready when I stood up for my connexion. I wer going to come down strong on what Eusa said after the show. That about getting the hevvyness off his back. I wer going to end up with: 'The man as got the hevvyness took off him wer ready to take on some mor.'

I startit out slow. I said, 'Las nite wylst they ben doing the front patter when Eusa hadnt come up yet I ben looking at the back clof. There it is you seen it so many times may be you dont even noatis it no mor. Smoak and flames paintit on it. When Eusa comes up hes got smoak and flames behynt him same as that 1st Eusa him as wrote the *Eusa Story*. Weve all of us got smoak and flames behynt us thats why theyre paintit on the back clof. To keap all that in memberment. So les not lose it out of memberment in this connexion.'

Going on like that I wer and the rain stil dumming on the thatch the same when there begun a crackeling and like a roaring in the air or in my head I dint know which. Such a bigness of it. I kep talking like I ben doing but I wernt thinking on what I wer saying I wer thinking on Eusa how he come up all slow and scanful and terning his head this way and that. I wer seeing him and afeart he myt start biggering up and bigger bigger. I had to tel my self he wernt nothing only a woodin head on Goodparleys finger. Mynd you there wernt no Eusa figger for me to see. Goodparley & Orfing ben gone since the day befor and all the figgers in ther fit up with them. Nor I wernt dreaming nor I hadnt ben smoaking I wernt acturely seeing Eusas head it wer jus *there* for me I cant say plainer nor that. Which it wunt stop getting bigger I cud smel the wood and the paint of it and the finger hoal so big it wer over all of us as big as the roof. Such a blackness. Not jus over us and all roun it wer coming up inside me as wel. Not jus wood and paint I smelt the blood and boan the redness in the black. The thot come to me: EUSAS HEAD IS DREAMING US.

1ce I said that I knowit there wer a many in it only I had to wait for the diffrent shapes of it to shif a part so I cud work be twean. Which they done then I did work in be twean and seen the shapes of it. I wer going to tel the shapes but that seamt foolish all I had to do wer show them when they movit pas. Which I done I poyntit to each 1 the woal thing wer as plain. I dint even bother to say it to my self I knowit I cudnt lose it out of memberment.

When I lookit agen it wernt there. I thot: At leas it ben all ready showit. I lookit roun and every body looking at me. I said, 'At leas it ben all ready showit.'

They all said, 'What ben showit?'

I said, 'You know. The shapes of EUSAS HEAD IS DREAMING US.'

Some said, 'You never.' Others said, 'Whats that?'

I said, 'That ben my woal reveal.'

They all said, 'You never spoak it out you jus ben stanning there and we ben waiting.'

I said, 'What ben the las thing I said?'

They said, 'About the back clof.'

I said, 'Wel you all know its Eusas head is dreaming us.'

They said, 'No. Be that your reveal?'

I said, 'The shapes of it. What I showit.'

They said, 'You never.'

Lorna Elswint said, 'You done a trants reveal. Only it let you out too soon. Parbly you lookit 2ce when you only shudve lookit 1ce. Aint no use talking about it it wants keaping qwyet til it joyns up with the res of its self if it ever does.'

So every 1 wer lef hanging. Me and all. My 1st connexion.

10

Nex morning when I 1st come a wake I wer $\frac{1}{2}$ thinking may be it ben a dream. Like when some thing harbel happens in a dream then you wake up and it aint nothing only a dream what a releaf. But when I woak up all the way there it wer and no dream. Not that it wer all that harbel it wernt nothing only I ben took strange in my very 1st connexion but I fealt like my Luck gone from me. I fealt like I rathert not come a wake that day.

I wer a wake tho so I stuck my head outside. Sky all hevvy and grey. Nothing moving no wind jus all col and stil. Littl Nimbel Potter and that lot waiting for a site of me and singing:

> 'Riddley Walker wernt no talker
> Dint know what to say
> Put his head up on a poal
> And then it tol all day'

Wel you know 1ce the kids start singing at you thats a cern kynd of track youre on nor there aint too much you can do about it. Making the kids stop singing wont help its too late by then youve jus got to clinch your teef and get on with it.

In the divvy roof at breakfas I wer sat at the top tabel which I only ben sitting there since I took the scar I wernt all that use to it. I had Lorna on 1 side of me and Fister Crunchman on the other side. Him what I ben on the weal with that morning when my dad got kilt. Girt big red hairt bloak 1 of Empys nexters he lookit jus like his name he lookit like he cud bus rocks with his bare hans and walk thru fentses without noatising. Lorna wer hanging over me in a special

63

way like no 1 only her in the woal worl knowit how it wer with me since I done my trants reveal. Fister Crunchman he kep sqwinting at me with his littl sharp blue eyes and nodding his head I wer jus waiting for him to lif up 1 of them hevvy fisses of his and drive me in to the groun.

Finely Fister stil nodding his head and sqwinting at me he said, 'Wel Riddley.'

I said, 'Wel Fister.'

He said, 'Wel Riddley you know if I wer you.' And noddit some mor.

I said, 'What if you wer me Fister? Whatwd you do?'

He helt up 1 finger and kep nodding. He said, 'Mynd you I aint qwick Im jus a woar out old hevvy is all I am.'

I said, 'Every body knows you aint a bit woar out plus youre as qwick as the nex 1.'

He said, 'Which is you nor I aint no where near as qwick as you. Youre myndy dont you see. You ben lernt to read and write and all ways thinking on things. Trubba not nor I aint staring but I wunt want to be like that it aint no way for a man to be.'

I said, 'No Trubba but you wer saying if you wer me.'

He said, 'There it is you see. Which I aint becaws Im slow nor I aint myndy so how cud I be you. Yet if I *wer* you and praps youwl let me give a word and to the whys.'

I said, 'Im craving for it Fister.'

He said, 'Riddley what Im going to say I Trubba not your dad it ben a diffrent time when he come a man this ben stil a moving crowd back then. May be a connexion man cud stil help his crowd to keap a littl bit a head of the cow shit plus may be he bint give no syn which you ben.'

I said, 'Fister whatre you getting at youre going roun by such a long track Im afeart Iwl dy on the road.'

He said, 'Riddley youre the qwick 1 how can you be so slow. Here come that dog at you dint he. Old woar out leader old woar out guvner which you steppt forit like a man and took him on your spear. Nex you do your 1st connexion and you come up with Eusas head is dreaming us. Which it is if

64

you keap on connecting them cow shit shows and pontsing for the Ram which thats all it is and you know it. Innit time to sharna pax for Eusas head you take my meaning. Leave the telling to the women and connect with a mans doing.'

I said, 'Youre mor the man for that nor me aint you Fister. I aint no kynd of a hevvy.'

He said, 'You aint no hevvy but youve got the follerme and I aint. You going to use it or not?'

I said, 'Iwl have to think on it wont I.'

He said, 'Dont think too much youwl grow hair on the in side of your head.'

Wel I cernly growit a head ake right then and the day only jus begun.

Weare off to Widders Dump then nor we hadnt no moren sydlt on the hy groun sholder when heres the Bernt Arse pack come out of the woodlings like it ben ther rota to show us the way. And heres that black leader with his ears prickt up and waiting for a staytmen.

I cud feal my self getting humpyer by the minim I cud see why they callit getting the hump I fealt like I wer growing 1. All my bother hevvy on my back and tingling and like coming to a poynt. That dog wer looking at me that cern way I uppit bow but the clevver sod wunt even move he knowit he wer out of bow shot.

Straiter Empy wer out with the forage rota it wer Fister Crunchman the 1stman of us that day. He said to me, 'That dogs looking this way like hes got some thing on his mynd.'

I said, 'Theres no knowing what a dog myt have on his mynd.'

Durster Potter said, 'Not without youre dog clevver.'

Fister said, 'Not that Ive numbert off that pack by colour but I never noatist that black dog til after he come leader.'

Durster said, 'I never seen that dog til after Brooder Walker dyd.'

I said, 'Whatre you getting at Durster?'

He said, 'Wel you know theres some wil tel you of peopl dying in the Ful of the Moon and then theres 1 mor in the

Black Pack. May be you shud ask that dog to show you hows your father.' He begun to larf he wer killing his self with it.

I ben carrying 2 throwing spears and a fighting spear like all ways. I ternt them roun and shovit the foot of them in Dursters belly. The wind gone out of him: Hoo! Then I swung them 3 spears and clubbit him on the head with the shafs of them. Down he gone. He come up with blood running down his face and come for me with his fighting spear poynt 1st. Fister grabbit the spear and back handit him 1 acrost the meat hoal and he gone flying.

Dursters all of a heap in the mud but he aint interstit in moving til hes sure its all clear with Fister.

Fister says to him, 'Durster Trubba not but wud you mynd if I call Plomercy right there? Im afeart if you and Riddley settl some 1 myt get bad hert. All right?'

Durster hes got 1 or 2 teef less in his mouf but he says, 'All right Fister no Trubba.'

On we gone then and I tryd to let my self go easy but I wernt easy. Becaws Id noatist the same as Fister and Durster and it ben working on me. Id never seen that black dog til after I kilt the old leader. I dint think my dad gone in to no black dog but it did seam to me that dog musve come special from some where or ben sent to tel me some thing some how. I never heard of no such thing but thats the fealing I had. Plus I pernear did think it myt tern in to some 1 in front of my eyes. Not my dad nor I dint know who but it wuntve snuck me at all to see that dog tern in to a man. Lorna Elswint tol me some thing 1ce the others mus neverve heard it or some 1 wudve brung it in sure:

3 black dogs and 1 says, 'The Pry Mincers dead I jus come from the berning.'

Up jumps the bigges of the 3 then on his hynt legs he says, 'I bes walk tall Im No. 1 now.'

Coming a long the hy groun sholder where it wer hevvy woodit on the hy side the dogs run on a head of us and gone out of site amongst the trees.

I wer walking fastern I ben you know how youwl do some times youwl put a space be twean your self and some 1 as ben giving you bother. Walking with my head down not looking a roun. You perwel all ways know what youre doing is my beleaf. I wuntve livet to be 12 years old walking that way but that day I musve wantit to give some thing a chance to happen.

Littl by littl getting farther a head of the others I come roun a ben oansome and all on a sudden theres the black leader stanning oansome in front of me. He aint no moren 2 spear lenths a way from me and his yeller eyes ful on me.

I said, 'What?' and going tords him. Not liffing spear nor making no move with my hans.

We wer stood there looking at each other then I heard the others coming. I throwt my self to 1 side and a arrer hisselt pas me. I ternt and I seen Durster Potter with a emty bow in his han and 2 dogs on him. Theyre in and out like a flash and theres Durster on the groun with his froat and his pryvits toar out and blood sperting all over and the dogs dispeart. They done it qwickern it takes to tel of it. I ternt roun agen and where the black dog ben it wernt nothing only emty space. No dogs in site at all. There hadnt even ben no noys nor not 1 scream from Durster hed never had no time for that. Nor I hadnt had no time to help him.

Durster ben about as far in front of the others as I ben in front of him. They come roun the ben then the other 17 of them. Wel you know there wer a big hulla bulla every 1 talking at 1ce nor no body never seen nor heard nothing like it. Broad in the day time and 5 days pas Ful of the Moon.

Coarse the upper asking mos in every 1s mynd were: Why Durster? Why not me? I ben the oansome 1 coming roun that ben 1st and the others not in site. Whynt they jump me whyd they wait for Durster? Peopl wer looking at me funny and Iwdve lookit at me the same ben I them. Becaws it lookit like them dogs ben watching when Durster and me had that littl rumpa and they contrackt my nemminy ther nemminy.

I bes put the red cord strait here becaws looking back over what I ben writing it looks like may be Durster ben shooting that arrer at me not at the black dog. I wont never know for cern but I dont think he ben shooting at me. Jus like Id uppit bow at that black leader when I ben fealing humpy I think Durster ben kean to hit some thing after getting flattent 1ce by me and 1ce by Fister. May be he thot coming suddn roun that ben he myt get his self a dog skin. Or may be he ben looking to miss the dog and hit me I dont know.

A nother asking in some peopls mynd and you cud see it in ther eyes wer why hadnt I done nothing. It lookit bad a nuff them dogs hadnt jumpt me but at leas I cudve got some blood on my spear when they ben pulling Durster down. Every body knowit how fas the dogs wer and how clevver but stil I cudve ben a littl qwickern I wer I knowit that. Fister said, 'No use moufing it over we cant make it be no other way. Theres blame on all of us but mos on me becaws Im 1stman nor I shuntve had no wandrers out in front.'

It snuck me a littl I dint have no fealings 1 way or a nother about Dursters dying. It ben mor to me when that las boar come on to my spear or the old leader dog. I never had nothing agenst Durster that rumpa ben jus 1 of them things jumps up on its oan sholders all on a suddn. But then I never had nothing for him nyther. I wer jus as glad to have his space as have him. Dead with his cock and balls toar off and his head near toar off his neck and his face gone grey and the wet leaves trampelt roun him and his eyes looking up to the grey sky over him.

Diffrent 1s stanning roun him. This 1 and that 1 ben his frend and mummelt this or that but you cud see it drawt them same as flys to honey. It give us all jus that littl thril. Watching Durster do it with Aunty. She took him in stead of us and us what wernt dead fealt that much mor a live.

We wer closer to hoam nor we wer to Widders Dump. We cut a drag and put Durster on it and back we gone to fents and there gone the death wail yet agen. Littl Nimbel Potter he lookit at me and made the Bad Luck go a way syn. His mum and some others as seen him do it they lookit at me that cern way you dont want no crowd never to look at you. Col iron in that look and heads on poals.

That nite we done the berning and thinet hans and the res of it. Wording roun and it come to Jobber Easting he ben a frend of Dursters he said, 'Bye bye Durster theres some of uswl keap it in memberment how you got dog kilt nor no 1 to lif a han for you.' He ben in that same rota when Durster got kilt. He come roun that ben with the others when Durster ben all ready dead so he knowit there bint no 1 only me there to lif a han. Nex wordit Coxin Shoaring a nother frend of Dursters. He said, 'Bye bye Durster theres others may be shudve give you crowd on that long road you gone.'

Id tol Lorna Elswint how that black leader and me ben looking at each other befor Durster lucet his arrer. She said, 'Wel did you get any 1st knowing this time?' Wel it bint til we ben coming in to fents with Durster on the drag when it come to me all on a suddn how I ben that close to a dog for the 2nd time and looking in them yeller eyes nor never even *thot* of 1st knowing. Hadnt ben thinking of nothing at all. Jus looking in them yeller eyes.

When Lorna done her tel she said, 'Whatd I tel las time about that old woar out leader took by Riddley Walker? Whatd I say did you keap it in memberment? 1st knowing in that dog I said dint I. Here it come agen dinnit. 1st knowing in the new dog the black leader. Whatd Durster Potter do? Tryd to kil 1st knowing dinnee and his self got kilt in stead. If you ask me is that a syn Iwl say yes its a syn and take it the same and thats my tel.'

When Lorna finisht I wer looking a roun and lissening a littl here and there I heard some 1 say, 'That old woman ben telling too long.' It wer Farner Salvage said it. 1 of Empys nexters. I lookit to see who he wer talking to and it wer Skyway Moaters. A nother nexter. Empy had 3 nexters. Them 2 and Fister Crunchman like Ive said.

It come to me all on a suddn may be I hadnt ben making connexions I shudve ben making. Mos of the time the peopl youwl talk to are the 1s as think the same as you. If youre easy in your mynd you aint all ways counting up how many think the arper sit way. Them in our crowd I mosly drunk with or chattit to they ben mosly agenst the forms and the diggings and that. Agenst all them new idears of moving things frontways like Goodparley ben talking of. They dint want Eusa to get his head back they wer mor for fynding back that 1st knowing Lorna kep on about. All the peopl I wer frendy with they rathert be a moving crowd and foraging ful time nor stop in 1 place jobbing on a form.

It use to be mor peopl in our crowd thinking that way nor the other way. Now all on a suddn I wernt sure how it wer. I fealt like when youre sleapy on look out and trying to stay a wake and suddn you catch your self nodding you wunner if youve droppit off and mist some thing.

What with 1 thing and a nother I dint qwite feal like sleaping in my shelter that nite. Lorna had the same fealing so we slyd up on top of the gate house when the lookouts wernt looking. If the skyd ben clear it wudve ben the failing moon littling tords the las $\frac{1}{4}$ but it wer cloudit over solid. Looking at the candls and the nite fires in the divvy roof and littl glimmers here and there from candls in the shelters. Lissening to the crowd shutting down for the nite. Coffing and farting and belching and peeing 1 place and a nother.

Foot steps and mummering now and then thru the nite. Nothing else.

11

Raining agen it wer nex morning. Theres rains and rains. This 1 wer coming down in a way as took the hart and hoap out of you there wer a kynd of brilyants in the grey it wer too hard it wer too else it made you feal like all the tracks in the worl wer out paths nor not a 1 to bring you back. Wel of coarse they are but it dont all ways feal that way. It wer that kynd of morning when peopl wernt jus falling in to what they done naturel they had to work ther selfs in to it. Seamt like a lot of tea got spilt at breakfas nor the talk wernt the userel hummeling and mummeling there wer some thing else in it. Like when you see litening behynt the clouds.

Soons we startit off for Widders Dump you cud feal how every 1 wer on the lert and waiting for some thing. Fister said, 'Les see if we can get there and back without losing no 1 this day.'

Coxin Shoaring said, 'May be wewd do bes to lose some 1 befor we start.'

Fister said, 'Coxin dyou want to name a name? Be there some 1 youre staring at?'

Coxin said, 'O no Fister I know bettern that. Roun here when you stare at the littl you settl with the big.'

Fister said, 'Which we all know you dont do no settling only with the littl dont we Coxin.'

Coxin said, 'Trubba not Fister I never said I wer in your class.'

Fister said, 'No Trubba Coxin no Trubba at all.' It gone qwyet then no 1 wanting to get Fister as cited. We gone talkless then jus lissening to our feet on the leaves and the rain peltering down.

We hadnt seen no dogs yet that morning nor we dint see none on the hy groun sholder. No dogs but it wer then in the soun of the rain I begun to see them yeller eyes agen. They begun to be there for me in the greyness. It wernt nothing to think on it wer jus the yellerness of them and the black of the dog in the soun of the grey rain falling. I begun to cry I dint know what I wer crying about only the yellerness of them eyes. I had my hood up any how parbly no 1 noatist and if they did what diffrents does it make now.

Dint see no dogs nor dint nothing happen going to Widders Dump. When we got there 10 of us gone to the timber crew and the res of us in a new hoal what jus ben markt off and startit.

Boggy groun it wer and hevvy muck. We roapit off in sqwares and sorting thru it befor we draggit with the big buckit and the winch. We begun to fynd bodys and parts of bodys from time back way back. That happent some times in that kynd of muck in stead of rotting a way they got like old dark levver. Them bodys that morning they wer littl kids the yunges mytve ben 6 or so and the oldes may be 7 or 8. It takes you strange digging up a littl dead kid like that. From so far back and dead for so long and all the time they ever had ben jus that littl.

I put my han in the muck I reachit down and come up with some thing it wer a show figger like the 1s in the Eusa show. Woodin head and hans and the res of it clof. All of it gone black and the show mans han stil in it. Cut off jus a littl way up the rist. A groan up han and a regler show man he ben becaws when I wipet off you cud see the callus roun the head finger same as all the Eusa show men have.

This here figger tho it wernt like no other figger I ever seen. It wer crookit. Had a hump on its back and parper sewt there in the clof. For a wyl I cudnt think what it myt be then when it come to me what it wer I cudnt hardly beleave it yet there it wer nor no mistaking it. It wer a hump and it wer meant to be a hump. The head wernt like no other head I ever seen in a show nyther. The face had a big nose what hookit down and a big chin what hookit up and a smyling mouf. Some kynd of littl poynty hat on the head it curvit over with a wagger on the end of it.

I ben so interstit in the figger and the dead han I hadnt ben taking no noatis of no 1 roun me. I lookit up and there wer that littl witey bloak Belnot Phist stanning by the hoal and his littl pinky eye on me I fealt like making the Bad Luck go a way syn.

Phist says, 'Whats that youve got there?'

I dint say nothing. We wernt allowit to keap nothing we foun in the digging some times they use to serch us tho not all ways.

He says, 'You bes anser me I said whats that youve got there?'

I said, 'Whynt you have a look for your self.'

He says, 'All right I wil then give it here.' He come to the edge of the hoal and stuck out his han.

I put the figger and the dead han in my pockit then qwick I grabbit Phists han in boath of myn and wirlt roun fas and slung him over my sholder head 1st in to the muck I cudnt do nothing else to save my life.

Out of the corner of my eye I seen his feet sticking up out of the muck and kicking and Chalker Marchman the 1stman of the digging coming after me.

I uppit out of the hoal with my feet sucking and sqwelching and up the moundit dirt to the hy walk and over the fents befor I knowit what I wer doing. It wer my feet done it by ther selfs I never give it no thot at all.

Come down with a thump on the out side of the fents and slyding down the slippy bank in to the ditch which I come up out of it soakit and sopping and there wer that black leader waiting for me with his yeller eyes. Jus stanning there in the rain and waiting for me.

Dint see no other dogs jus only him. Looking at me and wagging his tail slow. Then he ternt and gone off easy looking back over his sholder like he wantit me to foller so I follert. I ben waiting for it so long when the time come I jus done it.

He wer heading for Bernt Arse. I dint have no reason for going there I dint want no bother with Ram hevvys from the out poast crowdless like I wer nor I wernt even the qwipt man for roading let a loan fighting. I dint have no weapons nor no bundel I dint have nothing only the knife in my belt and the roady in my pockit plus that hump back figger and the dead han. I lookit back tho and there wer the woal Bernt Arse Pack strung out behynt me like Ive seen them strung out behynt a deer. It wer like magic how 1 minim they wernt there and the nex they wer it wer like they come out of no where. I tryd if I cud catch up with the black leader and may be get a littl a head of him I wer hoaping to draw him a way from Bernt Arse but how ever much speed I put on he put on mor and kep a head of me. With them others hot behynt me like they wer I wunt take no chance on forking off oansome I wer afeart Iwd be just so much running meat to them. I cudnt do nothing only keap going and hoap my fear pong wunt drive them mad. Even with the fear tho it wer a hy fealing it wer hyern any thing I ever fealt befor. Running oansome with them dogs. In that 1 look back I seen heads sticking up over the top of Widders Dump fents but no 1 overing and after me. No they wunt them careful cow shit barsets. Wel realy why shud they what diffrents wud it make to them what happent to me. In my mynd I heard them saying, 'He jus over the fents and off with the dogs!' And I thot: Yes thats what I done you sorry sods I over the fents and off with the dogs and thats the las youwl see of Riddley Walker in your cow shit diggings.

You cud see the smoak coming up from the out poast in Bernt Arse only you cudnt see the out poast. They dint have no hy look out no tower nor nothing to give them a clear site over the low groun I wer on they wer jus in amongst the dead town stannings which there wernt nothing very hy.

Wunnering what wer coming when we got inside the dead town. I thot if them dogs ben going to eat me theywd parblyve done it all ready. Wunnering what that black leader had in mynd becaws he cernly had some progam he wernt jus randeming.

The black leader gone in to Bernt Arse mazy ways and parbly keaping down wind of the out poast them dogs pong hevvy even when theyre dry but when theyre wet it pernear knocks you over. That smel plus the dead town pong it aint like nothing else. Dead towns they smel wet and dry boath even in a rain. Grean rot and number creaper on the stumps and stannings. Crumbelt birks and broak stoans all a jumbl and a parcht smel unner neath a smel of old berning. I hadnt ben in Bernt Arse since 3 or 4 years back when I use to sly in with the other kids. Now it lep up in my eyes like it ben waiting for this day to be its self for me for the 1st time.

We come to a littl hump of groun with a wood vennylater sticking up it dint have no rain cover on it. The black leader sticking his nose down the hoal and ruffing then he lookit over to me and ruffing some mor. I gone over and looking down inside I cudnt see nothing plus it stunk some thing terbel. There come up from be low a kids voyce then wel you cudnt say for cern it wer a kids voyce he parbly soundit as old as me only it wer some thing in how he soundit made me think it wer a kid he said, 'You jus going to stan there and breave or be you going to say some thing?'

I said, 'What dyou want me to say?'

He said, 'You dont have to say nothing jus get me out of this.'

I said, 'How?'

He said, 'Theres a trap doar then a nother doar with bars on it.'

I said, 'We mus be close to the out poast. Aint there hevvys all roun here?'

He said, 'They dont never put foot outside the out poast all they ever do is smoak and play cards they wont give you no bother without you bus up the game.'

I lookit roun til I foun a woodin trap doar I liffit up and gone down some conkreat steps. Come to a nother doar then with 2 bars. That part of the shelter wernt from time back way back it ben peast in where the old walls ben cavit in.

I all ready had boath bars slid out and the doar ½ open when I thot: How do I know whats coming out of there how do I know that kids oansome in there? For all I know it cud be open the doar and arga warga. Any how I opent the doar.

1st thing come out wer the stink. The kid said, 'That aint my blame the stink they wunt give me no shovvel to burry my dirt with.' I dint see him at 1st my eyes had to get use to it in there the onlyes lite come from the vennylater. The black leader pressing nex to me looking in thru the doar. The other dogs keaping back.

I seen some 1 move a way from the far wall then I seen like a wite shadder on that old conkreat wall. Like when you make a fire agenst a stoan and it gets black all roun where the flame ben only jus where the flames ben there its bernt clean. This wite shadder wer in the shape of a figger you cudnt tel if it ben man or woman it wer jus some 1 stanning with legs a part you cudnt make out no arms parbly the hans ben covering the face.

The kid come forit then in to the lite from the vennylater and looking strait at me. Only not realy looking he dint have no eyes to look with he dint have no parper face. It wer like it ben shapit qwick and rough out of clay. No eyes nor no hoals for eyes there wernt nothing where the eyes shudve ben. All he had for a face wer jus a bit pincht out for a nose and a cut for a mouf and that wer it. Dint have a woal pair of ears jus 2 littl blobs like they ben startit but not finisht. Nor he dint have no hair on his head. He wer as tall as me. Looking at him you cudnt tel if he wer a kid or ful growt only he soundit like a kid.

When he come tords me I dont know why I done it I helt up the dead han and the hump back figger in front of me.

He said, 'You dont have to make no Bad Luck go a way syn I aint no Bad Luck Im whats lef after the Bad Luck ben. Im pas the tern and on the way to Good Luck.'

I said, 'Yes wel I dont feal all that Lucky if you want out of here les go I rather not hang a bout.'

The kid had his doss bag all ready roalt like he ben waiting for the poynty time. Weare jus going up them steps when that black leaders up and pas us like a jaggit bolt of litening.

Up of us we hear a littl scuffl and nex thing theres some 1s legs inside the trap doar kicking then they stoppit. Blood and pee running down. I pult him in he had his head near toar off and they gone for his pryvits sames they done with Durster Potter. Only this wernt no Durster Potter it wer a hevvy from the Ram. I thot: Wel thats it theres no way back now. We lissent a littl nor dint hear nothing so I up and out in a rush. All clear and 2 dogs with bloody moufs stanning by looking to the black leader and the black leader looking to me like it wer front stations every body and les get moving. The dead bloaks bow wer on the groun with a arrer near it and his spears a littl way off he musve had a arrer on the string when they jumpt him. He bint too big a man I cud use his bow wel a nuff. I took his knife as wel I emtit his pockits too I thot I myt as wel hang for a ram as a lam.

The kid said, 'Its parbly Keaper. If hes got some stoans in his pockit thems my fealys he took from me.'

I give the kid back his fealys and we vackt our wayt out of there. We fas leggit out of Bernt Arse senter in to the outers in amongst a jumbl of stannings and rubbl jus to be out of site then we stoppit a littl to talk summit. The black leader and his 2 nexters stoppit with us the other dogs kep going. What they wer doing wer shaking foller for us. When I come to know them better I seen they dint do nothing random they had tack ticks.

There we wer then in amongst the broakin stoans the grean rot and the number creeper with the rain all drenching down and peltering on them dead stoans stumps and stannings. Spattering on crumbelt conkreat and bustit birk and durdling in the puddls gurgling down the runnels of the dead town. A kynd of greanish lite to that day from the rain the grean rot and the number creeper and the dead town pong wer going up all grean smelling in that greanish lite. Dog pong as wel a black smel in the grey rain. It wernt til then I even give a thot to why the kid mytve ben in the hoal. It wer like I jus ben progammit to go there and get him out. Now that wer done I wunnert what it wer all about. I said to him, 'Whyd they have you in that hoal?'

He said, 'Doing the askings bint we. We done Horny Boy and Widders Bel and Fathers Ham and nex come Bernt Arse dinnit. 1 day in 1 and 2 in 2 and 3 in 3 then it wudve ben 4 in the 4th. Come 9 it wudve ben the senter and helping the qwirys. Only Iwl get there without him Iwl channel the Senter Power my self where theres all the many and no end to me.'

I said, 'Who ben doing the askings? What ben they asking? I dont know what youre talking about.'

He said, 'Goodparley ben doing it bint he. Sharna pax and get the poal. *He* never ben the Puter Leat he never ben the Power Leat him and his Mincery. Pontsery is what he come out of and shitful servis. O yes the Mincery myt have ther red cords all wrote out and let them we know what ben time back way back. Iwl do it too see if I dont. I pult the dog and the dog pult you Iwl do the res of it as wel.'

It jus come tumbling all a jumbl out of him like that I stil dint have no idear what it wer all about but soons I heard the name of Goodparley I come the lert. I said, 'Wheres Good-parley right now and whats he doing?'

He said, 'I tol you dint I hes in Bernt Arse. We done the askings 1 time which it ben 3 to go.'

I said, 'Dyou know how many hevvys hes got with him?'

He said, 'Its 50 the same as he all ways roads with I heard Keaper say that. Plus the out poasts all ways have 6 on regler.'

I tryd to plot the parbeltys of it and progam what to do nex. I knowit we bes put a farness behynt us qwicks we cud only we dint have no hoap of going sly by day. Not 2 peopl crowdless and cernly not 2 peopl with 40 dogs or so. Lookouts on every hy walk and a pigeon fly in every form and dead town with a Mincery man working it. We use to see them talking over our heads be twean ther selfs and to the Ram. It dint look like Belnot Phistd bothert to pigeon Goodparley about me becaws if he had there cernly wudve ben moren jus the 1 hevvy to rumpa with. Say Goodparley dint know I wer in Bernt Arse. Theywd fynd the dead hevvy and for all they knowit him and the kid boath ben jumpt by dogs when he unbart the doar and the kid ben draggit off the sames theywl do with a calf or a lam. I thot we myt have a chance of no foller at all and Goodparley myt just get his self some 1 else to do his askings with. I said to the kid, 'How much does it matter to Goodparley if youre gone?'

He said, 'Wel Im the Ardship of Cambry enn I.'

I thot he wer making a joak. I said, 'Thats about it and you bustit out befor the 1st chop too. So now its some 1 elses tern inside the circel innit.'

He said, 'Thats right. 12 mor years or so and Goodparley can have his self a nother Ardship.'

I said, 'Whatre you talking about?'

He said, 'Im talking about how long Goodparleywl have to wait for a nother Ardship whatre you talking about?'

I said, 'What dyou mean a nother Ardship?'

He said, 'Wel its jus only a littl wyl since a son of myn ben beartht nor he cant be Ardship til he comes 12 and gets a boy his self can he.'

I said, 'How old be you then?'

He said, 'I jus come 12 this las Ful of the Moon din I.'

I said, 'So did I that makes us moon brothers.'

He said, 'Dark of the Moon as wel.'

I said, 'Be you telling me theres realy such a thing as the Ardship of Cambry?'

He said, 'Why dyou think I wantit out of that hoal?'

I said, 'Why?'

He said, 'Wel its sharna pax and get the poal innit. 1st the easy askings then its helping the qwirys then its Chops your Aunty and your head on a poal. Dont you know the rime?'

I said, 'What rime dyou mean?'

What he done then he sung *Fools Circel 9wys*:

Horny Boy rung Widders Bel
Stoal his Fathers Ham as wel
Bernt his Arse and Forkt a Stoan
Done It Over broak a boan
Out of Good Shoar vackt his wayt
Scratcht Sams Itch for No. 8

Gone to senter nex to see
Cambry coming 3 times 3
Sharna pax and get the poal
When the Ardship of Cambry comes out of the hoal

The way he sung it made my blood run col. I cud see like in a dream a figger running running in a kynd of dream space. I said, 'Thats *Fools Circel 9wys* thats jus a game.'

He said, 'O yes its a game right a nuff if you like to call it that only it aint too much fun for the Ardship what gets his head took off at the end of it.'

I said, 'Whats it all about why do they do it?'

He said, 'Its about what its all ways ben about and they do it for the knowing whats in us.'

I said, 'What knowing? In who?'

He said, 'Dont you know about the Eusa folk?'

I said, 'Who myt they be?'

He said, 'O dear o dear o dear you dont know nothing do you.' Then he begun to tel me. This what Im writing down here it wernt said all in 1 peace like its wrote. Wewd talk a littl and lissen. Talk and lissen. And all ways with 1 eye on the black leader and his nexters for any lerting any blips of foller which there wernt none. It stayd qwyet all day wylst we waitit there in Bernt Arse outers for it to get dark.

He said, 'Time back way back who ben the Puter Leat who ben the Power Leat in Cambry? Eusa folk is who it ben. Us the same and us to blame. Who run the Power Ring who ben too close to Power who gone Badstock crookit and seed of the crookit? Us the same the Eusa folk. Who ben bernt out after Bad Time all the clevver 1s bernt out with all the clevverness? Us the same. Who ben the 1st Ardship of Cambry? Eusa. Which the hardship be come the Ardship you see. They kilt Eusa but they dint kil all the Eusa folk they dint bern them all out did they. No they savit out some to keap in memberment that clevverness what made us crookit. Savit a breeding stock in Cambry so therewd all ways be some of us o yes theres all ways ben Eusa folk and wil be. And the knowing whats in them the

Ardship wil know. Roun the circel of the dead towns to the senter which is Cambry. Becaws weve kep the memberment you see. Kep the memberment of what we done time back way back the knowing of its in us. Dint you never hear of Eusa?'

I said, 'Coarse Ive heard of Eusa every bodys heard of him.'

He said, 'Then you know he wer crookit.'

I said, 'You bes tel me about Eusa as wel I parbly never heard the woal of it.'

He said:

> He wer crookit he wer Badstock
> He wer not boath sides the same
> Which the knowing brung the doing
> And the doing brung the shame

I said, 'Did Eusa go crookit from what he done?'

He said, 'Eusa gone crookit from Bad Time. He made his self that way with the clevverness he done and brung the same on others. Crookit he wer and playg soars on him he wer running from the bernings. The Ram wernt sepert from the res of Inland then it wernt a nylan. Eusa stood at the gate and the dogs licking his soars. Them on the gate they wer afeart they said, "If you want in why dont you say Trubba not?" Eusa said, "I cant say that."

'Them at the Ram they said, "You bes tel us your clevverness so we can make the 1 Big 1 agen befor some 1 else does. We bes be the strong 1s its the safes thing." Eusa wunt do it he said, "I know all about strong 1s I ben with the las lot it dint help them nothing all ther strongness. You bes stay how ever you are dont look for no exter strongness. Bes thing you can do is take me in and keap me til my times out. Show me for a lessing and a lerning Iwl tel every 1 my story so theywl know that road I took wrong and what harm I done."

'Them at the Ram they wunt lissen to Eusa. They kep asking for the clevverness and how to make the 1 Big 1. When he wunt tel them they beat him to death with col iron then they took his head they put it on a poal for telling. Eusas head tol them, "You had a chance to do a right thing but you done a wrong thing. Youve took my head youve took it on your self itwl be with you from now on." Thats all his head tol it wunt say no moren that.

'No soonerd that head stop talking nor there come a jynt wave it wer like a wall of water hyer nor a mountin. Dint it come tho. It come rushing it come roaring it come roaling down it cut acrost the lan right thru from Reakys Over down to Roaming Rune. It cut the Ram off sepert from the res of Inland that wer the day the Ram be come a nylan.

'Them at the Ram they wer afeart that head wunt res they dint know what they mytve brung down on ther selfs they dint know what myt be coming nex. They wisht theyd done like Eusa tol them only it wer too late for that becaws Eusa wer dead. They cudnt show Eusa for a lessing and a lerning like he tol them so they begun to make the figger of him then. Begun to make the Eusa figger. They made it littl so they cud work it on ther han they made a fit up so they cud carry the woal show on ther back. Trying to do like Eusa tol them which they wer going to show him. Show the idear of him any how. Thats when they stoppit killing off all the Eusa folk they startit keaping some of us in the dead towns. For a lessing and a lerning is what they say. Nor the Ram musnt want no 1 to have that lessing and lerning only ther selfs becaws they ben keaping us hid long a nuff aint they. The Eusa show men they come roun some times they do the juicy with the Eusa women which the Ram dont allow that only the hevvys keap it dark becaws they do it the same. The Ram dont want no other seed to mix with ours they dont want to straiten the crookit they want us kep jus like we are. They dont want the knowing sparsit out and scattert it dont make no odds tho you cant get a babby on a Eusa woman only with the Eusa seed I knowit my father right a nuff. When his time come to help the qwirys I bint no moren 3 monce old nor dint know nothing but the marks of it come out on me when they hung him up by his hans tyd

82

behynt him. I can feal him in me when its moving I can feal him in me when its stil.'

I said, 'When whats moving and stil?'

He said, 'What ever there is. I aint going to mouf over it you go somers else and do your moufing oansome if you have to keap on doing it.'

He gone qwyet for a wyl then. Peopl with eyes you can see them move back from the front of ther eyes when they dont have no mor to say. This kid tho being he dint have no eyes in his face you cudnt see nothing when he movit back he jus dispeart. There come out of him a sylents with a roaring in it like when you put your ear to a sea shel.

The black dog wer sitting qwyet with his yeller eyes on the kid his 2 nexters wer on look out. I closd my eyes and wunnert if Iwd know that dog wer black if I cudnt see him. Becaws I sust the kid knowit the dog wer black. Looking at that black leaders eyes they myndit me of gulls eyes. Eyes so fearce they cudnt even be sorry for the naminal they wer in. Like a gull I seen 1 time with a broakin wing and Dad kilt it. Them yeller eyes staret scareless to the las. They jus happent to be in the gull but they dint care nothing for it.

I said to the Ardship, 'Trubba not I have to keap asking becaws theres things I nead to know.'

He said, 'No Trubba.'

I said, 'Whyd they hang him up by his hans tyd behynt him?'

He said, 'Dyou not lissen or what? Im wording it all out for you til my joars ake nor you wont take it in. I tol you dint I its the easy asking 1st then its helping the qwirys then its head on a poal and whats it all about I tol you that as wel its the knowing what the Ardship knows. Him and the Eusa folk. Which thats the knowing of what Eusa done.'

I said, 'Every 1 knows that.'

He said, 'I mean the knowing of how to do it.'

I said, 'You mean the 1 Big 1 and the Master Chaynjis and that?'

He said, 'Thats it.'

I said, 'Dont tel me you know the Nos. of it.'

He said, 'I dont know them here but Iwl know them in the senter when we gether.'

I said, 'The senters where you come from tho innit. How come you never got the knowing befor this?'

He said, 'I have got it befor this and manys the time tho Ive never tol Goodparley of it. But its only there when we gether.'

I said, 'Whynt you write it down?'

He said, 'Even if any of us cud write I wunt have that. The 1 Big 1 and the Master Chaynjis aint some thing you littl in to writing.'

I said, 'Cant you keep it in memberment?'

He said, 'It goes.'

I said, 'Cant you work it wylst you know it? Work it on Goodparley and them?'

He said, 'There aint nothing I can do with it. I dont know what it means nor nothing. Why dyou think they keap doing the woal thing over every 12 years. Becaws Goodparley and them they dont know how to do nothing with it no moren I do. They jus keap hoaping some time some Goodparley wil ask the right asking and some Ardship wil say a anser whatwl break them thru the barren year. He ben doing the easy askings ever so gennl slow and careful. I dont know what its like to have eyes but I can feal when peopl look at me. I cud feal his eyes like trying to dril in to my skul and hewd say ever so sof, "Wel here we are in the cruciboal and waiting for that radiant lite hey?" Or hewd say, "Salt and saver. Think on that hey? Whats that salt for? Salt 4? Salt No. 4?" Hewd go on and on like that hewd say to me, "You myt jus only be the leas littl lef over part of it but the woal is in the part you know. The woal is in the part." Iwd like to work the woal of it on him Iwl tel you that.'

I said, 'There dont seam to be no foller on us he mus think you ben dog kilt. Which that means you cant show your self no where no mor if you want to keap wide of him. Wherewl you go?'

He said, 'Cambry is where Im going Im going to have a nother go at that Senter Power Im going to gether with the Eusa folk Im going to try for deaper nor I ben.'

When he said, 'Im going' there come a craving in me for him to say, 'Weare going'. We dint say nothing for a wyl. I dint ask him how he progammit getting pas the Cambry hevvys I dint want to think about it. We jus sqwattit there talkless unner a over hang. I wer lissening to the rain dumming in the puddls and looking at that black dog what brung me to the Ardship of Cambry.

That dog. I wunnert what the name of him myt be. Which I dont mean name like my name is Riddley or formers myt call a pair of oxen Jet & Fire. I knowit he dint have no name the other dogs callt him by nor I wunt try to put no name to him no moren Iwd take it on me to name the litening or the sea. I thot his name myt be a fraction of the nite or the numbers of the black wind or the hisper of the rain. A name you myt play on the boans or reckon up in scratches on a stoan. The Ardshipd said he pult the dog and the dog pult me. Which I cud feal that right a nuff. I wantit to be pult too. I dint know where to nor what for but I wantit to go with it. I thot of all the years I ben afeart of dogs. I said to the Ardship, 'Howd you get dog frendy?'

He said, 'Im frendy with any thing if it comes in right. Im the Lissener you know. Im all ways lissening thats how I know about every thing. How I pult the dog I lissent him in. You know when I begun to lissen like that?'

I said, 'When?'

He said, 'When the Other Voyce Owl of the Worl begun saying the sylents.'

I said, 'Wil you tel me about that?'

He said, 'All right Iwl tel you. This is about when the Lissener wer a kid.'

This is what he tol:

The Lissener and the Other Voyce Owl of the Worl

There wer the Other Voyce Owl of the Worl. He sat in the worl tree larfing in his front voyce only his other voyce wernt larfing his other voyce wer saying the sylents. He had a way of saying them. He said them wide and far where he begun them he said them tyny when they come close. He kep saying the sylents like that in his other voyce and when he done it the sylents wer swallering up the souns of the worl then the owl wer swallering the sylents.

No 1 knowit he wer doing it. He wer trying to swaller all the souns of the worl then there wunt be no mor worl becaws every thing wud foller the soun of its self in to the sylents then it wud be gone. What the owl had in mynd wer to get it all swallert then fly a way. He only done it at nite he thot hewd get some of it swallert every nite and til he gone the woal worl a way.

No 1 knowit what the owl wer doing only a kid. He dint have no eyes he lissent all the time. When he heard the owl saying the sylents in his other voyce he heard the sylents swallering up the souns of the worl littl and big from the wind sying in the trees to the ants crying in ther hoals. The kid knowit the owl wer trying to say the woal worl a way and he knowit wer on him to stop the owl so he begun to lissen every thing back. He lissent them far and wide where he begun them he lissent them tyny when they come close. The eye of the goat and the dants in the stoan and the beatl digging a grave for the sparrer. He lissent them in to his ear hoals he kep them all safe there. The foot steps of the mof and the sea foam hissing on the stran he lissent every thing back.

The kid dint keap the souns of the worl in his ear hoals only at nite he kep them safe til morning. When the cock crowt in the middl nite it never foolt him nor when it crowt agen befor 1st lite. He kep them souns safe in his ear hoals til the day stood up and the cock of the morning crowt every thing a wake. Then the kid unheard the souns and they gone back where they livet. The kid wer larfing at the owl but the owl dint know it he thot he done a good nites work. He sat in the worl tree grooling and smarling all day thinking he wud get the woal worl gone only he never done it.

The rivvers run
My storys done

I said, 'That owl tho he keaps trying dont he.'

The Ardship said, 'O yes he keaps trying and hewl do it 1 day too. All it takes is for no 1 to be lissening every thing back. Hewl go the worl a way and his self with it and thatwl be the end of it. But may be not for a wyl yet. Lissener is my calling name you can call me that.'

So we past the time til it come dark. That black leader he had that pack in good shape there come back 1 of them and bringing him a hynt leg of a goat nor there wernt no wyld goats roun there some form had a hoal unner the fents and 1 goat short that day. Which he offert us nor I wuntve beleavit that hadnt I seen it. Lissener and me we et a littl jus to show meat brothers only we dint fancy it raw nor dursnt make a fire. We made do with some of the roady I had in my pockits which I had some I brung from fents and some I got out of the pockits of that bloak the dogs kilt. I give some of it to the black leader and the 2 nexters.

Going in to my pockits for that roady I brung out the dead han and that hook nose figger. I put that old blackent figger on my right han and it movit qwick and fearce waving its arms and looking all roun sharp. It pickt up a stoan and begun banging on the wall with it. I said, 'Wutcha wutcha' then I put him back in my pockit. The dead han 1st I thot about it 1 way then I thot about it the other then I throwit over the wall. I lookit to see if any of the dogs wud eat it. They dint.

12

Like Ive said it stayd qwyet all day we dint hear nothing nor there wernt no lerting from the dogs. A littl *too* qwyet I thot it wer. Qwyet with may be eyes and ears in it waiting for us to make our move. The rain hevvit on by the end of the day it wer coming down in buckits plus it blowt up a hevvy wind out of the Norf and Eas you cud perwel lean on it.

It come dark early we waitit til it wer solid nite and filfy dark it wer you cudnt hardly see your han on the end of your arm. We slyd out slow and easy we had the woal Bernt Arse pack with us. I had the black leader nexy bumping agenst me now and agen and I wer leading Lissener by the han. Soons we come out of the outers and clear of stumps and stannings he pult his han luce and ternt his self a roun this way and that. Poyntit his self in to the wind and he said, 'Cambrys this way innit?'

I said, 'Thats it right a nuff.'

He said, 'Wel Im on my way then. Thanking you for getting me out of the hoal. Good Luck to you where ever youre going.'

I said to him, 'Whatre you on about? Be you out of your mynd or what? You think youre going to Cambry oansome?'

He said, 'I can fynd it by insterment. Ive got a knife and spear plus Ive got the dogs to look after me dont you worry over me.'

I said, 'Dont you want me to go with you?'

He said, 'Back there when you brung me out of the hoal you dint say, "Wherewl *we* go?" You said, "Wherewl *you* go?"'

I said, 'Wel now Im saying, "Wherewl *we* go?" Any where you go its the 2 of us going.'

He said, 'You know how it is with me I wunt ask you to come. Me I dont have nothing to lose they ben going to put my head on a poal any how. It aint the same for you parbly you can stil go back to your fents and Blobs your nunkel.'

I said, 'No odds. If the Ram aint after me all ready for what I all ready done theywl be after me soon a nuff for some thing else. We myswel joynt the effert.' When I said that I thot on Fister Crunchman what he said about connecting with a mans doing and how I had follerme. Yet there hadnt no 1 follert me and here I wer follering the Ardship nor I dint care what kynd of doing it wer.

So off we gone. I pirntowt we bes not go the straites way. Keap off the main tracks where we cud. I wer jus going to say les Eas roun by Monkeys Whoar Town and Norf up a long the Nellys Bum when I had like a mynd flash of colourt lites with clicking and bleaping it wernt like nothing I ever acturely seen nor heard only in dreams. I cud like feal the woal circel of the dead towns in me and see a line of grean lite sweeping roun that circel from the senter.

Lissener said, 'What is it?'

I said, 'What dyou mean?'

He said, 'Im lissening some thing nor I dont know what it is. And youre lissening me.'

I said, 'Dont break the circel yet.' The words jus come out of me by ther selfs I bint thinking them at all.

He said, 'What dyou lissen else?'

I said, 'I dont know its jus a line of grean lite sweeping and there come up blips.' Which Id usit that word times a nuff but never til then did I ever think of putting the word *blip* to a blob of grean lite.

He said, 'Blips where?'

I said, 'I dont know.'

He said, 'Say *Fools Circel 9wys*.'

I begun it:

Horny Boy rung Widders Bel
Stoal his Fathers Ham as wel
Bernt his Arse and Forkt a Stoan

Thats where I stoppit. Fork Stoan be come sharp in my mynd. I said, 'Fork Stoan.'

He said, 'Why cud you lissen me nor I cudnt lissen my self?'

I said, 'May be it aint nothing.'

He said, 'No its true foller I can lissen that much. If we go to Fork Stoan weare keaping the circel which thatwl be axel rating the Inner G you know. Thats what you do when you Power roun a ring. Which it looks like we bes ful that circel on a wyl yet.'

So we Souf and Eastit then for Fork Stoan which that put the wind on our lef side in stead of in our faces. That wind it jus kep fulling on and the rain like sling stoans in our faces. I wer thinking how it mus be out at sea. Which I wer beartht at Crippel the Farn near Fork Stoan and the sea is all ways somers in my mynd no matter where I am. I said, 'I wunt want to be out this nite.' Then I had to larf and shake my head calling to memberment Durster Potter and how he said them same words that rainy nite after the Eusa show which it seamt so long pas yet it wernt no moren 3 nites back. Now I wer wel gone out in to that rainy dark he dint want to be in and where wer he?

Nearing on to Bernt Arse outers we come thru some old bernt over common it use to be a fents there long time back but long since emty gone to scrub and runty woodling they callit Hagmans Il. I pickt up a stoan and put it in my pockit for memberment I said, 'Les hoap Aunty lets us get on top.'

Lissener said, 'She ever do that?'

I dint tel him the story then it wer too hard talking in all that wind and rain plus I wantit to keap on the lissen but now Iwl write it down here which it like stans for some roading time. I had it from a Eusa show man Wayman Footling.

The Bloak as Got on Top of Aunty

Every body knows Aunty. Stoan boans and iron tits and teef be twean her legs plus she has a iron willy for the ladys it gets red hot. When your time comes you have to do the juicy with her like it or not. She rides a girt big rat with red eyes it can see in the dark and it can smel whos ready for Aunty. Even if they dont know it ther selfs the rat can smel if theyre ready.

Time back way back after Bad Time there come playgs in the towns and they wer berning out the Badstock and the clevverness and that. Aunty she wer here and there and every where on her rat. She wer larfing and singing she wer doing the juicy right lef and senter she never got a nuff of it. Every 1 wer hiding out from her the bes they cud what ever hoal or shelter they cud fynd. It dint help them nothing that rat smelt them all out any how. Bloaks even if they dint think they cud get it up for Aunty jus 1 look from her and they wer ready. Theywd have ther go with Aunty but they never done it moren 1ce. 1ce Aunty clampt down with her bottom teef it wer Bye bye all bes no mor Trubba in this worl.

There wer a bloak his wife and childer dead from the playg and them what wer berning out the town wer after him with torches. Flames jumping up behynt him he dint have much chance but on he run from 1 hoal to a nother. He wer so much out of Luck his numbers all gone randem and his progam come unstuck he startit in to crave for Aunty he cudnt think of nothing else. He fealt ready only he dint see no red rat eyes nor he dint hear Aunty coming.

He gone looking for her then and calling to her he wer yelling, 'Come on Aunty Im ready for you and I want it now.' He mus not have smelt ready tho becaws the rat dint come after him. He begun to foller on the rat then. He wer faslegging it thru the berning looking for jynt rat shit til he cawt up with Aunty. He said, 'Drop your nickers Aunty you are for me.'

Aunty larft she said, 'Whyd you come running after me do you have a iron willy or what?'

He said, 'I dont have nothing special Im jus dying hard.'

Aunty said, 'All right then but you mus let me get on top thats how I all ways do it.' When Aunty got on top of any 1 her stoan boans and iron tits wud crush them down and her bottom teef wud finish the job.

This bloak tho he said, 'Not this time Aunty. Every thing else has got on top of me but I wil get on top of you.'

Aunty larft and let him do it becaws she liket how he come running after her. That bloak never had any thing like it he dint know if he wer dead or a live he said, 'Am I dead now or what?'

Aunty larft she said, 'No youre not dead becaws you got on top of me and I pult in my bottom teef for you. I done that becaws you dint hide you come running after me. Off with you now and keap in mynd nex time its arga warga for you.'

Off he gone then he come to that place which now its callit Hagmans Il. He seen a woman there she wer the 1st he seen since he ben with Aunty. He said to her, 'I done the juicy with Aunty and Im stil a live.'

She said, 'Prove it.'

He said, 'Iwl prove it right a nuff but wud you tel me 1st what do they call this place?'

The woman tol him, 'Hangmans Hil.'

The bloak said, 'Wel les call it some thing else now becaws Ive ben with Aunty and Im stil here. Jus a littl wyl back I ben ready to dy but now Im ready to live a littl and in joy with you so les call this place Hagmans Thril.'

The woman said, 'If thats the name wewl do the same.' There wernt much else to do in that place it wernt nothing only smoaking runes dead bodys from the playg and nothing to eat.

The bloak went with her then he went agen he went all day and all nite he woar his self out and tirely he cudnt put out no mor input.

The woman fealt him going she said, 'Dont you fancy me no mor?'

He said, 'It aint that its jus Ive overwent my self I think Iwl res a littl now.'

She said, 'I think youwl res a littl longern you think.'

He said, 'Whyre you looking at me that way who be you and whats your name?'

She said, 'Who I am is Auntys saymling sister and my name is Arga Warga.'

When the bloak heard that he tryd to run but he wer that woar out he cudnt move and she jumpt on him and et him up. From then on they callit that place Hagmans Il.

Hagman Hogman big or small
Thats the end Ive tol it all

Time back when Wayman Footling tol me that story I askit him, 'Be that realy how that place got its name?'

He said, 'No not realy. There use to be a fents there it ben Hogmans Kil Fents befor it be come Hagmans Il.'

I said, 'Why wer it callit Hogmans Kil?'

He said, 'Bloak namit Hogman he wer the Big Man they use to make pots there. Hogmans Killen wer what it wer but every body callit Hogmans Kil.'

I said, 'Howd it get to be Hagmans Il tho?'

He said, 'Hogman had a fight with his wife and she kilt him.'

I said, 'O that musve ben why they callit Hogmans Kil then.'

He said, 'No it ben callit Hogmans Kil befor she done him in. After she done it they callit Hagmans Il. Becaws she ben a rough and ugly old woman and it come to il he marrit her.'

I said, 'Then whered the other story come from? The 1 of the bloak as got on top of Aunty.'

He said, 'It come in to my mynd.'

I said, 'You mean you made it up.'

He said, 'Wel no I dint make it up you cant make up nothing in your head no moren you can make up what you see. You know what I mean may be what you see aint all ways there so you cud reach out and touch it but its there some kynd of way and it come from some where. That place Hagmans Il I use to wunner about it every time we come by it til finely that story come in to my head. That story cudnt come out of no where cud it so it musve come out of some where. Parbly it ben in that place from time back way back or may be in a nother place only the idear of it come to me there. That dont make no odds. That storys jus what ever it is and thats what storys are.'

1ce we got a good offing from Bernt Arse we come down be twean Brabbas Horn and Sel Out Form. They ben manooring ther arrabl we wer smelling cow shit on all sides of us. We come on to the A20 then which the Ram hevvys all ways roadit that track be twean Bernt Arse and Fork Stoan but I wernt looking for nothing to be moving on it this nite.

After a wyl the wind easit off and there come thunner and litening. Meat smoak in the rain and fires we cudnt get warm at. It snuck me how soon that come to seam the naturel way of things it felt like I ben roading in the rainy dark with Lissener and them dogs for years. Yet when the litening flasht and Iwd see all them dog backs wet and shyning in the rain then it wer like a dream.

1ce Lissener said to me, 'Dyou have the gethering dream?'

I said, 'Whats that?'

He said, 'Its where theres all the many nor there aint no end to you there aint no place where you begin nor leave off. Mountins of us valleys of us far far lans and countrys of us. Tits and bellys it wud take you days to walk acrost. Girt roun bums and arms and legs all jynt big and long and long and girt jynt man and woman parts all mullerplying back to gether all what ben de vydit. No mor oansome in the gethering. No mor edge where you leave off and the nex begins jus all of us as far as you can see with all the eyes of us it dont matter whose eyes youre looking out of you dont nead none of your oan. You have that dream?'

I said, 'No we have the ½ dream.'

He said, 'Whats that?'

I said, 'It aint a parper dream realy its a fealing comes on you when youre falling a sleap. Youre jus going off easy when suddn its like a bersting in you like youre bersting in 1000 peaces then you come a wake with your hart going fas.'

He said, 'Funny. It ben the Puter Leat give you that dream yet we dont have it our self.'

It realy glitcht my cool how he said that. He dint even have no parper face on the front of his head. Him the Puter Leat. I said, 'What ben the Puter Leat any how?'

He said, 'What Goodparley calls Eusas head which it ben a girt box of knowing and you hook up peopl to it thats what a puter ben. We ben the Puter Leat we had the woal worl in our mynd and we had worls beyont this in our mynd we progammit pas the sarvering gallack seas WE PROGAMMIT THE GIRT DANTS OF THE EVERY THING. WE RUN THE BLUE THE RED THE YELLER WE RUN THE RED THE BLACK WE RUN THE SEED OF THE RED AND SEED OF THE BLACK. WE RUN THE MANY COOLS OF ADDOM AND THE PARTY COOLS OF STOAN. HART OF THE WUD AND STOMP YOUR FOOT. 1 AND 2 AND SHAKE OF THE HORNS AND 1 AND 2 AND SPLIT OF THE SHYNING . . .'

That wer when I clappt my han over his mouf it wer giving me the creaps how he wer going on. He wer stomping in the mud he wer dantsing and shouting and his face all wite with no eyes in the litening flashes. He begun to groan then like some terbel thing wer taking him and got inside him. He startit to fall and I easit him down I knowit he wer having a fit I seen that kynd of thing befor. I stuck the clof part of the hump back figger be twean his teef so he wunt bite his tung. I wer on my knees in the mud and holding him wylst he twissit and groant and that hook nose head all black and smyling nodding in the litening flashes. The dogs all gethert roun and them close to him grovvelt with ther ears laid back. Holding Lissener I cud feal how strong he wer tho he wernt putting out no strenth agenst me he wer sturgling with what ever wer inside him. I wunnert what wud happen if it got pas him and out. It dint tho. It roalt him roun and shook him up it bent him like a bow but finely it pult back to where ever it come out of. When it gone he wunt do nothing only sleap nor I cudnt get him to walk 1 step.

By then wed come off the A20 we wer on what they call the Iron Track tho there aint no iron to it only some times in the summer youwl see red dus coming up. I put Lissener over my sholder and forkt off the track and looking for some shelter. Come the nex litening flash I seen a old stoan rune I knowit the place they callit Rose & Power it ben from wel befor time back way back. It wer mosly jus a jumbl of stoans ben dug out here and there for sheltering 1 time and a nother.

I got Lissener inside and covert him up with his doss bag then I huddlt in with all them wet dogs. Warm and coasy it wer plus that pong wer some thing you cud get hy on you dint nead to smoak. After a littl I thot may be there wer a nother smel in there as wel I cudnt say what it wer tho. I stayd sharp and scanful long and long then I thot I myswel catch a littl sleap my self.

When I woak up it fealt like the nite mus be about ½ gone. The storm wer pas the raind littlt off to a girzel. I got Lissener on his feet and off we gone. It wernt no moren a 6fag and we wer in Fork Stoan outers. Its only be twean 4 and 5 faggers from there to the senter so I begun to think on what we myt be going to do when we got there. Suddn it come down hevvy on me how many things I dint know. Dint even have no idear of. Me with my grean lites and my blips. I said to Lissener, 'How many Eusa folk be there in Fork Stoan?'

He said, 'There aint none there jus now. When its time for Goodparley and the Ardship to do the askings roun the circel they put all the other Eusa folk in Cambry and they keap the dead town hoals all emty for the Ardship.'

I said, 'How many Eusa folk be there all to gether?'

He said, '45 counting me. Which they axel rate it roun the circel you see. Counting from Horny Boy its 1 in the 1st then 2 in the 2nd and so on til you have 9 in No. 9 which the pirntowt is 45. They all ways breed us up to moren a nuff and then they kul us down to that.'

I said, 'Be you telling me there aint no moren 45 Eusa folk in the woal of Inland?'

He said, 'Thats right.'

I thot: 45 Eusa folk. 40 bleeding 5. Wunt you know it. Some how wylst we ben roading to Fork Stoan Id begun to see in my mynd me and Lissener with 100s and 100s behynt us and stomping the Ram flat. There it wer tho. Which ever side Im on theres all ways mor on the other side. I begun to wish I dint know nothing moren I knowit befor I come to Bernt Arse that morning. Iyther you dont know nothing or you know too much it dont seam like theres any thing in be twean. Lissener dint seam to have no worrys tho. He jus roalt a long with a easy kynd of sylents coming out of him I have to say it over loadit my serkits jus that littl bit. I said to him, 'You dont seam worrit nor nothing.'

He said, 'Why shud I be? When I ben in that hoal it lookit like there cudnt only 1 thing happen. Now it looks like any thing myt happen.'

I said, 'Yet it mus be hard for you with no eyes you cant even see what youre walking in to.'

He said, 'No 1 can. Onlyes diffrents is them with eyes they *think* they can.'

I tryd to ease up a littl. I myndit my self itwd parbly be a nother 6fag befor we come in to any bother so why not in joy that peace of time the bes I cud. Stil it takes you strange walking in your old foot steps like that. Putting your groan up foot where your chyld foot run nor dint know nothing what wer coming. All them ins and outs and ups and downs of Fork Stoan outers ben my vencher place when I ben littl. Me and my kid crowd. Some of them dead befor they ever growt up. Follery Digman dog et. Ender Easten kilt in a digging. Belgrave Moaters dead of the coffing sickness. Ferny Carpenter took off by a feaver. And here come Riddley Walker walking thru that dead town dark with his blyn moon brother. Smelling the dead town smel of old grean rot old berning old piss on the stoans. Old littl Riddley Walkers from time back running a head of me and follering behynt. Yelling ther sylents and singing ther rimes and clyming over old walls stumps and stannings.

We kep getting closer to the senter. I hadnt never seen the out poast but I knowit about where it wer and wewd perwel be in it in a minim or 2. I said to Lissener, 'I know I ben the 1 as said Fork Stoan but here we are coming in to the senter of it nor I dint have no progam what about you?'

He said, 'Im lissening enn I.'

I said, 'Youwl lissen us right in to Grabs your Aunty in a minim if we keap on walking dont you have nothing in mynd?'

He said, 'I dont know til I get there do I. Youre all ways worrying your self with littl myndy askings. Dont you know if you keap getting a head of your self youwl jus only fall over your self when you get to where youre going?'

I said, 'I thot may be you being such a telling head you myt even know some thing befor they acturely put your head on a poal.'

He said, 'I know you dont have too much balls but if you cud jus suck your thum qwyet for a wyl and stop giving me inner fearents I cud tune in better.'

I said, 'I had balls a nuff to get you out of that hoal when you neadit me tho dint I.'

He said, 'Yes you did after I pult the dog and the dog pult you. Hadnt he come for you youwd parbly stil be shovveling cow shit or what ever you done at that form.'

I said, 'Cow shit with them or bul shit with you there aint much in it is there.' What hed said it realy hert me tho. Here I ben thinking how wel I done going over that fents and oansome amongst them dogs and he wer trying to make it be nothing. I said, 'Any how whatve you done whats so ballsy?'

He put his han on my sholder I fealt like when he took it a way itwd leave a wite shadder behynt. He said, 'I know I soun like Im trying to littl you down but that aint what Im doing Im trying to bring on that seed of the red in you Im trying to strong it on Im trying to rise your hump. Dyou lissen me? Im trying to get you to be your oan black dog and your oan Ardship.'

I said, 'Why?'

He said, 'Becaws you wont all ways have me wil you.'

I said, 'Why not?'

He said, 'Becaws thats how itwl be nor les not mouf it roun no mor jus keap that in you. Be your oan black dog and your oan Ardship.'

We gone a head on the qwyet slow and easy nor no lert from the dogs no soun only the hisper of the rain. We wer farther in nor ever I ben when I ben littl we kep on thru hevvy rubbl til we come in unner some thing and out of the rain. Cudnt see nothing at all in there. Gone a littl farther and come to big steps going down and warm air coming up. I said to Lissener, 'You cern you aint ben here befor?' Becaws he wer moving like a dog on hot foller.

He said, 'No but weare coming strong on some thing. Be ready to move qwick.'

He neadntve tol me that I wer ready for any thing and wivvering all over with it. That place wer a Power place you cud feal it all roun you. *Smel* the Power even with the dog pong. Breave it in to your arms and legs. I cud feal a terning and a rushing in it so strong and Lissener the same. Lissening to our foot steps eckoing in that ringing dark.

We seen a feabl shaky glimmer like from a far off candl it wer jus a nuff so we cud see the edges of the steps. Slow and easy slow and easy. From there on it wer only the black leader and his 2 nexters with us the others ternt roun I gest they wer poasting ther selfs back at the top of the steps I fealt sorry for any body coming that way on our foller. Wunnering at the same time why the dogs hadnt give us warning of no lookouts yet. Lissener said, 'The out poasts dont keap sharp they dont think no 1s ever coming in on them.'

From there on it wer mosly cavit in rubbl we had to sqweaze thru then it opent up big you cudve lissent the diffrents even without looking. The lite wer coming from behynt some girt mouns of rubbl unner where the over head ben barmt out. It cudntve ben no moren a cuppl of candls or lanterns jus a feabl glimmer and the jynt shadders wivvering on the stanning walls and broakin stoans and rubbl and what ever over head wer lef. The jynt shadders wer from girt machines o they wer guvner big things and crouching all broakin but not dead they cudnt dy there wer too much Power in them. Where we wer stanning you cud hear the sea beyont us in the dark. Breaving and sying breaving and sying it wer like them machines wer breaving and sying in ther sleap.

Lissener hispert me, 'What is it? Be they terning be they moving?'

I hispert back, 'Its broakin machines they aint moving.' It wernt nothing like when you dig up old rottin machines out of the groun these wer in ther parper working place nor nothing rottin they wer some kynd of iron dint rot it wer all shyning all catching that shaky glimmer. Some of them ther shels ben broak open you cud see girt shyning weals like jynt mil stoans only smoov. Id all ways usit the word *shyning* same as any 1 else myt. The sun is shyning or the moon is shyning. Youwl see a shyning on the water or a womans hair. When you talk of the Littl Shyning Man its jus the middl word of what hes callt there aint no real meaning to it. Suddn when I seen the shyning of them broakin machines I begun to get some idear of the shyning of the Littl Man. Tears begun streaming down my face and my froat akit.

Lissener hispert, 'Whats the matter?'

I hispert back, 'O what we ben! And what we come to!' Boath of us wer sniffling and snuffling then. Me looking at them jynt machines and him lissening ther sylents. Right then I dint know where I wer with any thing becaws all on a suddn I wernt seeing any thing from where I seen it befor. Up to then I ben agenst Goodparley and I ben agenst what ever he wer for. I dint like him for his littl eyes and his big sqware teef nor I dint like all that Eusas head rubbish nor the res of it. The way he talkit of putting the Littl Shyning Man to gether and that. Now all on a suddn Eusa and Eusas head and the Littl Shyning Man be come some thing woaly diffrent in my mynd to what they ben befor. How cud any 1 not want to get that shyning Power back from time back way back? How cud any 1 not want to be like them what had boats in the air and picters on the wind? How cud any 1 not want to see them shyning weals terning?

All what Ive wrote jus now gone thru my head in a flash that nite and wylst thinking it I wer scanning sharp and lissening hard. Stil dint see no 1 nor nothing moving only them jynt shadders shaking and me shaking with them. Not from fear it wer as citement. Some peopl can feal ther mooning in them some cant. The moon of ther bearthing I mean. Parbly the moon of ther getting and all. Which I know I can. Some times Iwl feal the cross over in my sleap and it takes me strange. I ben got in the las thin sickel of the failing moon and I ben bearcht in the Ful. When Im in my ful bearthing moon Im wide on and sharp strung. When Im coming off it to my getting moon Im reaching on and hungering for that nex Ful. That nite in that Power place in Fork Stoan I cud feal that hungry moon what I cudnt see. Feal it thin. Feal it craving. Feal the tide making for the hy I dint have to see it I knowit wer hy water coming on. Feal it neap and craving for its big hy in the nex Ful. I hispert to Lissener, 'O yes we done right to foller the circel here its fulling on so strong.'

He dint say nothing I sust how it wer with him some times when we wer boath lissening hy 1 of us wud starve the other like when 1 boat puts a nother in its wind shadder. Becaws I begun to know by then I wer some kynd of lissener as wel. Being with Lissener brung it out and brung it on. I wunnert how I ever cudve fealt real up to then. How I ever cudve fealt a live befor I begun to take things in like I wer now. I wantit to move I wantit to do I wantit to happen with what ever wer happening roun me. Like it says in *Eusa 5*: 'Evere thing blippin & bleapin & movin in the shiftin uv thay Nos. Sum tyms bytin sum tyms bit.'

Thinking on from there. *Eusa 6:* 'Cum tu the wud in the hart uv the stoan.' I knowit I wer there in a way. Right then I wer in the wud in the hart of the stoan. Or the stoan in the hart of the wud it dont make no odds. Youre all ways there only you dont all ways know it.

We movit roun easy for a scan behynt the rubbl where the lite wer coming from. There wer a shelter it lookit to be about a 6 peopl 1 it wer the userel thing baskit and gunge with a thatch roof. Them as bilt it theyd movit rubbl so they cud put the shelter unner the hoal in the over head where it wer open to the sky. Big big that Power place wer you cudve stood 10 men 1 on top of the other nor they wuntve reacht the over head.

The black leader wer looking the same way I wer. I movit my head and han a littl like you wud out foraging and giving some 1 the syn to move up closer. That dogd all ready be come so much like regler crowd I jus done it without thinking. No soonerd I give the syn nor off he gone like we ben foraging to gether our woal lives. Big and hevvy as he wer he dint make no soun he jus slyd like a shadder getting longer til he come to the shelter then he easit to the doar way and lookit in. He lookit back tords Lissener and me with his ears up and waving his tail then he startit on beyont and looking back agen showing all clear as plain as any 1 cud.

Lissener and me follert on then and the 2 nexter dogs with us. I lookit in to the shelter with a arrer on the string. 3 pairs of up and down sleapers 2 benches a tabel with 3 candls lit and a fire place with the fire going. Pots and gear but no weapons in site. I had to smyl at the candls I knowit them Fork Stoan hevvys wer afeart of coming back in to that big place in the dark. I wudve took a doss bag only I dint want to leave no foller.

Follering the black leader we gone down some steps in to a tunnel and you cud hear the sea stronger. We come out in to the open nite and the littl girzel on our faces agen the sea wer beating loud on the stoans it wer hy water right a nuff. Where we come out then it wer some where a long the snug I think it wer jus inshoar of the lite house stump.

Lissener and me wer boath on the lissen and boath waiting for some thing we dint know what. Working our way a long the shoar then tords Do It Over we seen a fire and figgers black agenst it. 1st look I got I cudnt be cern how many it wer but I gest it wer all 6 Fork Stoan hevvys parbly changing the look out.

Looking beyont the fire and the figgers looking in to the dark a long the shoar then looking out to the sea dark and

Lissener hispert to me, 'The littl come big took by the far come close.'

I fealt like putting my 2 hans roun his froat and sqweazing hard. I hist back at him, 'Why in the worl did you have to say that? Whatre you trying to put on me?'

He hispert, 'Trubba not I wernt saying it to you I dint even know I said it out loud it wer jus some thing come in to my head.'

We workit up on to the top of the clif behynt the hevvys til we wer over where they wer. They had ther fire about $\frac{1}{2}$ way down on some kynd of stanning. Looking over the edge I cud see the woal 6 of them. We kep back out of the fire lite then and we lissent a littl.

Mosly they wernt talking they wer passing a flask roun. Which what they did say mos of it got los in the soun of the sea beating on the stoans. We did hear a littl of it tho. 1 of them said, '. . . Goodparleys boy and ben throwt over. He cud wel be . . .'

A nother 1 said, '. . . do any how?'

The 1st 1 said, 'His dad ben 1 Stoan Phist bint he. Iwl give odds there ben knowing . . . Iwl give odds that littl witey bloakwl go . . .'

Lissener pult me back he hist, 'Come on theres some thing else here les get to it befor some 1 else does.'

I hist, 'What is it?'

He hist, 'I dont know til we get to it.' He wunt even hol back 1 minim so off we gone a long the clifs tords Do It Over.

We come to where the clifsve fel in to the sea time back way back its broakin groun there all a jumbl we use to go there our crowd of kids when I ben littl. That place stil had its old name from way way back it wer callit The Warnings. Coming on to it I thot: Here!

The sea wer stil chopping and beating on the stoans but there come a nother soun it wer that holler bonking soun of a boat knocking on stoan. Looking hard I cud make out the shape of it black agenst the foam. Lissener said, 'There!'

Stanning on The Warnings looking at that boat out of the dark! Never ben befor. Never be agen.

O that water wer col. I pult the boat on to the stoans it wer
½ ful of water and hevvy. Sail dragging in the water the
marsed bustit itd come down on the bloak what ben sailing
the boat he wer stil unner it dead with his head smasht in.
Musve happent in the storm parbly he ben blowt Souf of
Fork Stoan then with the tide terning he ben driffing back
the other way a long the shoar tords Do It Over.

That dead bloak wer from other side dark as it wer I cud tel
by his boots. What ben he doing out there any how? Cawt in
the storm parbly and nitefel on the water. Ben he stearing for
that fire on the clifs when the marse come down on his head?

Nothing in the boat only oars and a bayling skoop. Hooker
roap and hook. Bow and arrers and spears. The bloak had a
knife on him he had some roady and some drowndit bread in
1 pockit. In a nother pockit he had flint and striker and
makings and a candl stub. About a ¼ cut of hash and some
rizlas. Plus a bag of littl stoans all wet and crummly. Not hard
at all you cud break them with your thum nail. There wernt
nothing else on the bloak nor nothing else in the boat I got my
self good and wet looking every where I even lookit inside
the drobber case. It wer only a littl open boat there wernt that
many hidey places.

Lissener took that littl bag of littl crummly stoans in his
hans he said, 'This is what I ben lissening. Hol it in your hans
and you can feal it in them stoans and scrabbling to get out
you can hear it hispering to its self and clacking like a skelter
of crabs.'

I said, 'What is it?'

He said, 'I tol you I dont know nothing only when we
gether but I know theres Power in it. And where theres
Power theres foller. We bes not ful this circel on no farther
we bes get in to Cambry qwicks we can with this here bag of
stoans Im going to gether deap Im going to work that Power.'

I had that bag in my han I begun to feal like it wer liting up
the dark like a torch and bleaping follerme all over Inland.
Suddn I wantit the nite to get darker I wantit dark a nuff to
smuvver it qwyet. I thot a littl on our suching waytion and I

done what I cud to dark it down a littl. We roalt mos of the water out of the boat so I cud row it then we put the bloak and every thing else back in it only kep out what ben in his pockits and the bow and arrers for Lissener plus I cut off a good lenth of sail roap it wer boun to be neadful some time. Then I got in and pult out to where it wer deap a nuff even at low water. I tyd the hooker roap short roun the dead bloaks leg then over the side I droppt the hooker and him boath. Thinking wylst I done it: That Powers working me all ready nor I dont even know what it is.

Pult back tords shoar and when I come to where some big rocks wer sticking out in to the water I clum out on to them and ternt the boat over and lef it floating up side down and driffing how it wud.

Then we vackt our wayt out of there and roading for Cambry.

13

Heading for senter then. I never ben to Cambry befor but I knowit wer a bit farther from Fork Stoan to there nor it wer from Bernt Arse to Fork Stoan. I reckont we had dark a nuff to las our road out if we kep on steady.

Out thru the Norf part of Fork Stoan outers we gone and Norfing on the A260 track by the Frogs Legs. Going thru the outers the 2 nexter dogs forkt off to the lef and by the time we come to Stickit Flats they wer back and the others with them we had the woal pack with us agen. I kep wunnering how long wewd have them I knowit they ben long pas ther markings and far off ther groun.

Peopl talk about the Cambry Pul theywl say any part of Inland you myt be in youwl feal that pul to Cambry in the senter. May be its jus in the air or may be where the Power Ring ben theres stil Power in the groun. You tern your self that way and it comes on so strong you cud beam your self in with your eyes closd. Or with no eyes thats how Lissener gone. He dint go slow and easy like a blyn man on strange groun which that wer about the only kynd of groun there wer for him he hadnt never ben no where in his woal life only 1 hoal to a nother from Cambry roun the circel 9wys to Fork Stoan. No he dint go slow nor easy. He stayd with that black dog some times with a han on his neck some times not he leggit so fas I cudnt hardly keap up with him. Hewd stummel and fall in to hoals hewd go arse over head down suddn drops it dint matter nothing to him. It wer like he had a winch inside him with a roap going right the way to Cambry and him winching his self in. All ways lissening and out of him there come a farring voyce with no soun going a head in to the dark.

I said to Lissener, 'Howre we going to work it so you can gether with them Eusa folk in Cambry? Have you got that progammit?'

He said, 'Not yet.'

I said, 'With the woal 44 of them to gard therewl be moren 6 hevvys wont there?'

He said, 'Theres all ways 12 in Cambry plus theyve put on a exter 6.'

I said, 'Be them Eusa folk all in 1 hoal to gether?'

He said, 'Yes.'

I said, 'Wel we bes progam some thing hadnt we?'

He said, 'There you go agen getting in front of your self. We dint progam nothing in Fork Stoan and we come out of that all right dint we?'

So I dint bother him no mor about progamming nothing. I said, 'How dyou do that kynd of gethering what youre going to do? Do you all set down and pul datter or dyou jus think to gether or what?'

He said, 'We do some poasyum.'

I said, 'Whats poasyum?'

He said, 'It aint jus poasyum you all ways say *some* poasyum. You ever seen a nes of snakes?'

I said, 'Yes.'

He said, 'I never but 1 of the hevvys tol me they do the same theywl get all in a tangl slyding and sqwirming and ryving to gether. Which is how we do it all the many rubbing up to 1 a nother skin to skin and talking vantsit theary. Which is a kynd of hy telling and trantsing. Thats when the singing and the shouting come the many cools of Addom and the party cools of stoan. The strong and the weak inner acting and what happent in the cloudit chaymber.'

I said, 'Is that where the seed of the red and the seed of the black come in to it?'

He said, 'Yes howd you know that?'

I said, 'When you ben having your fit you ben talking vantsit theary. If you cud do it then and you can do it now may be you dont even nead to gether may be you can get them Nos. oansome.'

He said, 'No when I talk in a fit or what Im saying now that dont mean nothing thats jus only the outers of it. It never comes the woal thing realy without the all of us gethering. Weare jus like scattert peaces of a broakin pot them peaces wont hol water without theyre gethert nexy and glewt ferm in the shape of holding dont you see. I cant make the shape of holding oansome.'

I said, 'What is that fit you get is it some thing coming in to you and you going out of your self?'

He said, 'Im mosly out of my self Im mosly elser lissening like I do. Thats what brings on the fit some times Iwl lissen some thing in too strong then the vy brations of it move in on my emty space and I have to sturgl back to my connexion.'

I dont know for cern what put it in my mynd then may be it wer the word *connexion* or him talking of scattert peaces but suddn it come to me we wer like Eusas 2 boys we wer going to have to go 2 diffrent ways some time I dint know why nor how nor when but it fult me sad it come like a weaping inside me. In the dark beside me Lissener begun to cry.

I said, 'Whatre you crying about?'

He said, 'Im crying for what ben Im crying for whats going to be.'

I said, 'Whats the use of that?'

He said, 'Whats the use of not?'

I said, 'May be it dont have to be.'

He dint say nothing he jus let my words littl off and dwindl stupid on the air. The black dog bumpt agenst my leg like he wer showing me at leas his part of the dark wer frendy.

I said, 'I wunner where they gone them 2 boys of Eusas?'

Lissener sung:

1 to live and 1 to dy 2 boys gone
1 to lite and 1 to dark roading on
Never did the Good Luck brother
Tern a roun to help the other
Never did the other 1
Ever have the sents to run

I said, 'Whats that then? I never heard that song is it about Eusas boys?'

He said, 'I dont know what it is its jus a bit of a old song nor I dont even know the res of it.'

I said, 'Did you ever hear any story of Eusas boys tho?'

He said, 'No I never. Whats the diffrents any how it wunt help us nothing knowing what be come of them.'

I said, 'Why do we have to go to Cambry why do we have to go for that gethering?'

He said, 'What else is there to do? Wait for Goodparley to close his han on us?'

I said, 'It dont look like there ben no foller on us parbly he dont have the leas idear where we are.'

He said, 'Thats what Mr Mouse said jus befor he be come owls meat.'

I said, 'You lissen hes on to us then?'

He said, 'Thats what I ben lissening for a wyl now.'

I said, 'Since when?'

He said, 'I aint sure only it wer some time after I had the fit.'

Then I membert that smel back at Rose & Power and it come to me what it ben. If that dog pong hadnt ben so hevvy over it Iwdve knowit right off. Partly it ben that wax they dip hard clof in to keap the rain out and partly it ben hash smoak and sweat and mud and meat smoak and torch smoak and beer. What it ben wer Goodparley & Orfing with ther fit up. They cudve ben there befor us they cudve gone a head to Fork Stoan thatwd be like Goodparley to suss which way wewd jump. I said to Lissener, 'You think theyre in front of us or behynt?'

He said, 'I lissen them in front.'

I said, 'Whynt you say nothing befor this?'

He said, 'What diffrents does it make? Be they follering behynt or leading on a head weare going where weare going any how aint we.'

I said, 'Even if they ben right on our backs they cudntve seen us take them stoans off that dead bloak. At leas they dont know nothing about that.'

He said, 'If I have any Luck gethering in Cambry theywl know soon a nuff.'

Thats when it come to me what them hevvys roun the fire ben talking about. I said, 'Belnot Phist.'

He said, 'What Belnot Phist?'

I said, 'Thats the littl witey bloak them hevvys ben talking about wylst you ben lissening the boat and the stoans.'

He said, 'What about him?'

Which I tol him then how Phist wer coming the do it man at Widders Dump plus I myndit him what them hevvys said about him being Goodparleys boy and ben throwt over and how his dad ben 1 Stoan Phist and parbly past on knowing. I said, 'It wunt sneak me if hes got knowing hewl use agenst Goodparley nor it wunt sneak me if Belnot Phist is out to be Belnot Goodparley.'

He said, 'Iwl give odds youve sust that right and you know what the nex thing is.'

I said, 'What?'

He said, 'Split up and dubbl our chances. Iwl go on to Cambry with ½ the stoans and gether how ever I can. May be Goodparleys waiting there may be not. May be I can work some thing with them stoans its a chance any how. You go to Belnot Phist with the other ½ and see if you can put some thing to gether with him. If hes Goodparleys nemminy he cud wel be our frend.'

I said, 'And yet you know may be weve boath got it wrong. May be Goodparley aint on to us may be Belnot Phist dont have a thot in the worl agenst Goodparley may be the bes thing is jus vack our wayt over the border in to Outland and take our chance there.'

Lissener said, 'You can do what you like moon brother but my peopl ben the Power Leat when Goodparleys peopl ben the maggits in the iron. My peopl ben the 1s as bilt the Power Ring and sent the air boats out beyont the sarvering gallack seas. He aint nothing only rottinness growt out of rottinness nor I aint leaving Inland to him jus yet.'

Wel I wernt really too kean to split up I wernt realy on for what I wer getting in to. When I gone over the fents at Widders Dump it ben jus me throwing my self in to the black and taking my

110

chance what it myt do with me. Swaller me up or spit me out I dint care I dint have no 1 on my back only my self. Only my self! Looking at them words going down on this paper right this minim I know there aint no such thing there aint no only my self you all ways have every 1 and every thing on your back. Them as stood and them as run time back way back long long time they had me on ther back if they knowit or if they dint. I had Lissener on my back plus a woal lot moren him I cudnt even say what all it wer and mor and mor I wer afeart it wer coming to some thing I wernt going to be hevvy a nuff for.

I said, 'I know you all ways say every 1 goes in to every thing blyn but you know if you go in to Cambry oansome you aint got the same chance as a bloak with eyes.'

Lissener said, 'You know and I know Ive parbly got a better chance so dont try to bul shit your self out of it if youre afeart to go jus say it strait.'

I said, 'Im afeart and Iwl go but we myswel road on to gether a littl way yet. Iwl fork off in a few faggers.'

He said, 'Lissen me now Riddley we dont have no minims to spare. The sooner you piss off out of here the sooner Phistwl have them stoans working for us.'

There wernt no mor to say about it. We boath knowit cud jus as wel be arga warga at boath ends. I said, 'Im off then. The sooner I get to Phist the sooner Iwl get back to where you are.'

He said, 'Good Luck moon brother.'

I said, 'Good Luck to you the same.' O I dint want to leave him. We huggit each other and I ternt to go. The black leader bumpt his sholder agenst my leg. I dint even want to think if any dogs wer coming with me or not I wer progamming to go it oansome what ever. Soons I movit off tho the 2 nexter dogs movit with me and it lookit like ½ the pack follert on behynt so I wernt qwite oansome in the worl after all.

Lissener gone Norf and Wes tords Cambry then and I gone Wes and Norf tords Widders Dump. For a wyl I dint hardly know which 1 of us I wer with. I knowit I wer Riddley

Walker heading for Widders Dump but I wer mor with Lissener heading for Cambry. I never ben there I never ben no closern the Ring Ditch yet I cud feal it coming closer to me with every step I took the other way. No 1 uses the old place names now they ben unspoak this long time but mos of them are stil there in the places. You know Cambry ben Canterbury in moufs long gone. Canterbury. It has a zanting in it like a tall man dantsing and time back there ben foun there girt big music pipes as big as fents poals peopl said. You try to think of how it musve soundit when the Power Ring ben there and working not jus crummelt stannings and a ditch. It musve ben some girt jynt thing hy hy up and with a shyning and a flashing to it time back way back when they had boats in the air and all the res of it. Did it woosh and hum or ben it dumming and beating like the hart of the worl and what ben the music come out of them pipes? You dont know nor you wont never know. You can feal how there ben Power there. You go down 1 side of the Ring Ditch and up the other side you can feal it in your knees how youre walking tremmery and you can feal it in your belly. Feal it hy hy over you and overing you. Old foller in the air the after blip and fading of what ben. Fading fading dwindling on the air but the fading and the dwindl sending out ther sylents roun and roun that circel never slowing to a stilness. Wel realy there aint no stilness any where is there. Not 1ce you begin to take noatis.

When I forkt off from Lissener it musve ben about a 6fag after 1st seeing that boat with the dead bloak in it. I stil had plenny of time and a nuff to get to Widders Dump befor day lite. I begun to get in front of my self thinking how Iwd do when I got there. Even if Id sust it right as Belnot Phist wer agenst the Ram I dint know how things stood at Widders Dump. For all I knowit they cud all be hard Ram there and Phist permuch a persner amongst them. I neverd had much to do with any of them formers only Chalker Marchman at the digging and chatting some times to the bloaks at the reddy. I cudnt realy see my self stepping up to that gate and saying Trubba not. On the other han if I slyd in over the fents how wud I fynd Phists shelter befor some 1 foun me? And the woal time I wer thinking them thots part of me wer heading for Cambry with Lissener wylst a nother part wer wunnering when some thing wud come up to stop me. Realy I cudnt beleave I wer going to be let to walk all over Inland any where I fantsyt and partly I wantit some thing to stop me. Becaws I knowit by then any thing at all myt happen and parbly wud. 1ce that eye starts roaling itwl roal right off the board and gone so easy. So easy. You can go the worl a way so easy. This nite Im writing down here it wer jus only the same nite of that very same day I gone over the Widders Dump fents in the morning. Which that seamt time back years back and long long pas. Yet here I wer now coming back to that same fents and thinking how to get inside agen.

With my mynd going all diffrent ways stil my feet gone jus that 1 way. Them dogs and me we slyd a long thru dark and girzel by forms and fentses pas all them sleaping in ther doss bags and all them looking out on hy walks be twean Fork Stoan and Widders Dump. No 1 seen us no 1 heard us nothing stoppt us nor it dint seam no time at all til we come sydling that hy groun sholder and nearing on to Widders Dump. My face and hans wet with the girzel my cloes hevvy with the wet my feet slyding in the mud my boots and leggers sogging with it. Smelling the dog pong the rain the mud and the nite. Sylents in my ears only the rain hisper. Far far back behynt my eyes some other place some other time the dry dus rising and the hotness wivvering on the air. No me. Jus barrens and the dry dus blowing. I thot: Who knows? May be Goodparley is the Littl Shyning Man nor he dont know it his self. That thot come to me then sydling that sholder in the rainy dark so I write it down here now.

Looking down to the low groun in the farness I cud see candl glimmers in the gate house at Widders Dump. Where I wer then its where the hy groun sholder goes in and out theres a long deap holler its like a short valley its that place they call Mr Clevvers Roaling Place. They say some times when Mr Clevvers roading thru Inland he gets a larfing fit he cant help his self he jus has to let his self go he roals on the groun there. It wer stil common groun they use to forage there time back. Long befor my time the goats had et it bare and since then there bint nothing only granser rats. They use to say there ben the goast of a batcherd living there hewd come out and show fight when dogs come too close to where he use to play with his cubs when he ben a live.

I dont know what made me go down there may be I wer hoaping for a site of that goast batcherd or may be Mr Clevver wantit me to have a larf. Userly any crowd I wer with wewdve took the upper track the l what come down easer off the sholder by where Belnot Phistd put the crew to timbering. Any how I dint go down that way I gone thru Mr Clevvers Roaling Place. I wer thinking thinking how wer I going to get to Belnot Phist and wishing I wer clevverer that way. Thinking if I wer realy clevver I wunt be busting my head over it oansome Iwd sly in to How Fents and have a word to Fister Crunchman him asd wantit me to stop pontsing for the Ram and do a mans doing. There wernt much wind then jus a littl and freshening it wer fulling and lulling fulling and lulling. Come the nex littl ful and whatd it bring me but Fister Crunchmans very voyce. Its very qwyet and small thru the hisper of the rain its like it ben pickt up ever so delkit by the wind the way you myt lif a keepaways egg from a ledge on a clif and clym down with it only this here wind egg it hatches in my ear and littl qwyet words come out of it. 'I dont feal right about it,' says Fister Crunchmans littl voyce.

Nex voyce is Straiter Empy he says, 'For his oan good and all.'

Farner Salvage is the nex voyce he says, 'Fister you know they wont do nothing moren dock his fraction for the nex 14nt or so. You jus cant go sticking Mincery peopl in bogs when ever you feal like it. Weare living on burrow time as it is. Wunt take hardly nothing at all for them to largen us in the same as Dog Et done Littl Salting. If youre thinking of putting some thing to gether youre wanking man youre roaling a fools pair of dice.'

Then some 1s hushing them qwyet the talking stops and Im out of there. Thinking how clevver I ben to go down thru Mr Clevvers Roaling Place it cernly lookit like he wantit me to have a larf with him. That lernt me some thing about them dogs too they wernt all of them as fine tunet as that black leader. Hewdve give me warning and early. Even hadnt he smelt nor heard nothing hewdve col sust any body waiting a jump on that hy groun up of us and hewdve let me know. Thinking of Lissener roading in to Cambry blyn at leas he had that black dog. Plus I wer thinking how close I come to being jumpt and how stupid I ben not to know my crowdwd have the grabbers out for me. I dont think Fister Crunchman wer in it I think he ben keaping them talking so Iwd be lertit. I aint had a chance to ask him yet.

I kep wide of the regler track then and working slow and scanful tords Widders Dump and that littl candl glimmer. I knowit I dint have too long til day lite I cudnt realy wayst no time nor chance on wrong gesses.

I come out of the woodlings to the edge of the Widders Dump clearing. That candl glimmer I seen from up on the hy groun sholder lookit lovely and brite and ever so warm and coasy thru the col girzel it wudve ben nice to be abel to walk up to that gate and say Trubba not in stead of slying roun in the dark. Widders Dump Form is perwel spread out it aint no littl 40 peopl fents theyve got 200 and mor plus all ther stock and cattl which theyre all inside the main compoun at nite so its a big fents to walk roun and its a big fents to look out for as wel. Even a small fentswl have 4 lookouts on the hy walk so I thot they mus have at leas 6 at Widders Dump but them being formers and with the nite so col and all I thot there myt be emty spaces here and there with some bloaks keaping ther look out in the gate house with a nice cup of tea.

Its a big clearing I crost it fas then working roun the Norf side a way from the gate house its the side tords the rivver. Cruising roun the primmeter ditch trying to keap my self on for any kynd of nindicater which there come 1 to me then it wer the terbel sharp pong from the dy working where they boyl up the pig shit earf. I thot: Hewl be close to the dyers. Dint realy think it it jus come to me.

They dont have no poynty stakes at Widders Dump its jus only the ditch which its a wide 1 and it wer ful of water from the rains. I stript off and bundelt my cloes roun my spears then I throwit the spears over the ditch in to the bank on the other side. In to that col water then and swum acrost. Come out of there with my teef clattering loud a nuff to lert the lookouts 5 faggers off. Dryd off with my clout put on my cloes and lissent hard. Not a soun not a creak from that hy walk. I thot: Formers. There parbly aint a 1 of them on the hy walk. Throwit my roap over a fents poal and up I gone. All clear on the hy walk so Thump. Down to the groun and I wer over that Widders Dump fents 2ce that same day. 1ce going out and 1ce coming in.

No lites in any shelters only the 1 neares the dy working which I thot that mus be Phist. Jus then I wunnert if I cud be walking in to a trap and in that same minim with that thot some 1 grabbit me from behynt.

14

Wel Im telling Truth here aint I. Thats the woal idear of this writing which I begun wylst thinking on what the idear of us myt be. Right then when I got grabbit my 1st thot wer: Wel now may be I dont have to progam nothing for a littl.

Who ever had a holt of me clampt me in a strangl holt with a arm like iron and the other han stuck a knife agenst my belly. I thot: It aint even that long since I had my E cut in me I dont hardly have no parper scab on it yet.

Any how this hevvy in charge of me he pushes me tords the doar of the shelter and he says, 'Here he is Guvner.'

The doar opens and of coarse theres Goodparley sitting there who else wud it be. With his fit up. He dont have Orfing with him its jus him and Belnot Phist which Phists face is even witern userel. Looking at poor old Phist then I thot we myt even end up frends if the boath of us come thru this littl rumpa a live.

Goodparley he smyls his teef at me and his littl eyes theyre near dantsing wylst theyre peaping over the fents of his cheaks. He says to me, 'Wel Riddley yung Walker its ben a long day for you aint it. We bes change your name from Walker to Runner you ben moving so fas 1 place to a nother and back agen. All the way to Fork Stoan to meet a boat with a dead sailer in it. Funny thing to do in the middl of the nite and such a stormy nite and all. Dead sailer from the other side which he brung you some thing for our frend Phist dint he. O yes he brung some kynd of treats what myt they be myt they be honey sweets or what?'

I dint say nothing.

He says, 'You know Riddley Iwd cernly like to have a littl scan of them sweets.'

I dint say nothing I dint know what to say. The hevvy what brung me in begun to smyl.

Goodparley says, 'Wel you know Riddley weare going to tern your up side down weare going to emty your pockits so what ever youve got whynt you jus han it over.'

Funny thing. I dint want him going thru my pockits I dint want him getting his hans on that blackent figger whatd put me on the road to where ever I wer going. There wernt no way I cud hide that bag of stoans so I took it out of my pockit and I helt it out to him.

He jus lookit at that bag for a littl like he dint want that minim to go a way from him. He says, 'Riddley what dyou think is in there dyou think that myt be a littl salt now dyou think it myt be a littl saver what dyou think it myt be?'

Phist says to Goodparley, 'Abel he dont know nothing Ive tol you that all ready he aint clevver.'

Goodparley says, 'O no and in deed he aint hes bettern clevver hes a mover hes a happener. Now Riddley Runner you jus tel me what you think youve got in that bag. Iwd be interstit to know what you think it is.'

I said, 'Truth is I dont have no idear what it is.'

He says, 'No you dont know do you I know wel a nuff thats Truth. All you done wer grab it becaws youre a mover and a happener aint you. Youve got to move about and make things happen o I sust that right a nuff and early on. Realy I wunt have to do nothing only tern you luce and let you run and youwd persoon get every thing all happent out and moving I wunt have to stress my self and strain like I ben doing so long. Yes thats all itwd take to get us moving frontwards agen is you and me working to gether. Abel Goodparley and Riddley Runner. Riddley Orfing. Why cant I have you for Shadder Mincer in stead of that dretful littl Orfing on my back and dragging his feet all the time.'

He took me by the rist of my out stretcht arm and pult me to him. He took the bag out of my han he said, 'You can feal it in there pecking to get out cant you. Like a chick in a shel. Whatwl it hatch I wunner?' He put his han in to the bag and brung it out ful of stoans. I hadnt seen them in the lite befor. Yeller they wer. Broakin bits of yeller stoan.

Goodparley lookit over to Phist like he wer going to have his head on a poal right soon. He said, 'Wel you foun your self a sweets place did you and sweeter nor honey you foun your self the yellerboy stoan the Salt 4.'

Phist said, 'I dint fynd nothing Abel I aint no mover nor no happener.'

Goodparley said, 'No and for a true fack you aint my littl pink eyed frend you aint no kynd of a mover nor happener thats jus what I come plaining of this long time innit. "Tryl narrer," you tol me. "Thats the way to do it which wewl do it in the new working," you said. "Spare the mending and tryl narrer." And all the time you ben waiting on your boat with honey sweets your Salt 4 you clevver littl man you yellerboy stoaner you. Whatm I going to do with you I wunner howm I going to put you strait it looks to me like youve tyd your self in such a knot there aint no end to it.'

Phist said, 'Abel I bint waiting on no boat I never knowit nothing about no boat til you come in here with your hevvys and claiming Trubba on me. I know I aint the frendyes bloak in the worl I know theres some dont like me may be theres some in the Mincerywd like to put some Trubba on me. I dont know what others myt be doing but *I* aint ben running no stoans. Them Fork Stoan hevvys they can say what they like that dont put nothing on me. You start beleaving that kynd of thing and any 1 can bring down any 1 they like all they have to do is jus only sen them some colourt stoans or powders or what ever.'

Goodparley said, 'What powders Belnot? What kynd of powders myt you be talking about?'

Phist said, 'Eusas sake Abel you jump on every word I say and progamming for Trubba. I aint talking about no powders I dont have no powders I jus only said stoans and powders sames you myt say sticks and stoans it wernt nothing only a way of saying.'

Goodparley said, 'Yes wel leave it with me jus a littl Belnot this wants thinking on praps youwl be so kynd to leave us the loan of your shelter and have a nice cup of tea in the gate house wylst I have a word with this here dog frendy oansome travveler.'

The hevvy as brung me in took Phist out. Goodparley looking at me and smyling hard then he said, 'Howd you get dog frendy Riddley?'

I said, 'I dont know it jus happent. I gone over that fents without realy thinking it out I jus run with them dogs nor they dint arga warga.'

He said, 'You jus run with them dogs did you o youre a deap 1 theres mor and mor to you aint there tel me whyd you go to Fork Stoan with Lissener?'

I said, 'I keap saying I dont know but its Truth it jus like come in to my mynd I thot we bes not break the circel then.'

He said, 'O yes I beleave you parbly you dont even know your self what levvils youre working. *Horny Boy* which is what you are the same as any yung man. *Rung Widders Bel* Ive heard about you and Lorna Elswint shes out livet moren 1 husbin and manys the time youve rung her bel. *Stoal his Fathers Ham as wel.* Which you took over your dads connexion when he got took off. Thats 3 blipful roun the circel nex you done your 1st acturel. *Bernt his Arse.* Bernt your arse here in the digging then over the fents you gone and running with them dogs to Bernt Arse where you bernt *my* arse killing 1 of my hevvys with your dogs. I sust youwd parbly hoal up til dark and I sust you myt do a nother acturel so on I gone to Fork Stoan a head of you. I wer there by The Warnings when you come *and Forkt a Stoan* which is that same and very bag of yeller stoans you brung here roading blipful agen bringing them stoans to Belnot Phist like I knowit you wud you *Done It Over.* You gone over this here fents in the morning and back you come doing it over agen at nite. Only this 2nd time you like *broak a boan* dint you in a way of saying. You got cawt by your old Nunkel Abel.'

My head begun to feal like it wer widening like circels on water I dint know if it wud ever stop I dint know where the end of it wud be. The stranger it took me the mor I fealt at hoam with it. The mor I fealt like Iwd be long where ever it wer widening me to. I said, 'How can you work all that out of a kid rime? *Fools Circel 9wys* is a kid rime for a kid game.'

He said, 'O Riddley you known bettern that you know the same as I do. What ben makes tracks for what wil be. Words in the air pirnt foot steps on the groun for us to put our feet in to. May be a nother 100 years and kids wil sing a rime of Riddley Walker and Abel Goodparley with ther circel game.'

I said, 'What put *Fools Circel 9wys* in the air then?'

He said, 'Dint Lissener tel you who ben the 1st Ardship then?'

I said, 'He said it ben Eusa.'

He said, 'Dint he tel you how the Eusa folk stoand Eusa out of Cambry for what he done? How they crowdit him roun the circel of Inland 1 town to a nother? Every town they come to they tol them on the gate, "This is Eusa what done the clevver work for Bad Time." Them what wer lef in the towns them what wer the soar vivers of the barming they torchert Eusa then. Torchert him and past him on to the nex. Thats when the playgs come follering hot on Eusas road and wiping out each town he lef behynt him. 9 towns in the rime and 9 towns dead but Cambry shud be in it 2ce it ben the 1st it ben the las. Cambry where they stoand him out of starting him on to his circel and Cambry where they brung him back to blyn and bloody not a man no mor he ben cut off.

'To the gate they brung him lef a space all roun him come the dogs then and licking his soars. Them on the gate they wer afeart they said, "Why dont you say Trubba not if you want in?" Eusa said, "I cant say that." They beat him to death then with col iron becaws it ben col iron he done Inland to death with. Mynd you this wer his oan folk done it to him.

'They took his head off then they put it on a poal for telling. Eusas head tol them, "Onlyes part of Inland kep ther hans clean of this ben the Ram which is the head of Inland. You cut my head off my body now the body of Inland wil be cut off from the head." With that there come a jynt wave it wer a wall of water hyer nor a mountin. Dint it come tho. It come rushing it come roaring it come roaling down it cut

121

acrost the lan right thru from Reakys Over down to Roaming Rune. It cut the Ram off sepert from the res of Inland that wer the day the Ram be come a nylan.

'That head of Eusa said to them what put it on the poal, "Now throw me in the sea." Which they done that and the head wer swimming then agenst the tide it swum acrost that water from Inland to the Ram. Them on the Ram took in the head and this is what it tol them: "Make a show of me for memberment and for the ansers to your askings. Make a show with han figgers put a littl woodin head of me on your finger in memberment of my real head on a poal. Keap the Eusa folk a live in memberment of the hardship they brung on. Out of that hardship let them bring a Ardship 12 years on and 12 years come agen. Let the head of Inland ask the Ardship then. Let the head of Inland road the circel ful and to the senter asking what he wants to know for all of Inland. When the right head of Inland fynds the right head of Eusa the anser wil come and Inland wil rise up out of what she ben brung down to." Then the head roalt back in to the water it swum out to sea.'

Goodparley wer all as cited telling that his littl eyes wer shyning you cud see it wer hy telling for him. He said, 'Theres your Fools Circel Riddley its that ful circel Eusa gone his hevvy road on time back way back. Its that circel I ben roading looking for the anser as wil bring poor Inland up from what she ben brung down to.'

Dint say nothing for a littl nyther of us jus lissening to the hisper of the rain. Finely I said, 'Why wernt all this in the *Eusa Story* then?'

Goodparley said, 'It ben Eusa wrote the *Eusa Story* he done it befor they stoand him out of Cambry. After that he dint write nothing mor. Words! Theywl move things you know theywl do things. Theywl fetch. Put a name to some thing and youre beckoning. Iwl write a message if I have to but I wunt word nothing moren that on paper. Eusa ben fetcht by words on paper you know.'

I said, 'What dyou mean?' With my head widening in circels and my mynd sinking like the stoan what made the circels. Part of me where I wer and part of me with Lissener and coming in to Cambry. Thinking:

> Never did the Good Luck brother
> Tern a roun to help the other

With a sickish fealing as I myt be the Good Luck brother and I contrackt I *wud* help the other Iwd get to him soons I cud and what ever Trubba he wer in wewd boath be in it. Cursing my self for leaving him and coming to Widders Dump which I hadnt done nothing only put them yeller stoans in Goodparleys hans.

Goodparley had a peace of paper in his han and holding it in front of me. He said, 'Have a read of this.'

This is what I read wrote down the same:

The Legend of St Eustace

The Legend of St Eustace dates from the year A.D. 120 and this XVth-century wall painting depicts with fidelity the several episodes in his life. The setting is a wooded landscape with many small hamlets; a variety of wild creatures are to be seen and a river meanders to the open sea.

1. At the bottom of the painting St Eustace is seen on his knees before his quarry, a stag, between whose antlers appears, on a cross of radiant light, the figure of the crucified Saviour. The succeeding episodes lead up to his martyrdom.

2. The Saint and his family appear before the Bishop of Rome renouncing their worldly possessions and becoming outcasts.

3. His wife is taken off by pirates in a ship; on the right the father and sons stand praying on the shore.

4. St Eustace and his boys reach a river swollen by torrents. Having swum to the opposite side with one of the

children, he returns for the other. As he reaches the middle of the stream a wolf runs off with the child he has left. He looks back and beholds a lion in the act of carrying off the other child. We see St Eustace praying in the midst of the river.

5. Fifteen years pass by. St Eustace has recovered his wife and sons and is the victorious general of the Emperor Hadrian, who orders a great sacrifice to the gods in honour of his victories. Eustace and his family refuse to offer incense. We see them being roasted to death in a brazen bull. The Emperor Hadrian stands on the left with a drawn sword in his hand.

6. At the top of the painting two angels hold a sheet containing the four souls; the Spirit of God in the form of a dove descends to receive them into heaven.

The date of the painting is about 1480; the work is highly skilled in an English tradition and is a magnificent example of wall painting of this date.

Wel soons I begun to read it I had to say, 'I dont even know ½ these words. Whats a Legend? How dyou say a guvner S with a littl t?'

Goodparley said, 'I can as plain the mos of it to you. Some parts is easyer workit out nor others theres bits of it wewl never know for cern jus what they mean. What this writing is its about some kynd of picter or dyergam which we dont have that picter all we have is the writing. Parbly that picter ben some kynd of a seakert thing becaws this here writing (I dont mean the writing youre holding in your han I mean the writing time back way back what this is wrote the same as) its cernly seakert. Its blipful it aint jus only what it seams to be its the syn and foller of some thing else. A Legend thats a picter whats *depicted* which is to say pictert on a wall its done with some kynd of paint callit *fidelity. St* is short for sent. Meaning this bloak Eustace he dint jus tern up he wer sent. *A.D. 120* thats the year count they use to have it gone from

Year 1 right the way to Bad Time. *A.D.* means All Done. 120 years all done theyre saying thats when they begun this picter in 120 nor they never got it finisht til 1480 is what it says here wel you know there aint no picter cud take 1360 years to do these here year numbers is about some thing else may be wewl never know what.'

I said, 'What year is it now by that count?'

He said, 'We dont know jus how far that count ever got becaws Bad Time put a end to it. Theres a stoan in the Power Ring stannings has the year number 1997 cut in to it nor we aint never seen no year number farther on nor that. After Bad Time dint no 1 write down no year count for a long time we dont know how long til the Mincery begun agen. Since we startit counting its come to 2347 O.C. which means Our Count.'

I said, 'Dyou mean to tel me them befor us by the time they done 1997 years they had boats in the air and all them things and here we are weve done 2347 years and mor and stil slogging in the mud?'

He put his han on my sholder he said, 'Now youre talking jus like me I dont know how many times Ive said that. Now you see the woal thing what Im getting at its why Im all ways strest and straint Im jus a woar out man. *Riddley we aint as good as them befor us. Weve come way way down from what they ben time back way back.* May be it wer the barms what done it poysening the lan or when they made a hoal in what they callit the O Zoan. Which that O Zoan you cant see it but its there its holding in the air we breave. You make a hoal in it and Woosh! No mor air. Wel word ben past down thats what happent time back way black. You hear what I said? I said time back way *black*. You ever hear the story of why the crow is black and curses all the time?

Thru the smoak hoal I cud see the nite thinning out and the day coming on. I dint want to hear no storys about crows. I said, 'Wheres Orfing is he gone after Lissener?'

He said, 'Gone a head of him to Cambry.'

I said, 'Waiting a jump on him.'

He said, 'Keaping a eye and a ear on him til I get there.'

I said, 'Whatwl you do when you get there?'

He said, 'Iwl do what I *ben* doing Iwl go on asking wont I. Do some Cambry asking then its up to Horny Boy and begin that woal Fools Circel over agen becaws it ben broak this time.'

I said, 'You going to help the qwirys on him?'

He said, 'Whats the use of helping qwirys on him that poor simpo I dont think he knows nothing to tel no moren any of them ever do. I do like other Pry Mincers done befor me becaws thats what the Mincery wants. Im terning them frontwards in a woal lot of ways only I cant do it all at 1ce. We aint none of us what you cud call qwick but mos of them roun me theyre 2ce as unqwick as I am Iwl tel you that. May be you ben thinking Im your nemminy but that aint how it is. You think like I do you feal like I do we aint nemminys. Its them as cant think nor feal none of them things theyre the nemminy. Them peopl as jus want to hol on to what theyve got theyre afeart to chance any thing theyre afeart to move even 1 littl step forit. I dont care if its Mincery or forms or fentses its them as wont move theyre the nemminy. Riddley may be you dont know it but you dont have no better frend nor me?'

I dint say nothing.

He give me a littl shake and took his han off my sholder. He said, 'Wel never mynd les get on with this here writing. *XVth century* parbly thats old spel for some kynd of senter where they done this thing theyre telling of in this blipful writing. *Episodes* thats when you do a thing 1 part at a time youve got to get the 1st episode done befor you go on to the nex. Thats how youwl do if youre working chemistery or fizzics. Youwl do your boyl ups and your try outs in episodes, "*Wooded landscape with many small hamlets.*" Wel thats littl pigs innit then theres a *variety* which thats like a pack or a herd and *creatures* thats creachers parbly dogs. May be Folleree and Folleroo in that pack who knows. May be them littl pigs is the many cools and party cools weare looking for becaws this here is blipful writing it aint strait. "*Meanders to the open sea.*" Mazy ways to a open see meaning a look see is

126

what I take that to mean. Whatre we follering them mazy ways for? Have a look right here now weare coming on to the nuts and balls of the thing weare coming to the hart of the matter and the Hart of the Wud where them dogs is on the foller of them littl pigs. Whats at the bottom of the thing and whats this sent bloaks name? Wel it says right here: *"At the bottom of the painting St Eustace"*. That name mynd you of any other name?'

I said, 'Eusa.'

He said, 'Thats it. Its the very same name jus woar down a littl. Who ever this bloak wer what wrote our *Eusa Story* he connectit his self to this here Legend or dyergam and the chemistery and fizzics of it becaws this here Legend writing and the *Eusa Story* the 2 of them ben past down to gether in the Mincery. *"St Eustace is seen on his knees before his quarry."* Which a *quarry* is a kynd of digging. Whys he on his knees? What brung him down what knockt him off his feet? What come out of that digging? *A stag.* Wel thats our Hart of the Wud innit we know him wel a nuff. Whats he got be twean his antlers its *"a cross of radiant light"*. Which is the same as radiating lite or radiation which may be youve heard of.'

I said, 'No I never.'

He said, 'Youve seen wite shadders on stannings cernly you seen the 1 in that hoal in Bernt Arse where you foun Lissener.'

I said, 'Yes I seen that wite shadder.'

He said, 'Wel it ben radiant lite as made that shadder. Radiant lite. Shyning. Wel we know from our oan *Eusa Story* where you fynd the Hart of the Wud youwl fynd a shyning in be twean his horns. Which that shyning is the Littl Shyning Man the Addom. Only in this Legend its callit *"the figure of the crucified Saviour"*. Figure is a word means moren 1 thing and 1 of the things it means is number. Number of the *crucified Saviour*. Now Iwl tel you some thing intersting Riddley Walker son of Brooder Walker you what put the yellerboy stoan the Salt 4 in my hans. Iwl tel you theres a working in this thing theres a pattren theres mor connexions nor wewl ever fynd reveals of. You know who put me on to what this woal things about? This woal blipful writing?'

I said, 'How cud I know that?'

He said, 'It wer your oan dad it wer Brooder Walker the same. It wer that reveal he done back when Dog Et largent in Littl Salting. Orfing and me we done a special show then your dad come a long Nex Nite he done a connexion and a reveal the woal thing took lessen a minim. I wernt there to hear it but I heard of it. Dyou have that 1 in memberment?'

I said, 'O yes I member that. "A littl salting and no saver."'

He said, 'Thats the 1. "A littl salting and no saver." Wel you know every now and agen youwl hear some thing it means what ever it means but youwl know theres mor in it as wel. Moren wer knowit by who ever said it. So that reveal stayd in my mynd. You see how it wer up to then I never thot this Legend ben anything moren a picter story about a bloak with a name near the same as Eusa. Nor I dint know nothing of chemistery nor fizzics then I hadnt payd no tension to it. Any how I wer reading over this here Legend like I use to do some times and I come to "*the figure of the crucified Saviour*". Number of the crucified Saviour and wunnering how that be come the Littl Shyning Man the Addom. Suddn it jumpt in to my mynd "A littl salting and no saver". I dint have no idear what *crucified* myt be nor up to then I hadnt give *Saviour* much thot I thot it myt mean some 1 as saves only that dint connect with nothing. Id never put it to gether with saver like in *savery*. Not sweet. Salty. A salt crucified. I gone to the chemistery working I askit 1 Stoan Phist that wer Belnots dad what *crucified* myt be nor he wernt cern but he thot itwd be some thing you done in a cruciboal. 1st time Id heard the word. Thats a hard firet boal they use it doing a chemistery try out which you cud call that crucifrying or crucifying. Which that crucified Saviour or crucifryd salt thats our Littl Shyning Man him as got pult in 2 by Eusa. So "*the figure of the crucified Saviour*" is the number of the salt de vydit in 2 parts in the cruciboal and radiating lite coming acrost on it. The salt and the saver. 1ce youve got that salt youre on your way to the woal chemistery and fizzics of it. Right up to your las try out which is the *brazen bull* which is to say your brazing boal and the chard coal. But thats all tecker knowledging realy you wunt hardly unner stan it nor I wont wear you out with it. Youve got to do your take off and your run off and your carry off. Which its wrote in the story its the wife took off by pirates and the wolf run off with 1 littl boy and the lion carrit off the other. The wife is the sof and the sweet you see which is took off by the sharp and the salty. Them pirates and wolfs and lions theyre all assits theyre all sharp and biting its all chemistery in there. Them 2 littl boys theyre what they call "catwl twis" which is what you put in to qwicken on your episodes. Right thru that part of it Eusa hes whats lef after the takings hes having his res and due. Finely after the brazing boal you get your *four souls* which is your 4 salts gethert. Man and wife and littl childer coming back to gether for the las time thats your new clear family it aint the 1 you startit with its the finement of it in to shyning gethert to the 1 Big 1. Mynd you all this what Im saying its jus theary which I mean we aint done nothing with it yet we cudnt cud we we aint had the parper salts and that. Wel now this here bag of yellerboy myt be the break and thru the barren year with a bang. I know itwl take tryl narrer and spare the mending but may be this time wewl do it.'

I dint say nothing I wer jus sitting there with my head widening in them circels spreading to no where. It wer broad day looking in thru the smoak hoal. Goodparley looking at me suddn then he says, 'We never did emty your pockits did we whats that bulging in there? Trubba not Iwl jus have a littl look.' Which he reaches in to my pockit and puls out that blackent hook nose hump back figger.

He looks at it and his eyes get big then nex thing he begins to cry. I dint know what to do I said, 'What is it?'

He wer snuffling and wiping his eyes he said, 'O how that takes me back o how it twisses my hart. I tel you theres a working in this it aint jus happening random theres too many things be twean us.'

I said, 'Whatre you talking about? Whats that got to do with that figger?'

'O,' he said. 'How them trees swayd in the morning wind that day and the smoak going up from the berning!' He wer pulling me to him and hugging me and slubbering on my neck. I dint know what to do I pattit his back like you wud with any frend took greavis. Knowing wylst I done it he wernt my frend tho he wantit to be. Some thing else as wel. Dint know how I knowit but I knowit I had the upper of him some how I wer the stronger 1. He myt have me kilt if it come on him to do it yet I had a Power he dint. He knowit and I knowit yet I cudntve said right then what it wer. I dont mean the Power you have when some 1 craves for you I mean some thing else.

He said, 'Here it is a nother morning and the sky all grey jus like that morning so far back when I ben a boy I bint a man like you I bint no moren 10 years old.'

I said, 'What happent?' Thinking on Lissener and thinking on Belnot Phist. Wunnering how it wer with them and suddn I wer scaret for the werst. Becaws Goodparley myt talk easy and smyl yet you never cud be qwite sure where you wer with him. There wernt no 1 else in the shelter with us jus then. I knowit wer going to be him or me some time some way. My weapons ben took a way from me I wer wunnering if it mytnt be the bes thing if I jus grabbit his knife out of his belt and stuck it in him. It cud wel be thatwd save Inland a woal lot of Trubba. Only soons that thot come to me it like ternt Goodparley in to the Littl Shyning Man. Which some thing as wantit to be 1wd be toar in 2. Plus even if it hadnt ben for that I wernt a qwick a nuff thinker to progam whatwd come nex. How to get Phist and me boath out of there. Any how the minim past nor I dint do nothing.

Goodparley movit a way and sat his self down agen. He had that blackent hook nose hump back figger on his right han it wer terning its head this way and that looking at him. Some times it wavit its arms wylst he talkit.

He said, 'This here figger his name is Punch which hes the oldes figger there is. He wer old time back way way back long befor Eusa ever ben thot of. Hes so old he cant dy is what Granser tol me. He wernt my Granser he wernt no kin to me that ben jus the name I knowit him by I never knowit his parper name he wunt tel me it.

'1st I ever seen of Granser I wer sitting up in a tree and the smoak going up from my fents berning. May be you think I ben beartht on the Ram beartht in to the Mincery. Wel I wernt nor I wernt beartht on no form nyther I wer beartht in a fents we wer a moving crowd sames your peopl ben time back. A border fents it wer Bad Mercy Fents you wont fynd it now its long gone. Bernt down that day in a raid from Outland. We dint have nothing for them to take only our groun and our women which they took boath. 1 time follers a nother the groun come back in a cuppl of years Weaping Form is what it is now they say you can hear the goasts of the childer what ben kilt there. The groun come back but the women never and my mum 1 of them.

'I ben out with a forage crowd that morning we wer coming back with pig when we seen the smoak going up we sust right off what it wer. We fasleggit back and right in to the jump they ben waiting. They wer too many we dint have no chance I seen my dad go down with a arrer in his hart and others dropping all roun I droppt as wel and slyd off in the hy grass. When they finisht killing the men I heard them taking the women. Hiding in the woodlings hearing that and smelling the smoak I can stil smel that smoak it wer peopl smoak as wel as wood. When it got qwyet I crep out. Cudnt hear nothing only the fire crackling and the crows calling 1 to a nother. Wite smoak and arnge flames upping in that grey morning and the dogs coming for the dead.

'I clum a tree and sitting up there smelling that smoak. Down be low me dogs wer grooling and smarling and the dead bodys jerking and flopping amongst them. I wer looking at the trees all roun. The way the tops of them wer swaying in the morning wind. You look outside right now beyont the clearing youwl see the tree tops swaying jus that very same way. They dont take no read of us we dont matter nothing to them. Time on far on wewl be dead and theywl be swaying in the morning wind the same. Any how there I wer and dogs all roun that tree that woal day and on in to the dark. Eat ther fil and come back agen they cudnt hardly walk ther bellys wer that swoal up. Parbly if Id come down out of that tree they cudntve run me down even if they bothert to try only I wernt going to chance it. I slep in that tree that nite I tyd my self in it. Stil summer it wer and warm.

'Nex morning I woak up it wer stil smoaking and the dew on the bernt brung the smel up strong. Some of the dogs wer a sleap and others crunching boans. Emty skuls and bits of boan all roun I wunnert which of them myt be my dad. Looking at the smoak stil driffing thru the trees and I seen a littl old wite hairt bloak coming a long he lookit permuch like this here figger only no hump. Hook nose and a hook chin and a wicket littl eye. He seen me and coming tords me he wernt bothert about the dogs. Some of them looking up and they ruft a littl. He just said Trubba not like you myt to any 1 and peed agenst a tree. The leader of the pack gone over to the tree he sniffit the old bloaks syn then he peed and the old bloak sniffit his syn and that wer that. No Trubba.

'He took me with him then I wer his boy til I come in to the Mincery 2 years after that. He showit me this figger which is Mr Punch. He dint have no fit up nor nothing the Mincery never has allowit no show of figgers only Eusa nor they wunt allow no 1 only Eusa show men to carry a fit up.'

I said, 'What kynd of a show wer it?'

He said, 'Iwl show you that show which he past it on to me the show and the figgers boath. Now Iwl pass it on to you the same thats how its meant to be you see. It aint like a Eusa show its meant to stay the same all the time.'

I dint have nothing to say about it all I cud do wer sit there and be a crowd of 1 to watch what ever he wer going to show. He fittit up all parper the same as if I ben 40 peopl. When he had his self all ready he said, 'Now you ask Mr Punch if hes ready.' Goodparley wer out of site in the fit up and I wer sat there staring at it.

I said, 'Wel Mr Punch this woal crowd is waiting for you.' Thinking on Lissener and Belnot Phist which I begun to feal not too easy. 'Be you coming up to show?' I said.

There come a littl salty voyce out of the fit up it wernt a voyce Id ever heard befor yet it wer a voyce I knowit some how it wernt no stranger to me. Salty and sharp like if a game cock wud talk. It said, *'Showing right now. Wot a beauty.'*

A littl hy womans voyce said, 'Cor! Whatre you going to do with that girt big thing Mr Punch?'

Mr Punchs voyce said, *'Come a littl closer and I wl show you.'*

I said, 'Mr Punch whynt you show your girt big thing up here so every 1 can see it?'

Punchs voyce said, *'Do my bes showing down be low. Rrrrrrr!'* He made a noys like a cock fessin taking off.

I said, 'Cant you get your down be low up here?'

Punchs voyce said, *'I can all ways get it up you bes stan wel back here I come.'* Up he shot then and zanting a bout with a longish flat stick it wer paintit red and wite and it wer split flatways so it wer a dubbl flat stick. You cud hear the whack of it and feal the smack of it jus looking at it. My Mr Punch what I dug out of the muck he wer all black with rot but this 1 wer all brite and sharp colourt. Face all pinky rosey and brite blue eyes he wer swanking in red and green and yeller cloes and a poynty red hat with a yeller wagger on it. Zanting a bout and saying, *'Ah putta putta putta ah putta putta way.'* Looking roun all sharp and brite and waving his stick.

I said, 'Is that your girt big thing?'

Punch said, *'Yes this is my 1 Big 1 its good for every il. If youre sick itwl make you wel.'*

I said, 'What if youre wel?'

Punch said, *'No bodys wel or I wunt have this stick wud I. Its a neadful stick you see so every 1 mus nead it.'*

I said, 'Its not what I thot itwd be.'

Punch said, *'Thats what they all say til they get use to it. All it takes is a littl getting use to. Ask Pooty.'*

133

I said, 'Whos Pooty?'

Punch callt, *'Oy! Pooty!'*

The littl hy womans voyce said, 'Whats happening?'

Punch said, *'Dont talk stupid its happent all ready.'*

Pootys voyce said, 'If its happent all ready you dont nead me do you.'

Punch said, *'Gennl man wants to see you.'*

Pootys voyce said, 'If hes a gennl man he dont want to see me and if he wants to see me he aint no gennl man.'

Punch said, *'Hes a frend.'*

Pootys voyce said, 'Frends all ways want it for nothing I ratherwd have a clynt.'

Punch said, *'Whats a clynt?'*

Pootys voyce said, 'Clynts are binses and binses comes befor pleasur.'

Punch said, *'Whats your pleasur then?'*

Pootys voyce said, 'Binses.'

Punch said, *'And whats your binses?'*

Pootys voyce said, 'What ever theywl pay for.'

Punch said, *'Whatwl they pay for?'*

Pootys voyce said, 'What ever they can think of.'

Punch said, *'What can they think of?'*

Pootys voyce said, 'Its mosly the same thing.'

Punch said, *'What thing is that?'*

Pooty comes up then she says, 'Swossage!' Shes a sow she dont have no cloes jus pink and nekkit only a littl frilly cap tyd unner her chin. Shes carrying some thing looks like a iron sossage only its got a dubbl fish tail. Like if youwd fevver a arrer up and down and crossways boath. The other end has like a nippl sticking out of it. 'Swossage!' says Pooty.

Punch has a good look at it he says, *'Theres a parper banger for you les have a fry up.'*

Pooty says, 'Iwl fetch the babby and the frying pan.'

Punch says, *'Never mynd the babby there aint a nuff swossage to go roun.'*

Pooty says, 'You know how he likes a bit of swossage.'

Punch says, *'Hes too yung for swossage give him the tit.'*

134

Pooty says, 'Boan dry.'

Punch says, *'Give him the boan then.'*

Pooty says, 'Et it our selfs dint we. Cruncht the boan and suckt the marrer.'

Punch says, *'Then tel the babby no suck ter day. Suck ter marrer.'*

Pooty says, 'You mynd the swossage wylst I fetch him.'

Punch says, *'Yes I wil Iwl mynd that swossage.'*

Pooty looks at me then she says, 'Now I want you to keap a eye on Mr Punch I want you to give me a shout if he has a go at that swossage.' She puts the sossage on the play board.

I said, 'All right Iwl do that.'

Pootys down then Punch grabs the sossage he terns his back to me and arga warga. I yelt, 'Pooty!' but its too late becaws Punch terns roun agen and that sossage is all gone.

Punch is rubbing his hans in joy of it he says, *'Um. You cant beat a good banger.'*

Up comes Pooty with the frying pan and the babby which its a littl pink piglet. Pooty says to Punch, 'Youve et that swossage havent you.'

Punch says, *'No I dint.'*

I said, 'O yes you did.'

Punch says, *'O no I dint.'*

I said, 'O yes you did.'

Pooty says, 'Never mynd Iwl see if I can fynd a nother swossage.' She hans the babby to Punch she says, 'You look after him wil you wylst Im gone.'

Punch is running his eye up and down that piglet he says, *'O yes Iwl look after him hewl be in good hans. You bes be off now after that swossage its a long time since Ive had any.'*

Pooty says to me, 'Youwl give me a shout wont you if theres any nead.'

I said, 'O yes Iwl do that.'

Pootys off then and Punch is holding the babby. Punch says, *'Youwl be good wont you. You wont cry wil you.'*

The babby dont say nothing.

Punch says to the babby, *'Les walky walky.'* He puts the

135

babby down and backs off a littl. Hols out his arms and says, *'Walky walky.'*

The babby that littl pink piglet slyds tords him like it wer on a string. Grey morning lite and candls stil lit in there. Shadders wivvering and wayvering on the smoak and flames paintit on the back cloth. Punchs head wer 1 solid peace of wood but looking at him I begun to think his joars myt open wide. *'O wot a good babby,'* says Punch. O how I hoapit that babby wer going to stay good nor not give him no bother.

Punch puts the babby back where he startit. He says, *'Walky walky'* agen.

'Wah!' says the babby.

Punch whacks the play board with his stick. *'Dont cry,'* says Punch to the babby. *'You look so terbel juicy when youre crying.'*

'Wah!' says the babby. 'Wah wah wah!'

Punch grabs that littl pink piglet and I yelt, 'Pooty!'

Pootys up then and grabbing the babby as wel. Shes pulling on 1 arm and Punch on the other it looks like theyre going to tear that littl pig in 2 peaces. Punch lets go of the babby he grabs his stick and hes beating Pooty and the babby. Pootys yelling, 'Ow ow ow!' and the babbys screaming, 'Wah wah wah!' til Punch beats them qwyet. Theyre boath dead then Punch has beat the life out of them. He puts them boath in the frying pan they dont fit too wel and hanging over the sides but hes frying them the bes he can.

Up comes a ugly bloak he dont look like any kynd of good news for Punch. Hes got a hang tree which he sets it up on the play board. He says, 'Jack Ketch is who I am which Im the Loakel Tharty roun here I thot I heard a woman frying.'

'My wife,' says Punch.

'Shes a beauty,' says Jack Ketch. 'Iwl have a bit of that.'

'Shes myn,' says Punch, *'Eat your oan wife.'*

'I heard a babby frying and all,' says Jack Ketch. Hes got his nose pernear in that frying pan he dont $\frac{1}{2}$ look hungry.

'My babby,' says Punch. *'Fynd your oan.'*

'You bes share with me or Iwl have you up for it,' says Jack Ketch.

'*Im hy a nuff all ready I dont nead no upping,*' says Punch.

'You shudve thot of that befor you come hitting piggy side,' says Jack Ketch hes readying the roap on his hang tree.

'*You mean bacon side,*' says Punch.

Jack Ketch says, 'If a dead pig is bacon whats a dead Punch?'

Punch says, '*You wont never see no dead Punch Im too old to dy.*'

'This heres a magic tree itwl make you yung a nuff,' says Jack Ketch hes patting his hang tree.

'*Im too ripe for that,*' says Punch. '*The fruit dont go from the groun to the tree.*'

Jack Ketch says, 'Youwl get back to the groun soon a nuff I wont keap you long jus only til youre dead dead dead.' He takes his hang tree in boath hans and trying to catch Punch in the loop of the roap.

'*You wont keap me at all,*' says Punch. '*Becaws Iwl whack you on the head head head.*' Hes whacking Jack good with his stick he finishes him qwick he says, '*Nor I wont keap you nyther*' and he flings him a way.

'Oy!' says a voyce and up jumps Mr Clevver he looks jus the same as Mr Clevver in the Eusa show hes got the same red face and littl poynty beard and the horns and all.

Punch looking at him sharp and scanful he says to Mr Clevver, '*Who myt you be?*'

Mr Clevver says, 'I myt be the Pry Mincer of Binland and I myt be the Hard Bitchup of Cantser Belly only I aint. Who I acturely am is Drop John the Foller Man which they call me Mr On The Levvil as wel.'

Punch says, '*Dont let me keap you parbly youve got binses elser.*'

Mr On The Levvil says, 'O no my binses is right here Ive come for a littl sumfing from Pooty.' He hasnt took noatis of the frying pan yet.

Punch says, '*Going to give you a littl sumfing is she?*'

Mr On The Levvil says, 'For my swossage you see.'

Punch says, *'That big hard swossage you mean?'*

Mr On The Levvil says, 'Thats the 1.'

Punch says, *'That girt big banger you mean?'*

Mr On The Levvil says, 'Right you are Guvner thats the very.'

Punch says, *'Youre looking to get sumfing for it?'*

Mr On The Levvil hugs his self a littl he says, 'Um um Im craving for a littl of that Pooty sumfing. Thats what I give her the swossage for din I.'

Punch says, *'You mean you give her that swossage befor she give you the sumfing?'*

Mr On The Levvil says, 'Thats what I done.'

Punch says, *'Then youve stil got sumfing coming to you here it is its frying now.'* He shows Mr On The Levvil Pooty in the frying pan.

Mr On The Levvil says, 'Now I call that a frying shame becaws a dead Pooty aint much good for sumfing.'

Punch says, *'Every man to his oan tase. Have a side of bacon.'*

Mr On The Levvil says, 'What Iwl have is my swossage back. No sumfing no swossage.'

Punch says, *'What if you dont get your swossage back?'*

Mr On The Levvil says, 'Iwl have my sumfing out of you then it dont make no odds to me.'

Punch says, *'You aint too fussy how you have it longs you have it?'*

Mr On The Levvil says, 'Im easy longs I have my sumfing.'

Punch terns his back and poynting his arse at Mr On The Levvil he says, 'Be you ready?'

Mr On The Levvil hes wynding his self up for it he says, 'Ready for it and ramping for it and here I come.'

'And here it comes,' says Punch. Which that iron sossage comes zizzing out of him and in to Mr On The Levvil. BANG! Flattens him dead.

'Hooray!' says Punch. *'Punch has done for Mr On The Levvil now every 1 can do as they like.'*

'Hooo,' says some 1 coming up then. Its a goast its got a skul face and all in wite. That skul has horns and a littl poynty beard. 'Hooo,' says the goast agen.

'*Whos that?*' says Punch. He dont look easy at all.

'Who do I look like?' says the goast.

'I ratherwd not say,' says Punch.

The goast says, 'Do you get like a dropping fealing in your belly when you see me?'

'*Yes,*' says Punch.

'Thats why they call me Drop John,' says the goast.

'*O dear o dear o dear,*' says Punch. '*How do I make that fealing go a way?*'

'It wont go a way,' says the goast. 'Itwl be with you longs Im with you.'

'*How longwl that be?*' says Punch.

'From now on,' says the goast. 'Thats why they call me the Foller Man.'

Punch dont look too easy when he hears that. He says, '*What dyou want to foller me for?*'

The goast says, 'I dont want to only I cant help it. When you done for Mr On The Levvil you put me on to you. Mr On The Levvil he ben the out side of me which you knockt him off and now Im nekkit enn I. I dont have nothing I dont have no l to live in only you.'

Punch says, '*Cant live in me theres no room.*'

The goast says, 'O wewl fynd room some time Iwl jus ride on your back til then.'

Punch says, '*O dear o dear o dear l hump is a nuff. I bes be off and put a littl farness be twean us.*'

'O dont leave me Mr Punch,' says the goast. 'I dont have nothing nor no body only you. The worl is emty for me only you.' With that it hops on to Punchs back its clinging to him all prest up agenst his hump with boath arms roun his neck.

Punch is off then with the goast on his back and the goast is singing:

Drop John the Foller Man
Roal him over throw him down

1 for you and 1 for me
Roading hoam to Do It Over
Roading hoam to Dover

I stayd sat there looking at the emty space and the paintit
smoak and flames on the back clof. I knowit Goodparleywd be
out of the fit up in a minim and this daywd go on from there. Iwd
have to say things and do things which I dint want to say nothing
nor do nothing I wantit to think on that goast what ben living in
Mr On The Levvil 1st then it wer on Punchs back and going to
live in him soons it got the chance. I never seen that show befor
nor never heard the names of Punch and Mr On The Levvil and
that goast befor yet now as I seen them and heard what they had
to say it seamt like I musve all ways knowit about them. Seamt
like I knowit mor about them nor I knowit I knowit.

Goodparley come out of the fit up he stil had Punch on his
right han and the goast on his lef.

I said, 'Who done the Nex Nite for that show?'

He said, 'There wernt no Nex Nite for it. Granser said this
show dint have no connexion nor no reveal. Dyou beleave that?'

I said, 'Theres all ways a connexion aint there.'

He said, 'Thats what I tol Granser. He said thats as may be
only there bint no connexion nor no reveal hed ever heard of for
this show. He said it ben jus only a fun show.'

I said, 'What dyou mean fun show? Bint it done by Mincery
bloaks?'

He said, 'Granser tol me this show never had nothing to do
with no Mincery it ben jus to make peopl larf. Give peopl a bit of
fun.'

I said, 'Thats a funny kynd of show to do. Who done it then?
What kynd of show men?'

He said, 'I dont know nothing about that nor Granser dint
i. 'ther. Whats the diffrents any how it aint a show no 1 wl see no
mor. I never knowit any 1 know it only Granser and me. Hes
dead nor I wunt show it to no 1 only you.'

I said, 'Punch and Eusa. 2 shows.'

He said, 'The 2 be come the 1.'

I said, 'Whats that Drop John song about? Roal *who* over? Throw *who* down? What is that 1 for you and 1 for me? Why is every thing in 2s? Whys Drop John singing about going home to Do It Over?'

He said, 'I dont know nothing about that song only its about some thing else. Which every thing is innit. Every thing is about every thing. And what evers in 2wl be come 1. The 2 of Granser and me be come jus only the 1 dinnit. You know how I partit from him?'

I said, 'How?'

He said, 'I kilt him.'

I said, 'How come?'

He said, 'It wer the nite of my 12th naming day. The day I be come a man.'

I had a suddn fealing I said, 'What day is your naming day?'

He said, 'Its the 2nd Ful. Whens yours?'

I said, '2nd Ful.' We wer boath shaking our heads and thinking on that. I said, 'What happent that day?'

He said, 'We ben talking about that day long befor it come. I ben watching that moon fulling on. We ben roading all roun like userel. Granser he wer what they callit a knowing man he knowit herbs and roots and mixters he done deacon terminations he done healing and curing plus he knowit dreams and syns. We roadit 1 fents to a nother clinnicking and national healfing we done forms and all. He never tol no 1 he wer dog frendy we mosly roadit with crowd like any 1 else. When we roadit oansome we all ways joynt up with some road crowd befor a riving any where. Wewd come roun a hil or thru the trees and Granserwd say we seen them from a farness and forkt off from the crowd we ben with. Some times they dint beleave him they thot he wer a Magic man they made the Bad Luck go a way syn but they let us road with them. Some said theyd seen him running with the Black Pack.

'Wel befor my naming day Id tol Granser Iwd be moving out for my self soons I come a man. I tol him that daywd be the end of my boy time. He larft and said O yes. We wer overing the nite at Good Mercy Form we ben roading with a

trade crowd. Some of them from Bollock Stoans up near Horny
Boy and they wer joaking how they had the mos bollocks and
they wer the hornyes boys in Inland. Getting pist and talking
juicy. How they wer dying for a littl. Tiret of husbinding ther
hans nor you cudnt get near them form women. Wel they
begun looking at me and putting ther hans on me. Granser
then he tol them being we wer at Good Mercy he wer going to
give them good mercy plus itwd be a bye bye party for the end
of my boy time so he give them me for the nite. 7 bloaks had
me 1 after the other on the nite of the day I be come a man.
Hevvy bloaks all of them I cudntve stood up to 1 let a loan 7.
He had to do that he had to put his mark on that day he cudnt
leave it a loan. Then after they all had good pleasur and good
measur that nite he tol me Iwd have to wait a nother year befor
I begun to man for my self becaws I ben boying on my 12th
naming day. Larfing his wicket larf and he said he wer going to
keap me with him 1 year mor thats when I stuck my knife in
him. He cudnt leave a thing be come what it wer going to be
nex. Thats what it wer made me kil him it wernt the 7 bloaks. I
wantit to man for my self and he made me boy for him 1 time
too many. I overt that fents and off oansome tho I bint dog
frendy and scaret to death I took my chance I put a farness
behynt me I Norft up the A28 keaping close to trees for
clyming til there come a long a road crowd they wer Mincery
bloaks I gone with them and to the Ram.'

When Goodparley said that about wanting to man and being
made to boy it made me think on *Eusa 13*:

13. Eusa wuz angre he wuz in rayj & he kep pulin on the
Littl Man the Addoms owt strecht arms. The Littl Man
the Addom he begun tu cum a part he cryd, I wan tu go I wan
tu stay. Eusa sed, Tel mor. The Addom sed, I wan tu dark I
wan tu lyt I wan tu day I wan tu nyt. Eusa sed, Tel mor. The
Addom sed, I wan tu woman I wan tu man. Eusa sed, Tel
mor. The Addom sed, I wan to plus I wan tu minus I wan tu
big I wan tu littl I wan tu aul I wan tu nuthing.

Goodparley said, 'Every thing wants to man dont it. Wants

to go from littl to big. Wants to be whats in it to be.' He stil had the figgers on his hans and Punch pickt up the bag of yeller stoans. Goodparley said, 'This here yellerboy stoan the Salt 4 it wants to be whats in it to be.' He stept back inside the fit up. BANG! Punch and the goast gone flying. He made the noys with a clapper he workit with his foot.

I said, 'It wants to be the 1 Big 1.'

He said, 'Thats it. 1 Big 1.'

I said, 'Thats going to move Inland frontways is it? Thats going to get us out of the mud? Thats going to get us boats in the air and picters on the wind?'

He said, 'Them boats in the air it seams like they ben hevvy on my back longs I can member. What wer it put them boats up there in the air dyou think? Power it musve ben musnt it. Youve got to have the Power then befor youwl have the res of it havent you. Which theres Power in this here Salt 4 we know that much. Its 1 of the Nos. of the 1 Big 1. All weve got to do is put it to gether with the others. Weve got to work the E qwations and the low cations weve got to comb the nations of it. We ben looking for Eusas head 1 way and a nother this long time. We ben digging in the groun for it we ben spare the mending we ben tryl narrering for it we ben asking roun the circel for it. We never come this close befor we never had no Salt 4. Weare closing in is what weare doing Riddley it aint going to get a way from us this time. Where ever it is Iwl fynd it. Iwl fynd Eusas head and Eusas knowing. Iwl get it out of Belnot Phist if its in him Iwl get it out of the Ardship of Cambry if its in him.'

I said, 'You said befor hes jus only a poor simpo he dont know nothing.'

He said, 'Tryl narrer is what it takes you dursnt miss out nothing youve got to try every thing. Try the clevver try the simpl.' His face begun to go sharp. He said, 'You never know what levvils it myt be moving on you never know what common nations you myt be missing. May be Eusas 2 littl sons 1 ben clevver 1 ben simpl. "Off thay gon 1 with Folleree & 1 with Folleroo. 1 hedin tords the rivvr 1 a way frum it &

143

each with ½ uv the Littl Shynin Man."'' He wer looking at me
diffrent from how he ben looking at me befor. He said, '2 littl
sons. 1 of them not qwite clevver may be. 1 of them not qwite
simpl. 1 heading tords the rivver which the Rivver Sour runs
thru Cambry dunnit. 1 heading a way from it. Tords Widders
Dump may be. Each littl son with ½ a pack of dogs. Folleree
and Folleroo. Each littl son with ½ the Littl Shyning Man.' He
pickt up a bag of yellerboy stoan and shook it. '½ the Littl
Shyning Man,' he said agen. 'Whats that Littl Shyning Man
say in *Eusa 26*? "Yu ar lukin at the idear uv me and I am it.
Eusa sed, Wut is the idear uv yu? The Littl Man sed, It is
wut it is." You see what I mean Riddley? "*It is wut it is.*"
Diffrent things at diffrent times may be. Its what ever it
wants to be.'

I said, "Eusa wut is the idear uv yu?"

He said, 'You know what the idear of Eusa is. Hes the 1
what goes thru chaynjis. If hes chemistery or if hes a man.
Thats what hes for thats the idear of him.'

I said, 'He endit up with his head on a poal tho dinnee.'

He said, 'Riddley my heads ben on a poal this long time.
My head ben cut off from the res of me it ben oansome and
greaving in a hy place. Iwd like to get my head down off that
poal is what Iwd like.'

I said, 'You dont have to be Eusa do you.'

He said, 'Coarse I have to be Eusa you do as wel and every
1 else weve all got to be Eusa and get him thru his Chaynjis.
Dont you see its on all of us to be every thing. There aint
nothing only us to be Punch and Eusa boath. Nothing only us
to be Drop John and all and manys the time I ben him and
riding on my oan hump.'

I said, 'Whatre you going to do now?'

He said, 'May be its time to put that Eusa family to gether.
4 souls in the brazing boal.'

I said, 'Whos Eusas wife then?'

He said, 'You know who she is Riddley shes that same 1
shows her moon self or she shows her old old nite and no
moon. Shes that same 1 every thing and all of us come out of.

Shes what she is and the woom of her is in Cambry which is the senter. It all fits you see. Old beleaf and new. Thats where the Spirit of God is coming down in the form of a dove.'

I said, 'Whats the Spirit of God?'

He said, 'Thats chemistery and fizzics and all its what the 1 Big 1 come out of realy theres so many ways of saying it you see. A dove is a kynd of pigeon which a pigeons a messenger innit. Which this message aint being sent its *de-scending* or you myt say unsending its going back where it come from which is Heaven. Now Heaven thats where hevvyness comes from innit. So that message or you myt say the trants mission its unsending its self back in to the hevvyness plus its *receiving* them 4 souls. Receiving is what you do with a trants mission you read it you take it in but this here trants mission its the other way roun its doing the taking in its taking in them 4 souls back in to the hevvyness. Thats how you get your 1 Big 1 which is the hevvyness made hevvyer with the 4 souls.'

He wer talking so many levvils at 1ce I dint all ways know what he meant realy I wisht every thing wud mean jus only 1 thing and keap on meaning it not changing all the time. I thot wewd be going to Cambry tho I dint know what wer going to be when we got there. I wunnert what wer happening with Belnot Phist and afeart to ask.

I dint have to ask. There come a yel. 'Daddy!'

Goodparley says, 'Ah! Talky talky.'

I said, 'You cunt.'

He said, 'Funny what peopl wil use for a hard word. The name of a pleasur thing and a place where new life comes out of. There ben times nor not too far back nyther when they use to offer to that same and very 1 what has her woom in Cambry. That same and very Nite and Death we all come out of.'

I said, 'Dont you push words at me you rat cunt.'

He said, 'Youre hard took by that yel are you. You dont want no 1 to suffer. Wel my boy I dont like herting no 1 but I

145

wont be tol lys and you bes keap that in memberment. I cant
stan lying I realy wont put up with it. It ben jus only a littl wyl
back our yung Belnot said right here in this very same shelter
he dint know nothing about that yellerboy stoan only I think
hes parbly saying diffrent now. I cudve tol them to take him
some place where you wunt hear nothing but you see what it is I
wunt ly to you I wunt set up for no sof nunkel. Im what I am and
youre seeing me how I am.'

I dint anser him nothing I jus shook my head.

> Never did the Good Luck brother
> Tern a roun to help the other

Thats what wer saying its self in my mynd nor I wernt going to
let it happen like that. Phist wer some kynd of brother may be
even a moon brother like the other 2. Cernly a Trubba brother
nor I wernt going to leave him in the shit. How come he wernt
in that Eusa family Goodparley ben talking of I wunnert.
Nothing for him to be. The Littl Shyning Man may be only
Goodparley hadnt said nothing about him coming in to it with
the brazing boal.

Wylst thinking that I ternt and run for the gate house. In my
mynd I seen Phist with his arms out stretcht like the Littl
Shyning Man. In my mynd he wer hanging black agenst a
redness. Redness like a berning.

I gone up the ladder and in to the gate house no 1 stoppt me
the hevvys wer all stood back from Phist and a clear space lef all
roun him. His arms wernt out stretcht he had his hans tyd
behynt his back and they ben pult up with a roap over a beam
so he wer hanging by them with his feet off the floor. His head
wer down and his wite hair hanging over his face. I grabbit a
knife from 1 of the hevvys I helt Phist up and cut the roap then
I cut his hans luce. He seen it wer me and he knowit me. He
like pult me to him with his eyes and he hispert:

> When the yeller boy
> Fynds the pig shit
> In the hart of the wood

He said it so qwick and qwyet I wernt even sure if Id heard him say it or if it ben jus only in my mynd. I waitit for the res of it but all he said wer, 'Thats my onwith its yours now.' He dint say nothing mor his pink eyes gone glazy and he wer dead.

1 of the hevvys it musve ben the 1stman of them he said, 'We never done nothing to him Guvner only hang him up. We never done him no greavis at all.' He wernt calling me Guvner it wer Goodparley behynt me.

Goodparley said, 'Whatd he say?'

The 1stman said, 'He dint say nothing only yelt for his daddy 1ce and jus now he hispert some thing to Riddley Walker here.'

Goodparley said to me, 'Whatd he hisper?'

I said, 'He dint say nothing only that yellerboy stoan wud be my onwith then he dyd.'

The 1stman said, 'You can see he aint ben bloodyd nor nothing we never done him nothing only hang him up.'

Goodparleys face lookit like he wer having a bad dream he cudnt wake up out of. He said, 'Who cud know he wer that delkit? I never wantit him dead.'

I said, 'Parbly thats what Eusa said when he pult the Littl Shyning Man in 2.'

Goodparley dint say nothing only shook his head. The hevvy Id took the knife from helt out his han for it and I give it back. Goodparley said to me, 'You can have your weapons back and go where you like I wont keap you.'

I near larft when he said that. Becaws I knowit we wer tyd to gether from then on and Belnot Phist like Drop John on boath our backs. Goodparley wer terning me luce to let me happen but he knowit I cudnt get a way from him no moren he cud get a way from me. We myt do our diffrent moves and try new 1s if we cud but there wer jus only so much doing to go roun and if 1 of us done 1 thing the otherwd have to do the other.

When they give me back my gear Goodparley said, 'You myswel have your onwith and all' which he give me the bag of yellerboy stoan. Then I did larf and off I gone.

I wer glad to be vacking my wayt befor the jobbing rota from How Fents ternt up I dint want to see none of them right then I jus wantit to road oansome to Cambry and my other moon brother qwicks I cud.

I lookit up at the gate house when I gone out and Goodparley wer looking down at me. He said, 'Iwl see to it Belnot gets a parper berning.'

I noddit and put my foot tords Cambry. Soons I crost the clearing them dogs wer all roun me agen they wer like my oan pryvit nite in the morning of the day.

15

Roading with *Eusa* 7 in my mynd:

> 7. Thay dogs stud up on thear hyn legs & taukin lyk men.
> Folleree sed, Lukin for the 1 yu wil aul ways fyn thay 2.
> Folleroo sed, Thay 2 is 2ce as bad as the 1 . . .

I cud feal it in the guts and barrils of me. You try to make your self 1 with some thing or some body but try as you wil the 2ness of every thing is working agenst you all the way. You try to take holt of the 1ness and it comes in 2 in your hans. Jus the same as the Littl Shyning Man done when Eusa took holt of him. Orfingd said the Littl Shyning Man wer what ever cudnt never be put to gether and I wer beginning to think he wer right. And yet it lookit to me like the Littl Shyning Man wer jus and very what *wantit* to put its self to gether and trying its bes to do it. Not Goodparleys Littl Shyning Man that wer a nother thing and tirely. What I thot the Littl Shyning Man wer I thot he wer right doing. I thot the Littl Shyning Man wer what I ben putting to gether when I brung that yellerboy stoan to Belnot Phist and look what happent. If Id kep wide of him he myt stil be a live. Poor Belnot Phist parbly his hart give out on him. Hart of the Phist Hart of the Wud. I ben the 1 as made that happen and now I wer coming in 2 with it. Saying in my mynd over and over: Whatd I do whatd I do?

Now I wer trying to hol fas to being 1 with Lissener and I knowit wel the 2ness wer hot on my foller it wer out to get its teef in me and arga warga. That 2ness be come jus as real to me as if it ben a pack of dogs. I wer frendy with the dogs now but I dint know how to get frendy with the 2ness. Trying to lissen in my mynd for Lissener but nothing come. My mynd wer all roylt and turbelt and muddy with every thing going roun in it. Trying to progam my self for Cambry yet at the same time trying not to get in front of my self.

Plus all the res of it it took me strange roading with them dogs by day pas all them lookouts be twean Widders Dump and Cambry. Dint realy matter nothing how many lookouts seen me dint matter nothing how many pigeons flew that message 1 form to the nex or to the Ram there wernt no body going to stop me longs the Pry Mincer wantit me luce and walking out my happenings. Stil and yet I dint want no 1 seeing me I wisht it wudve stayd nite. I dint want to be tol of every where. Riddley Walker the dog clevver or Riddley Walker running with the Black Pack. I kep out of site as wel as I cud but I knowit I wer seen time and agen becaws I wunt put no exter time nor faggers on to my road with going wide and slying roun I jus gone the straites way to Cambry trying to get to Lissener fas as I cud. Trying to get there befor the 2ness got me.

Coming up a long the rivver arper sit Good Mercy Form I seen the userel blue smoak hanging in amongst the aulders. I ben singing unner my breaf like youwl do some times roading a long I wer singing:

'When the yeller boy fynds the pig shit
  (Dont you wish he cud)
When the yeller boy fynds the pig shit
  In the hart of the wood'

I heard some 1 else singing and I stoppit to lissen. It wer a crackt old mans voyce and singing:

When the yeller boy comes hoam
Wewl make such a noys
Such a noys
Such a noys
When the yeller boy comes hoam
My good old boys

150

There come like a rushing and a tingling all thru me my head gone lite my legs gone wobbly. I stood there looking and I seen a littl old bloak zanting a bout on the out side of the chard coal berners fents. He stoppit singing then and he come out where I cud see him plain. Littl wite hairt bloak with a hook nose and a hook chin in his red jumper he lookit jus like Mr Punch only no hump. The dogs dint take no special noatis of him it lookit like they knowit him. The 2 nexters ruft and the littl old bloak said, 'Trubba not' and peed agenst the fents. The nexters sniffit his syn then they peed and he sniffit ther syn.

I said, 'Youre Granser youre that same and very littl old hook nose bloak what Goodparley kilt time back.' It wer like a dream.

He said, 'No I aint Im Drop John the Foller Man you tel Goodparley that nex time you see him. You cant kil Drop John hewl ride your hump hes the Foller Man.'

I said, 'That wer a good song you wer singing.'

He said, 'What song?'

I said, 'When the yeller boy comes hoam.'

He said, 'Ben that what I ben singing? I dint realy take no noatis my self.'

I said, 'Be there mor to it?'

He said, 'Mor to what?'

I said, 'That song.'

He said, 'O dear I realy cudnt say Im so old you know my memberment is mosly gone I jus have bits of this and that in my head like meat and vedgerbels in a stew Im jus a old stew head is all I am.' Looking at me like a ren out of a hedge.

I sung:

'When the yeller boy fynds the some thing
  In the some thing of the some thing'

He said, 'What kynd of a song is that?'

I said, 'Thats a How much do you know? song.'

He said, 'I dont know nothing like that realy I dont know nothing only what any chard coal berner myt know.'

I said, 'You wunt know who the yeller boy is?'

He said, 'No I wunt know nothing like that is he some 1s brother?'

I said, 'You know a song about brothers?'

He lookit at me all brite eyed and wicket and he sung:

When the other brother come
Stanning at the gate
When the other brother come
Then it wer too late

I said, 'That souns like the end of the song. What about the beginning?'

He said, 'Thats jus it you see thats why he wer too late he never come in to it at the beginning.'

I said, 'You never *sung* no beginning if youd sung it he cudve come in to it.'

He said, 'I never sung no beginning becaws you wont never fynd no beginning its long gone and far pas. What ever youre after youwl never fynd the beginning of it thats why youwl all ways be too late. Onlyes thing youwl ever fynd is the end of things. What ever happens itwl be what you dint want to happen. What ever dont happen thatwl be the thing you wantit. Take your choosing how you like youwl get what you dont want. Howd you get dog frendy?'

I said, 'I dint get dog frendy it wer the dogs as got frendy with me.'

He said, 'O I see youre a very special kynd of bloak then aint you. Parbly 1 day youwl be some thing big like Dog Pry Mincer.' He begun to kil his self larfing at that.

I dint know if I shud keap on talking to him or jus go my road. I fealt like if I kep stopping there I myt get los from what I wer going to Cambry for. I fealt like that old man myt make things happen on some other track. Wel I can put it plainern that. What I wer lissening wer Power. What ever it wer. The 1 Big 1 or the Spirit of God or the Littl Shyning Man or what ever. I cud feal that yellerboy stoan scrabbling to get out of it bag I cud feal how it wantit to get to that old man and I cud feal as he knowit what to do with it. Only I dint know who he myt be for and who agenst. Dint know if I shud show my han or not. The chard coal berners wer in with the dyers at the forms I knowit that much but I dint know if they wer Mincery men or what they wer. 1ce every year they come in to the forms for ther red clof then back in to the woodlings and ther blue smoak they gone. They kep to ther selfs they wernt frendy with no 1 nor no 1 never give them no Trubba. Every 1 wer a littl bit afeart of them they thot they mus be some way clevver.

And stil I aint said all there is to say about that littl old hook nose man. That day when I seen him for the 1st time and stanning there talking to him it wer like a dream I cudnt wake up out of. There wernt nothing terbel happening and yet there wer. Whats so terbel its jus that knowing of the horrer in every thing. The horrer waiting. I dont know how to say it. Like say you myt get cut bad and all on a suddn there you are with your leg opent up and youre looking at the mussl fat and boan of it. You all ways knowit what wer unner the skin only you dont want to see that bloody meat and boan. Never mynd.

That old man tho. That old man he ben the man to Goodparley when Goodparley ben a boy and here wer that old man stil going strong. Jus looking at him you cud see he wuntve ben kilt by Goodparley. Not him. Wel I wer afeart of him thats the Truth of it I wer afeart of what he myt happen. He drawt me. I fealt like he wer going to make me happen or I wer going to make him happen.

He said, 'Cheer up it may never happen.' I ben stanning there shrunk in my thots I musve ben looking down struck. He said, 'Wel you bes go your road Ive got my harts to look after. May be wewl sing songs agen some time I all ways like a good song. Keap in memberment to tel Goodparley you seen Drop John.'

I said, 'Wait a minim.'

He said, 'What is it then?'

I said, 'Never mynd.' I had my hans in my pockits. Fealing old blackent Punch with my right han and that yellerboy stoan with my lef.

Granser said, 'Right you are.' Opent the gate and in to the fents he gone and closd the gate agen. I heard him singing behynt the fents:

> Wewl make such a noys
> Such a noys
> Such a noys
> My good old boys

I startit off then I stoppit and looking back and going tords the gate agen. Them 2 nexters they begun grooling and smarling and showing toofy.

I said, 'All right then have it your way.' Off we gone tords Cambry then.

And stil I aint said all there is to say about that morning in the aulders. The bloody meat and boan of it. The worl is ful of things waiting to happen. Thats the meat and boan of it right there. You myt think you can jus go here and there doing nothing. Happening nothing. You cant tho you bleeding cant. You put your self on any road and some thing wil show its self to you. Wanting to happen. Waiting to happen. You myt say, 'I dont want to know.' But 1ce its showt its self to you you *wil* know wont you. You cant not know no mor. There it is and working in you. You myt try to put a farness be twean you and it only you cant becaws youre carrying it inside you. The waiting to happen aint out there where it ben no mor its inside you. That old man sung his littl song and he put that waiting inside me.

Coming pas Pig Sweet Form I seen them plowing with a 4 crowd plow and 8 oxin. 4 bloaks on the plow and 2 on look out. It wer stil early morning a dul day with the sun low behynt the grey and the way the lite come acrost the feal you cud see some kynd of old pattren unner neath of the new furrows. Strait lines and circels from time back way back. There wer a scare crow on a littl rise of groun it had a crow sitting on 1 arm. The other arm the strawd come out of the sleave and the wind wer moving the sleave a littl on the stick it lookit like the scare crow wer beckoning the plow men.

Lookit like the crow wer telling the scare crow to do it. The plow men come to the end of the feal and I heard ther voyces littl acrost the farness when they ternt the team: 'Wo Jooper! Go roun Klisto!' Coming the other way then 1 of them seen me and the dogs in a bare space be twean trees. He poyntit at me and the others made the Bad Luck go a way syn. The crow yelt, 'Caw caw caw!' and it had the right of me. The scare crow jus kep on beckoning.

On we gone tords Cambry. Dint see no other dog packs tho we wer far and a way beyont the Bernt Arse packs markings. It fealt to me like other packs wer keaping out of our path. Like every thing holding its breaf waiting for some thing special to happen.

So far that morning it hadnt ben raining only hanging over grey. Coming acrost the barrens the sky darkent on and hevvy. When we come to the Ring Ditch the stannings of the Power Ring stood up wite agenst the dark like broakin teef. I tryd to see the Power Ring in my mynd. Hy and shyning with the 1 Big 1 wooshing roun inside it. That story of why the dog wont show its eyes where it tels of putting the 1 Big 1 in to the Power Ring which the very 1st time they woosht it roun it ternt the nite to day then every thing gone black I dont beleave that. Looking at them stannings I knowit inside me they musve had that 1 Big 1 going roun there regler. I cud feal the goast of it hy over me farring roun and out of site going roun that circel and coming back and roun agen EEEeeeeee.

Black sky. Wite broakin teef. 'SPIRIT OF GOD,' I yelt. Becaws thats where Goodparleyd said the 1 Big 1 come out of. I dint know nothing about chemistery nor fizzics but I wer getting to where I neadit some thing hy to yel at. I cud feal it like a rushing hy over me roun the hy goast of the Power Ring. The dogs all laid back ther ears and grovvelt so I knowit they cud feal it over them and all. 'CANTERBURY,' I yelt. Becaws that wer the old name. The new name wernt no good it wer a stanning in the mud name it dint have no zanting to it. I run down in to the Ring Ditch and up the other side. Stanning on the barren groun I cud feal it coming up in to me thru my feet the Power of the goast of the Power what ben. 'IT STIL IS,' I yelt. Becaws it come to me then I knowit Power dint go a way. It ben and it wer and it wud be. It wer there and drawing. Power wantit you to come to it with Power. Power wantit what ever cud happen to happen. Power wantit every thing moving front-ways. The same as Goodparley wantit. The same as I wer wanting then.

Thinking back to that nite when I took the scar which it ben jus only 3 nites back it wer that same nite they done the Eusas head show and that same nite Goodparley tol me he wer looking for the Littl Shyning Man nor it wernt jus only the idear of him it wer some thing real. Now I wer beginning to get a idear of what he meant. Plus thinking agen on what Orfingd said. How the Littl Shyning Man wer what ever cudnt never be put to gether. Wel that wer Power wernt it. The Power of the 2ness trying to tear the 1 a part. What if you put the 2 and the 1 to gether tho? What if you put the 2ness inside the 1? Power inside of Power myt that be 1 Big 1 and Spirit of God? The 2 inside the 1 the Big inside the littl like thunner and litening inside a egg shel. Then what if you broak that shel. Parbly thatwd make such a noys such a noys such a noys. Or may be you cud work it so it jus come wooshing out like the Wind of the Worl. Myt that be the same what I cud stil feal the goast of rushing hy in the air roun the circel of the goast of the Power Ring? I begun to see why Goodparleyd ternt me luce hed parbly sust it myt come to me by its self if he lef me a loan.

I begun to get as cited then thinking on them things. I wudve liket to gether with Goodparley right then and pul datter wylst my mynd wer running hy like that. Thinking like that I begun to wish I hadnt progammit nothing with Lissener agenst Goodparley. Wunnering then why I ben so qwick to go in with him jus becaws that black dog brung me to him in that hoal in Bernt Arse and I fealt sorry for him. Now Orfing and his hevvyswd parbly have him and what wer I going to do about it? Cambry coming up in front of me nor I dint have a idear in my head. I begun to wish that black dogd never brung me to that hoal I jus dint want to have to bother with Lissener right then.

Thinking on Lissener and wunnering how much him and the Eusa folk realy knowit when they gethert. Membering what he shoutit when he ben took with that fit: 'WE PROGAMMIT THE GIRT DANTS OF THE EVERY THING. WE RUN THE BLUE THE RED THE YELLER WE RUN THE RED THE BLACK WE RUN THE SEED OF THE RED AND SEED OF THE BLACK. WE RUN THE MANY COOLS OF ADDOM AND THE PARTY COOLS OF STOAN. HART OF THE WUD AND STOMP YOUR FOOT. 1 AND 2 AND SHAKE OF THE HORNS AND 1 AND 2 AND SPLIT OF THE SHYNING . . .'

Then it come to me. Onlyes reason Goodparley ben giving Lissener bother wer becaws he wantit the knowing of how to do that 1 Big 1. Wel what if I put Goodparley to gether with Granser and give them the yellerboy stoan and they got the 1 Big 1. Then theywd tern Lissener luce they wunt help no qwirys on him then. Parbly that wer the bes thing I cud do for Lissener and the mor I thot on it the better it lookit. I ternt roun then heading back tords Goodparley but soons I done that there come a woal lot of grooling and smarling and ever so many sharp and toofy teef looking at me. It wernt jus only them 2 nexters then it wer all them dogs grooling low and deap it soundit like it wer coming out of the groun. I ternt roun agen tords Cambry and the grooling stoppit.

Coming in to Cambry outers and fealing the place rise up in me wylst I movit in to it. Jumbelt stoan and crummelt birk. Grean rot and number creaper. The old dry parcht smel and the wet grean smel to gether like in all the dead towns. No stilness like the other dead towns tho. Qwick it wer. All of it qwick and a qwickful hy moving coming up out of the groun and hyering hyering up thru the rain in to the dark what stans for ever on them broakin stoans with its hans over its face. Day time it wer then nor not raining but the rain wer in it and the dark is all ways there. The shape of the nite what beartht the day when Canterbury dyd. Hart of the Wud in the hart of the stoan. I cud feal that thing inside us how its afeart of being beartht. I cud feal how every thing is every thing. I fealt like if I stampt my foot therewd come horns on my head and the Littl Shyning Man nekkit be twean them.

Thinking on the Littl Shyning Man he be come mixt to gether in my mynd with Belnot Phist. Poor old Belnot he bint pult in 2 acturel peaces and yet in a way of saying he ben pult a part and it wer the Power of the 2 as done it. Now that 2 wantit to be 1 agen and moving me I cud feal it strong that Big Power what ever it wer. Spirit of God may be that same what woosht roun the Power Ring time back way back. I wantit to be the happener for that Big Power. I wantit to happen that 1 Big 1. I thot of the yellerboy stoan ½ of it with me and ½ of it with Lissener. Reaching out then with my mynd I tryd to lissen him. Cudnt lissen nothing only jynt sylents there wernt nothing of him in it I wer all a loan. Eusas littl son nor cudnt fynd the other 1.

'Be your oan black dog and be your oan Ardship. Becaws you wont all ways have me.' Thats what hed said. Now I knowit why hed said it. Becaws he knowit time to come wewd go 2 diffrent ways. I wantit that Hy Power back agen and wooshing roun the Power Ring not jus the goast of it. I wantit that Spirit of God moving Inland frontwards agen. I wantit the same as Goodparley I wernt agenst him no mor and that wer the hart of the matter. Lissenerd lissent that and pult his mynd a way so I cudnt lissen him nor where he wer. Boath of us looking for that 1 Big 1 but we wernt on the same side no mor. Suddn it flasht in to my mynd may be he wer the Good Luck brother not me.

So sad I fealt then. Sad and emty with a crying in me. I fealt like that Other Voyce Owl of the Worl musve lissent the woal worl a way and every thing gone. Every thing emtyd out of the worl and out of me.

Funny fealing come on me then I fealt like that Power wer a Big Old Father I wantit it to do me like Granser done Goodparley I wantit it to come in to me hard and strong long and strong. Let me be your boy, I thot.

Stanning on them old broakin stoans I fealt like it *wer* coming in to me then and taking me strong. Fealt like it wer the han of Power clampt on the back of my neck fealt the Big Old Father spread me and take me. Fealt the Power in me I fealt strong with it and weak with it boath.

And stil I fealt a nother way. Grean rot sweating on the old grey broakin stoans all roun me and number creaper growing on the rubbl. I knowit Cambry Senter ben flattent the werst of all the dead town senters it ben Zero Groun it ben where the wite shadderd stood up over every thing. Yet unner neath that Zero Groun I lissent up a swarming it wer a humming like a millying of bees it wer like 10s of millyings. I begun to feal all juicy with it. Juicy for a woman. Longing for it hard and hevvy stanning ready. Not jus my cock but all of me it wer like all of me wer cock and all the worl a cunt and open to me. The dogs begun running roun me all in a circel roun and roun with ther littl heads up hy and ther hy sholders up. They begun running on ther hynt legs. The sky wer black the stoans gone wite the dogs gone all diffrent shyning colours and the wite stoans shyning thru them. I tryd to hol it like that but I los it I wernt man a nuff right then. I cud boy for the other but I cudnt man for her what has her woom in Cambry.

The sky gone grey the stoans gone grey the dogs gone back to how they lookit befor and come down on to all 4s. It wernt a circel it wer a nother shape they wer running like a black rivver out and a roun out and a roun it wer a big shape they wer running in amongst the rubbl and a roun I begun to run it with them. It wer 2ce as wide acrost as the divvy roof at How Fents I run it 3 times roun befor I knowit jus what shape it wer. It wer a dolly shape it wer like the woman dollys they hang over where a womans bearthing. Which them dollys theyre the same shape as the woman cakes they bake. Not realy like a real woman shape its a bulgy body like a jug or a flask with a littl roun head.

The out line of that shape ben dug out of the broakin stoan and rubbl it wer the line of a old old wall in that woman dolly shape it wer that same and very 1 what has her woom in Cambry.

. . . Shes that same 1 shows her moon self or she jus shows her old old nite and no moon. Shes that same 1 every thing and all of us come out of. Shes what she is . . .

I cud feal all them millyings of bees humming in me but they wer humming the emtyness they wer humming what I cudnt hol when them dogs ben running shyning colours on ther hynt legs they wer humming what Id los. Yet Id knowit the shape of nite Id gone in to the nite in the day time. Not a nuff. Do your mos nor it aint a nuff. Miss your connexion nor you dont even know til its ben and gone.

The woom of her what has her woom in Cambry aint inside the out line what the dogs ben runnin its a littl to the Wes of that which its unner neath the groun. Thats where I gone sad and emty it wer the dogs took me to it. Old stoan steps going down to it. That wer the hoal where the Eusa folk ben I lissent that strait a way. It wernt dark there winders ben dug out of the rubbl it wer like that shaddery ½ lite youwl see amongst the trees on a grey day. When ever Id thot of a hoal with Eusa folk in it Id thot of some thing filfy with a terbel pong like the hoal in Bernt Arse where Id foun Lissener. This place wer clean tho nor it dint have no pong it smelt good it had jus the fayntes foller of a bernt smel like the goast of the blue smoak in amongst the aulders.

Seed of the littl
Seed of the wyld
Seed of the berning is hart of the chyld

I dont have nothing only words to put down on paper. Its so hard. Some times theres mor in the emty paper nor there is when you get the writing down on it. You try to word the big things and they tern ther backs on you. Yet youwl see stanning stoans and ther backs wil talk to you. The living stoan wil all ways have the living wood in it I know that. With the hart of the chyld in it which that hart of the chyld is in that same and very thing what lives inside us and afeart of being beartht.

The wood be come stoan in the woom of her what has her woom in Cambry. That place unner the groun where I wer it wer a wood of stoan it wer stoan trees growing unner the groun. Parbly that stoan ben cut and carvit by them as made them jynt music pipes I never seen. Roun trunks of stoan and each 1 had 4 stoan branches curving up and over Norf Eas Souf and Wes all them curving branches they connectit 1 tree to a nother. Stoan branches holding up the over head and growt in to it. Stoan branches unner a stoan sky. A stoan wood unner the groun the hart of the wood in the hart of the stoan in the woom of her what has her woom in Cambry.

I fel down on to my knees then I cudnt stan up I cudnt lif up my head. The 1 Big 1 the Master Chaynjis it wer all roun me. Wood in to stoan and stoan in to wood. Now it showit 1 way now a nother. The stoan stans. The stoan moves. In the stanning and the moving is the tree. Pick the appel off it. Hang the man on it. Out of the holler of it comes the berning chyld. Unner the stoan. See the bird boan. Thin as grass. Be coming grass.

I opent my mouf and mummering only dint have no words to mummer. Jus only letting my froat make a soun.

Becaws it come to me what it wer wed los. It come to me what it wer as made them peopl time back way back bettern us. It wer knowing how to put ther selfs with the Power of the wood be come stoan. The wood in the stoan and the stoan in the wood. The idear in the hart of every thing.

If you cud even jus only put your self right with 1 stoan. Thats what kep saying its self in my head. If you cud even jus only put your self right with 1 stoan youwd be moving with the girt dants of the every thing the 1 Big 1 the Master Chaynjis. Then you myt have the res of it or not. The boats in the air or what ever. What ever you done wud be right.

Them as made Canterbury musve put ther selfs right. Only it dint stay right did it. Somers in be twean them stoan trees and the Power Ring they musve put ther selfs wrong. Now we dint have the 1 nor the other. Them stoan trees wer stanning in the dead town only wed los the knowing of how to put our selfs with the Power of the wood the Power in the stoan. Plus wed los the knowing whatd woosht the Power roun the Power Ring.

May be all there ever ben wer jus only 1 minim when any thing ever cud be right and that minim all ways gone befor you seen it. May be soons that 1st stoan tree stood up the wrongness hung there in the branches of it the wrongness ben the 1st frute of the tree.

I put my han on a stoan tree trunk. There wernt no grean rot on it the stoan fealt clean and dry. In the $\frac{1}{2}$ lite in the grey lite it lookit like it wer stanning in its oan time not the same time I wer in. Cud it hear the music of them los jynt pipes I wunnert. Fealing the carving unner my hans it wer like shaller runnels cut in the stoan. The runnels come down strait and parrel 1 to the other. Then they ziggit then they zaggit then gone strait agen. Running my han over the strait and over the zig zag. Fealing how other hans done the same thing time back way back. Some 1 carvit that stoan with a chiswel and mowlit then they run ther han over it. That carving wudve took some time too. 1st that stoan trunk ben shapit roun then the runnels ben cut in to it. Then there wudve ben the fitting to do the measuring and the cutting and the pegging and the hoaling and the joyning when they fittit them curving branches on to the trunks. They wudve had to prop them branches with shapers wunt they. All of that to make that wood of stoan. All them hans digging and cutting and hoysting and joyning and carving. All of that to put the Power of the wood to gether with the Power of the stoan in that wood of stoan trees.

This nex what Im writing down it aint no story tol to me nor it aint no dream. Its jus some thing come in to my head wylst I ben on my knees there in that stoan wood in the woom of her what has her woom in Cambry. So Im writing it down here.

Stoan

Stoans want to be lissent to. Them big brown stoans in the formers feal they want to stan up and talk like men. Some times youwl see them lying on the groun with ther humps and hollers theywl say to you, Sit a wyl and res easy why dont you. Then when youre sitting on them theywl talk and theywl tel if you lissen. Theywl tel whats in them but you wont hear nothing what theyre saying without you go as fas as the stoan. You myt think a stoan is slow thats becaws you wont see it moving. Wont see it walking a roun. That dont mean its slow tho. There are the many cools of Addom which they are the party cools of stoan. Moving in ther millyings which is the girt dants of the every thing its the fastes thing there is it keaps the stilness going. Reason you wont see it move its so far a way in to the stoan. If you cud fly way way up like a saddelite bird over the sea and you lookit down you wunt see the waves moving youwd see them change 1 way to a nother only you wunt see them moving youwd be too far a way. You wunt see nothing only a changing stilness. Its the same with a stoan.

Theres a kynd of stoan its all mos like a mud stoan it aint hard. Some times youwl see 1 broak open all mos like it ben shapit with a ax. It looks like 1 cut then a nother making a poynt like a short beak. Owl beak or hawk beak some times you can see the eye bulge unner the skin of the stoan. Wel them stoans aint ben ax shapit theyve broak ther selfs open its that bird head in the stoan what peckt the stoan a part. Some times youwl see the 2 peaces stil to gether the bird head and the other to gether they look like a broakin hart.

Come back a nother time the bird head wont be there no mor nor it dint grow a bird body on to its self and fly a way. What it done it growit a man body on to its self and off it gone walking its self a way. Stoan men growt out of the bird head in the stoan 1 for every 1 of us. Where they are theyre up side down in the groun. Like youwl see a picter of your self up side down in the water theres a stoan self of your self in the groun and walking foot to foot with you. You put your foot down and theywl put ther foot up and touching yours. Walking with you every step of the way yet youwl never see them.

Theywl stay unner the groun longs youre on top of it. Comes your time to ly down for ever then the stoan man comes to the top of the groun they think theywl stan up then. They cant do it tho. Onlyes strenth they had ben when you ben a live. Theyre lying on the groun trying to talk only theres no soun theres grean vines and leaves growing out of ther mouf. Them vines getting thicker and pulling the sides of the mouf wide and the leaves getting bigger curling roun the head. Vines growing out of ther mouf. Vines and leaves growing out of the nose hoals and the eyes then breaking the stoan mans face a part. Back in to earf agen. Them stoans ben trying to talk only they never wil theyre jus only your earf stoans your unner walkers. Trying to be men only cant talk. They had earf for sky wylst you had air. Its jus only stoan men walking unner the groun like that. Women have some thing else.

Your other stoans your stoan stoans not earf stoans they talk ther oan way which is stoan talk. They ben there wylst you ben walking theywl be there when you ly down. The hart of the wud is in the hart of the stoan where the girt dants is.

That come to me in the Eusa hoal in Cambry with the dogs all roun me that day. From now on when I write down about the tree in the stoan Iwl write *wud* not wood. You see what Im saying its the hart of the wud its the hart of the wanting to be.

You cant all ways know when some things happent. Some times youwl think there ben some thing and realy it ben nothing at all. Other times you dont take no noatis til later it comes to you what happent.

This time in the Eusa hoal in Cambry I knowit wer some thing happent. Some thing come in to me. Some thing I lissent out of that place. Else how cud I have in my mynd how the saddelite bird a way way up over the sea looks down on the waves. I can stil see it in my mynd the blue water and the wite foam far far a way down be low me. Thinking then of when Goodparley ben terpiting of the Eusa Legend and there ben that part about the open sea which he terpitit that wer open *see*.

Thinking on that other thing that with the stoan men I cud see it in my mynd so plain that face with the vines and leaves growing out of the mouf. Them stoans like birds heads Id seen them times a nuff but the face with the vines and leaves Id never seen. I knowit that dint come out of my mynd it musve come in to it from somers. Where ever that mans face come from it fult me sad. It wer a thick kynd of face. Thick nose lookit like it ben bustit. Thick mouf $\frac{1}{2}$ open and the leafy vines growing out of boath sides and curling up roun his head. Lookit like he myt be wearing a hood as wel. The way his mouf wer open and how his eyes lookit it wer like he dint know what to make of it. Like he ben breaving and suddn the breaf coming out of his mouf ternt in to vines and leaves. Cudnt swaller them back and tryd to bite them off but theyre too hard and thick and pulling his mouf a part wider all the time. His eyes wide open with sir prize. Lite grean eyes open so wide.

The look of that face saying so many diffrent things only no words to say them with. Never seen that face befor yet it wer a face I knowit. Take a way the vines and leaves and it myt be Punchs face or it even myt be Eusas face. Which wud be on the front of Eusas head wunnit. Id never realy thot much on that befor. How Eusas face and headwd go to gether.

That face in my mynd with the vines and leaves growing out of the mouf I begun to see it wer the onlyes face there wer. It wer every face. It wer the face of the boar I kilt and the dog that old leader. It wer the face of my father what ben kilt in the digging. It wer Belnot Phist hung up by his hans tyd behynt him and it wer the Littl Shyning Man. Wer it the Ardship of Cambry and all? The Ardship dint have no eyes in his face. And yet myt it be him? I dint know I cudnt say. I cudnt put that face to gether with his face. And yet we wer moon brothers. Goodparley? Yes it wer Goodparleys face moren any bodys may be. Orfings as wel becaws Goodparleys face all ways had Orfings in it. What wer it made the Ardship odd 1 out then? Why wer it every bodys face only not his? I dint know.

Too many things coming in at 1ce. Like all ways. Mixt up I wer. Like all ways. Yet some thing happent there in Cambry. It happent where the dogs run them shyning colours on the wite stoans agenst the black sky. It happent in the Eusa hoal amongst them stoan trees. It happent in my head when I seen the changing stilness of the far a way waves and the face with the grean vines and leaves.

I wer progammit diffrent then from how I ben when I come in to Cambry. Coming in to Cambry my head ben ful of words and rimes and all kynds of jumbl of yellerboy stoan thots. Back then I ben thinking on the Power of the 2 and the 1 and the Hy Power what ben wooshing roun the Power Ring time back way back. The 1 Big 1 and the Spirit of God. My mynd ben all binsy with myndy thinking. Thinking who wer going to do what and how I myt put some thing to gether befor some 1 else done it. Seed of the red and seed of the yeller and that. That onwith of the yeller boy and the pig shit in the hart of the wood. Hart of the wud. Now I dint want nothing of that. I dint know what the connexion wer with that face in my mynd only I knowit that face wer making me think diffrent. I wernt looking for no Hy Power no mor I dint want

166

no Power at all. I dint want to do nothing with that yellerboy stoan no mor. Greanvine wer the name I put to that face in my mynd.

I cud feal some thing growing in me it wer like a green sea surging in me it wer saying, LOSE IT. Saying, LET GO. Saying, THE ONLYES POWER IS NO POWER.

There come in to my mynd then music or the idear of music I dont know what it wer if I try to hear it now I cant only I know I heard it then. It wer as much colours as it wer souns only if I try to see the colours now I cant. The souns and the colours they be come a moving and I thot I cud move with it.

I startit up out of that stoan wood. The dogs dint grool nor nothing only them 2 nexters black and yeller black and red ther moufs opent like larfing and ther eyes $\frac{1}{2}$ closd and up they gone on ther hynt legs agen. Soons they done it the woal res of the pack done it with them. They had ther littl heads up hy they had ther front legs liffit with ther paws dangling they wer running on ther hynt legs in and out of them stoan trees they wer moving with the souns and colours.

There come mor dogs then it wer the res of the Bernt Arse pack and the black leader with them. Him and them what ben with Lissener. All of them running on ther hynt legs with the others. Runnying a idear in and out of them stoan trees it wer the idear of Greanvine.

Then the black leader stil on his hynt legs he led a way thru the rubbl and the stumps and stannings not too far then down on all 4s and down in to a place dug out be low some fallin stoans. At the back of that place the black leader sniffing and scratching on a stoan with his paw and looking at me.

It lookit like he wantit me to shif that stoan. Which I done. It come out easy there wer a hidey hoal and some thing in it rapt up in a bit of red and black stripet hard clof it wer that same and very clof the Eusa show men use for ther fit ups.

I had a idear what it wer going to be when I unrapt it. I wer right. It wer Greanvine. Carvit out of wood and paintit it wer may be $\frac{1}{2}$ as big as a real face. The back of it flat and the front of it ful roundit it wer that same and very face I seen in my mynd. Them wide open grean eyes staring up at me wylst the vines and leaves growit out of his mouf.

Wunnering if it ben jus only this 1 dog foun that rapt up face or ben it past down 1 dog to a nother 1000s of years and 100s of dogs lifes. The clof wernt old but that face wer. Nothing blackent nor rottit I dint know how I knowit but I knowit. It wer his look he wer looking at me from time back way way back is how I knowit. I lissent it ben past down 1 dog to a nother 1 man to a nother as wel. Not a woman this wernt a woman thing. A woman in this place by the woom of her what has her woom in Cambry wuntve bothert hiding a way this face of a man with vines and leaves growing out of his mouf. This here man dying back in to the earf and the vines growing up thru his arse hoal up thru his gullit and out of his mouf. Not a woman thing. Becaws a woman is a *woom*an aint she. Shes the 1 with the woom shes the 1 with the new life coming out of her. You wunt carve a womans face with vines and leaves growing out of the mouf. A woman shewl dy back in to the earf but not the same as a man. You cud see the knowing of that in Greanvines eyes. A man myt get 100s of childer but the onlyes new life growing out of him wil be that dead mans vine at the end of his run.

Wunnering who ben the las to look at Greanvine befor me. That red and black stripet hard clof it wer old but not as old as Greanvine. Did it come from a Punch mans fit up or a Eusa show mans? Ben there Punch back then in what ever time Greanvine come from? How far back did Greanvine go? Ben he there when them jynt music pipes ben making ther music? There wer a broak off peg in the back of him. May be he ben peggit to a poast or he ben a kynd of head on a poal when all the broakin stoans of Cambry ben the parper town of Canterbury. Hummering girt and tall in some shape I wunt never know.

Them stoans come down when the wite shadder stood up over Canterbury. Parbly Greanvine come down with them and some Punch man foun him and savit him a way in this

168

hidey hoal. Dint walk off with him no he savit him a way in this hoal for who everwd be the nex to come a long and fynd him.

So there I wer then may be I wer 1 with Greanvine only it lookit like Id come in 2 with every 1 else. 1st I ben with Lissener agenst Goodparley then in my mynd I begun to go tords Goodparley and a way from Lissener. Now on a suddn I wer off the boath of them. I wernt on for no mor yellerboy stoaning nor all the res of it I dint care who wer doing it. Every body juicying for Power 1 way or a nother nor I dint want no part of it no mor. I realy fealt like the onlyes Power wer no Power nor I cudnt think of no 1 I wantit to be on the same side with no mor. Wel the dogs. And here they wer the woal Bernt Arse pack and the black leader all them dogs what ben with Lissener now they wer with me. Which that mus mean Lissener ben took by Orfing.

I dint like to think of him hung up like Belnot Phist ben. Nor coming to no harm for lack of me. Dint want to have to do nothing about it only I knowit I wunt have no res if I dint.

I said to the black leader, 'Wheres the Ardship gone?' By then I wer talking to him like you wud to a nother person you cudnt help it.

He showit which way with his head then he gone that way and I follert. It wer the out poast he took me to it wer close by. I gone slow and scanful but it wer emty. Tabels benches and sleapers cook pots and buckits but no weapons nor no doss bags. On a wall some bodyd drawt some thing with a bit of chard coal. What it wer it wer a joak picter of Goodparley. Rough done but you cud see it wer him easy a nuff. With his littl eyes and big chin and big teef he wer easy to do. Coming out of each side of his mouf wer vines and leaves the same as Greanvine. I wer holding the 1 face in my han and looking at the other on the wall. On the wall unner Goodparleys face wer wrote:

HOAP OF A TREE

Took strange a nuff by that I wer. Hoap of a tree! Coming

from them stoan trees like I wer jus then them words put me
I dint know where. Hoap of a tree! Hoap of a tree for what?
Hoap of a tree to grow out of Goodparleys mouf? Hoap of a
tree to hang Goodparley on? Greanparley? Goodvine? Grean-
good? Parleyvine? My head begun to go roun with it.

Goodparley had a long chin and the chin in the picter wer
even longer. At the top of that long chin the vines and leaves
coming out of the mouf lookit like stag horns and the long
chin lookit like the stags head. There ben a bit of chard coal
lef on the floor I pickt it up and drawit in the stags eyes and
nose and ears. There wer Goodparley in be twean the horns
of the Hart of the Wud then. Unner neath of it the words:

HOAP OF A TREE

What kynd of a tree wud that be then? The aulder? Never
mynd, I thot. Iwl parbly fynd out soonern Iwd like. I brung
my mynd back to the Ardship. From the 1st I come to
Cambry realy I ben fealing like I had the place to my self. If I
ben lissening every 1 gone then I thot may be I mytve lissent
where they gone as wel. I tryd to let it come to me.

I wer looking at that picter on the wall and the words unner
it agen. They dint look like they ben done by the same han.
The picter of Goodparley wer big and sprawly and the words
wer wrote littl and close kep. Tite face. Orfing. Hoap of a
tree. Tree in the stoan. Fork in the tree. Fork Stoan. I said to
the black leader, 'Wheres the Ardship now? Wheres Lissener?'

He lookit at me with them yeller eyes of his then he jus tost
his head and like give a sylent larf with his mouf.

Wel any how I dint have no other place in mynd only Fork
Stoan so thats where I wer heading for nex.

16

Wel I dint go to Fork Stoan strait off. Seamt like I kep fealing different ways 1 minim to the nex that day it come on me then I dint want to road no mor by day I wantit to go dark. I dint want no 1 to know where I wer no more even if Goodparley did want me running luce. Special I dint want him to know. I dint want him all ways knowing where he cud put his han on me.

Goodparleyd said hewd be coming to Cambry but I dowtit that. It seamt too simpl. I dint think Goodparley ever gone any where and foun it emty without he meant to fynd it emty. Parbly he knowit bettern me where Orfing and the Ard-shipwd be. What ever HOAP OF A TREE and that picter meant they wer agenst Goodparley some way I knowit that. Nor I dint think I knowit any thing Goodparley dint know. He wer a girt 1 for letting peopl run luce and til they run in to his han. If he pirntowt Orfing wer putting some thing to gether agenst him hewd be sure to tern up where itwd do him the mos good and Orfing the leas. Which I dint think thatwd be Cambry jus now.

I laid up in the out poast with dogs on look out. No sleap the nite befor and I wer ready for some kip. Nothing only bare sleapers there nor nothing to get warm with. The black leader come and floppit down on the floor and I floppit down with him I kep warm that way and off I gone.

Woak up with a lam leg in my face it wer that dog forage sqwad looking after me agen. Dint want to show no smoak so I cut some off and chewing it raw same as the dogs. I thot I myswel get use to it. Thinking that thot and suddn it come to me I dint know when Iwd ever be living like regler peopl agen.

171

I hung a bout there til it got dark I past the time with my old black Punch on my right han and Greanvine on my lef.

Punch said to Greanvine, 'Whats it all about then?'

Greanvine said, 'You dont nead me to tel you that do you. Youve put in your time this long time unner groun you know what its all about.'

Punch said, 'Whats that then?'

Greanvine said, 'Wel air is the short sky innit but earf is the long 1.'

Punch said, 'Balls my boy. Thats what you aint got a nuff of.'

Greanvine said, 'It dont matter how much balls youve got its all the same in the end.'

Punch said, 'No it aint the same its diffrent if youve got balls a nuff.'

Greanvine said, 'Hows it diffrent?'

Punch said, 'Its diffrent right the way up to the end and thats why the end is diffrent. If the way is diffrent the end is diffrent. Becaws the end aint nothing only part of the way its jus that part of the way where you come to a stop. The end cud be any part of the way its in every step of the way thats why you bes go ballsy.'

Greanvine said, 'Is that how you all ways go?'

Punch said, 'I am the balls of the worl I am the stoans of the worl. I am the stoans and I have my littl stick.'

Greanvine said, 'Is that your tree then is that your living wood?'

Punch said, 'Yes thats what it is its that same and very wood what never dys.'

Greanvine said, 'Wel then is there hoap of a tree?'

Punch said, 'Theres hoap of the wud in the hart of the stoan.'

Greanvine said, 'What stoan is that then?'

Punch said, 'Balls. Which thems the stoans what never dys.'

Wel of coarse Punch wud say that. Thats how he is hes that way myndit. Me I dint have Punchs balls nor I wernt all that sure them wer the stoans what never dys.

Any how when nite come on I put Greanvine back in his hidey hoal and my self on the road to Fork Stoan.

It come on to rain I dint mynd that I like the rain plus by then I wer out path myndit. Put me on a muddy track in a black nite with the rain pissing down and I wer hoam.

Roading with them dogs thru the dark it wer like I wer in a diffrent country from the res of Inland. Every 1 else the formers and them what jobbit or foragit or what ever they had the country of the day time. That same country I use to go in. In the day time there wer all ways things coming up in front of your eyes. In the nite you cud may be see other things. Other ways.

I stil aint qwite said how it wer. Not like a diffrent country. It wer mor like I wer behynt the back clof in a show. Thats how it wer. Thru the clof I cud see the other figgers moving I cud see the peopl watching only no 1 cud see me. If I wer a figger in a show what hand wer moving me then? I cudnt be bothert to think on that right then. Theres all ways some thingwl be moving you if it aint 1 thing its a nother you cant help that.

Fealing that black leader bumping agenst me roading thru the hispering rain and dark and Fork Stoan coming closer and closer. Nor I dint realy want to think about it. Dint want to get in front of my self. I cudnt lissen what wer happening but I cud lissen wel a nuff there *wer* things happening. In my mynd Fork Stoan wer like a hoal in a fents. It wer the place where some thingd come thru all ready nor you cudnt know whatwd come thru nex.

It wer stil fresh in my mynd from the nite befor I cudnt keap my mynd from showing me that big space with the girt sleaping machines in it. I cud see figgers moving in that space and ther jynt shadders wivvering and wayvering all roun. Not wanting to see no faces til I had to.

Closer closer the rain hispering down on the old stoans and my new foot steps going on top of my old 1s. Trying to lissen and not lissen boath at 1ce. Knowing the Ardship mus be lissening me as wel.

Closer and closer. No lookouts on the steps it wer like they wantit any body to come in as wantit to. There I wer then. By then I knowit what I wer going to see befor I seen it jus by lissening the regler way. The dogs helt back only the black leader come forit with me.

They had Goodparley hung up by his hans tyd behynt him sames hed hung up Belnot Phist. I thot I wer going to vomit when I seen that. It wer like that torcher wer all ways waiting and sooner or later every 1 wer going to have a tern. I cud feal it like it wer happening to me I cud feal my hevvyness pulling my arms out of ther sockits.

Goodparley wer twissing and terning on that roap he wer pulling up his feet like he thot he cud stan on air and ease his arms. There wer some twissit iron beams sticking out of the wall by them girt broakin machines theyd past the roap over 1 of them. There he hung and ternt and twissit and his jynt shadder twissing and terning with him and him crying and moaning with his head hung down.

Orfing and his hevvys looking on. The Ardship and the Eusa folk looking on as wel. Faces like bad dreams. Faces with 3 eyes and no nose. Faces with 1 eye and a snout. Humps on backs and hans growing out of sholders wer the leas of it they had every kynd of crookitness and ther shapes and shadders wivvering and wayvering on the wall with the shadder of Goodparley twissing and terning.

The black leader he laid back his ears and poyntit his nose up at the shadders and he begun to howl. Some of the hevvys uppit bow but the black leader stayd where he wer.

Orfing said, 'Down bows.' Which they done.

I said, 'What is it you want from him?'

The Ardship said, 'I want to hear him sing like that its a good soun to lissen to.'

I said, 'Orfing whyve you hung him up like that?'

Orfing said, 'I aint Orfing no mor Im Goodparley now.'

I said, 'Whats Goodparley then is he Orfing now?'

Orfing said, 'He aint nothing no mor.'

I said, 'Then whyve you got him hung up whynt you let him go?'

Orfing said, 'Now you know he aint a bloak you can jus let go of. Tern him luce and hewl be binsyern ever. He cant live qwyet you know hes all ways got to be doing and moving.'

I said, 'Stil you dont have to hang him up do you?'

The Ardship said, 'O yes we do we have to hang him up sames he hung up my father we have to hang him up the sames he wer going to do me.'

Goodparley said, 'Riddley dont you look at me like this o please dont look at me this aint me youre seeing this aint me no mor.'

The Ardship said, 'O yes it is and its the reales part of you. Its the Littl Shyning Man of you innit. Which thats what you ben looking for this long time Ive heard you say that times a nuff.'

I gone over to where the roap wer tyd to a iron ring on 1 of the girt machines and I untyd it I lowert Goodparley til his feet toucht the groun and his arms come down. He screamt when his arms come down. I cut the roap what tyd his hans. Dint know if I myt be the nex 1 hung up twissing and terning I had a suddn idear. Shaddery it wer and Goodparleys fit up right there by us. Wylst bending over Goodparley and helping him up I took the yellerboy stoan out of my pockit I slippit in to the fit up thinking theyd parbly sercht that all ready. Goodparley seen what I wer doing his littl eyes they sparkelt in the shadders.

No 1 else took no noatis. Eusa faces and strait 1s they wer all stil looking at Goodparley not me. Orfings limpit face and the Ardships no eyes face staring like a blyn owl. Stretching his self out tords Goodparley and the way he lookit made me think of the Other Voyce Owl of the Worl.

I said to Orfing, 'Is this HOAP OF A TREE then?'

He said, 'Yes it is. Which theres hoap of a tree if its cut down yet itwl sprout agen. And them tinder branches theyre of wil not seaze. Tho the root of it works old in the earf and the stick of it dead on the groun yet even jus only the smel of

water and itwl bud and bring forit bowing like the plan. Thats
ben the go word of the arper sitting in the Mincery year on
year it ben past down 1 shadder mincer to the nex. Inland
may be cut down yet them branches wil keap coming. Peopl
may try to kil them branches only itwl be the peopl what fall
down and dy them branches wil grow out of ther moufs which
thats our blip and syn.'

'Greanvine,' I said.

Orfing said, 'This aint no vine its the tree what never dys.'

I said, 'And youre 1 of them branches what keaps coming
are you.'

He said, 'Yes I am and growing seeds of the new.'

I said, 'Which Goodparley is that face whats dying out then
is he.'

He said, 'It looks that way dunnit. Whatre you then are you
the Asker of the Worl?'

I said, 'It seams like every body elses got ansers only I
havent got nothing only askings.'

He said, 'Now Iwl ask you some thing if youwl jus be so
kynd wud you please han over your littl bag of yellerboy
stoan.'

I said, 'I havent got it have I. Theres a Rivver Sour runs
thru Cambry which I sweetent it with that yeller boy.'

The Ardship said, 'Thats a ly if ever I heard 1 youve got it
hid somers I can lissen that.'

Orfing said, 'Les jus have a look then shal we.'

Wel I had to take off all my cloes then and Orfing his self
gone thru them. He lookit at my old black Punch for a long
time he put his finger in the head and all then finely he put
every thing back in my pockits and give me back my cloes.

The Ardship said, 'May be it aint on you but youve hid it
somers havent you.'

I said, 'No I never.' With my hart jumping in me.

He said, 'Whats the use of lying wewl jus hang you up the
sames we done your new frend here.'

I said, 'Lissen me if you think Im lying. When I come to
Cambry I lissent you joynt the effert with Orfing and I

throwit them stoans in the rivver I knowit I cudnt do nothing with them nor I dint want no 1 else to have them moon brother.' In my head I wer singing

Sharna pax and get the poal
When the Ardship of Cambry comes out of the hoal

hard as I cud hoaping he wunt lissen nothing only that.

Orfing said to the Ardship, 'Therewl be mor stoans soon a nuff weve got boatswl go where that 1 come from what we need is the knowing for our 1st try out with the stoans weve got. Have you got that knowing or not?'

The Ardship said, 'I tol you I dont know nothing til we gether.'

Orfing said, 'Wel you bes gether then.'

The Ardship said, 'What about these 2 then?'

Orfing said, 'They dont have no knowing nor no Belnot Phist nor no hevvys they cant do us nothing.'

The Ardship said, 'May be theres stil a littl some thing we can do them tho.'

Thats when the Eusa folk opent ther moufs and begun to sing:

Sharna pax and get the poal
When the Ardship of Cambry comes out of the hoal

Which the way they sung it wernt like nothing I ever heard befor.

Then I seen some thing flashing and like dantsing in the lite of the candls it wer a ax the Eusa folk wer passing it from han to han only it lookit like it wer zanting a bout all oansome.

Looking at that shyning ax nor I cudnt take my eyes off it. All them Eusa faces with ther eyes shyning. All of Orfings hevvys which they ben Goodparleys hevvys wester day ther eyes wer shyning the same. Orfings littl eyes shyning as wel.

That shyning ax zanting amongst the many agenst the few. Agenst the 2 of us. It wernt even Goodparley and me I wer thinking on jus then. It wer how that ax wer dantsing for the many. I knowit we wernt going out of that place the same as we come in. All this time Goodparley wer huddelt by me he wunt look up agen 1ce he seen that ax. I wer looking from the ax to the Ardship his face wer shyning pernear like that ax. He wer singing:

'Whatwl we take
Whatwl we leave
Whatwl we chop chop chop
Wherewl we start
Wherewl we end
Whatwl we lop lop lop'

Finely Orfing said to the Ardship, 'Les not be talking of no chopping we never progammit nothing like that.'

The Ardship said, 'O no we wunt chop the Pry Mincer like he choppt my father we wunt never do that. Onlyes thing wewl do is make him lissen bettern what hes done so far. Hes all ways telling and asking yet he dont never lissen to no 1 nor nothing.'

By then the Eusa folk had holt of Goodparley and passing him 1 to the nex like they ben doing with the ax. He showit fight then only it dint help him nothing. That black leader dispeart like magic there wernt no 1 on our side only the 2 of us. I jumpt in to it and trying to pul Goodparley out of it only I got clubbit on the head and every thing gone black.

When I come out of it there wer a howling coming and going a roun me. 1st I thot it wer the black leader then I heard a slubbering and a moaning in it I knowit wer some thing else. It wer Goodparley he wer running and falling down and getting up agen running in to stoans and rubbl falling down and getting up agen slubbering and moaning the woal time there wernt no words in it.

I gone after him and cawt him. He ternt his face to me it wer all bloody and blood stil running out of where his eyes ben.

He said, 'Is that you Riddley?'

I said, 'Yes its me Im here.'

He said, 'Wil you stay with me now?'

I said, 'Yes I wil Iwl stay with you its all right now.'

He musve ben in terbel pain but he stoppt his moaning and his crying then he gone all qwyet. Every 1 else wer qwyet too all of them wer looking at him like he wer magic now theyd made him blyn.

Goodparley said to me, 'Put me in front of them wil you please. Put me in front of the new Goodparley.'

I led him over and he poyntit to his blyn and bloody face and said to Orfing, 'This for you and what for me?'

Orfing said, 'You know that wernt for me Abel that jus happent befor I cud stop it.' Lissening to him I cudnt help noatising how ful fed he soundit. He said, 'Whats your asking?'

Goodparley said, 'Plomercy Erny I aint asking nothing only jus a littl Plomercy.'

Ording said, 'Wel what is it Abel?'

Goodparley said, 'Im broakin now Erny there aint no fight lef in me I jus only want to live qwyet wil you give me letshow?'

Orfing said, 'You mean you want to go on showing Eusa?'

Goodparley said, 'O no Erny Eusa is the Mincery show its the Pry Mincers show I wunt even ask to do no shadder mincer show o no not me I aint even arper sitting now.' He reacht in to my pockit and got that old blackent Punch figger on his han. He begun to zant him a bout and saying, 'Ah putcha putcha putcha. Ah putcha putcha way.' Terning his bloody face to Orfing and he said, 'Its jus only a fun figger Erny it wont be nothing only show for meat roading 1 place to a nother with Riddley here to lead me.'

It wer the terbeles strange thing how he wer then it got to me moren the moaning and the crying. He wer swaying back and forit wylst he talkit so easy them bleading woons musve ben tharbing like the sea pounding on the stoans. It seamt like hed come pas the werst now jus in them littl few minims hed come to a qwyet place where he wer man a nuff for any thing.

Orfing said, 'Abel you cudnt run a fun show to save your life. If I put you on the road with a fit up that figger on your

179

hans going to come the shadder mincer to Eusa and wel you know it.'

Goodparley said, 'Wel Erny are you afeart Iwl do a better show nor Eusa are you afeart Iwl bring down your Mincery with Punch? Are you afeart 1 poor old broakin blyn mans going to come the upper of your hoap and your tree? Erny dont you have no balls at all?'

Orfing said, 'All right Abel this is where weve come to now and wewl see where we come to after this. Iwl give you letshow for that fun figger only you wont be showing Eusa no mor Iwl have a drop or 2 mor of your blood Im putting the down stroak on your scar.'

Goodparley larft then he said, 'O youre a careful 1 Erny youre afeart Iwl sly a roun making Eusa say the wrong things are you.'

Orfing said, 'You jus mynd what I say Abel dont stress me now dont strain me.'

Goodparley said, 'Iwl be careful not to do that Erny I realy wil.' He opent his anrack and pult up his jumper and his vesses then. 'Here we go Erny,' he said. 'Take your littl knife and put the Z to my E.'

Which he steppit up to Orfing then with all them Eusa faces looking on and his hevvys from wester day. The Ardship now when he lissent to Goodparley you cud see even with his no eyes face he wer lissening him diffrent. The Ardship never ben afeart of Goodparley when Goodparley ben Pry Mincer but he wer afeart of him now. The woal lot of them wer that littl bit afeart they sust theyd put some kynd of Power in him when they blyndit him.

There wer Goodparley with his belly uncovert agen the same as when I took my scar from him. Which the scab wernt even off my E it wer only 4 days back I took that scar. Which the wood slid out from unner me that nite and I had to grab him and he said, 'Take that for a blip.' There wer them jynt shadders wivvering and wayvering. Orfings han with the knife poyntit at Goodparleys belly.

Theres words for down stroaking a scar as wel as putting 1 on. Orfing said, 'Wheres Eusa?'

Goodparley said, 'Hes gone from my belly like Im gone from his hart.'

Orfing said, 'Dont lissen for his voyce in you no mor.'

Goodparley said, 'Iwl have the sylents I know that.'

Orfing said, 'Dont talk for him out of your memberment. You cant talk for Eusa now hes going a head and leaving you behynt.'

Goodparley said, 'I know that I know Im the 1 whats lef.'

Orfing said, 'Its E to Z then.'

Goodparley said, 'My blame my shame.'

Orfing cut the down stroak then. Goodparley took some mud off his boots and prest it in to the cut he said, 'Inland be my healing.'

Orfing said, 'That aint in the wording.'

Goodparley said, 'It is now.'

Then we wer outside in the rain and the dark and Goodparley with a bloody clout roun his head. In my mynd I cud stil see that ax shyning and dantsing in the candl lite I wer a littl bit snuck wed come out of there a live. The handl of that ax ben what they blyndit him with. It all happent so fas and now there I wer with blyn Goodparley took on me. When I said Iwd stay with him I never give no thot to how long. A mooning? A year? The res of his life? I took his fit up on my back. The littl man all ways carrys the fit up the big 1 is the hevvy.

Goodparley said, 'Let me carry the fit up Riddley its me as put this woal thing on our backs.'

I said, 'Its me as took it on with you.'

He said, 'Dont you see it aint going to hevvy me down its going to hol me up.'

I let him take the fit up and I took his bundel. Here come the Bernt Arse pack then with the black leader. Goodparley said, 'I aint ben this close to dogs this long time.'

I said, 'You myswel get use to it theyre the onlyes hevvys weve got.'

He said, 'I dint noatis them doing no hevvying in there jus a littl wyl back.'

I said, 'I think they knowit bettern to get ther selfs trappt in there.' What I wer thinking tho it cud wel be them dogs wunt come in with Goodparley til hed paid some thing. They had ther oan progams.

We headit out of Fork Stoan going Norf. Goodparley said, 'Where we going?'

I said, 'You tol me Granser done healing and curing.'

He said, 'Gransers dead.'

I said, 'No he aint hes berning chard coal in the aulders acrost the rivver from Good Mercy. He tol me to tel you he wer Drop John the Foller Man.'

Goodparley dint say nothing to that he wer qwyet for a long time. Jus walking a long keaping nexy but not holding on to me. In the dark I cud see the clout roun his head moving he wer shaking his head and tsissing thru his teef. Finely he said, 'O yes why not. Why not him a live and riding my hump. I stuck that knife in him and I run. Looks like I dint have it in me to finish him. May be I never had it in me to start my self nyther.'

I said, 'No 1 never starts his self.'

He said, 'Yes they do. You dont start the life in you thats like a rivver running in you stil there comes a time when you push your oan boat out in to the middl of it.'

I said, 'Or you put your self on the road to the hart of the wud.'

He said, 'How dyou spel that?'

I said, 'W-u-d.'

He said, 'You think this is the road to the hart of my wud? You think I put my self on it?'

I said, 'Seams like it dunnit. Them as ben progammit to bring you down you let them run luce til they done it. Thinking on it now you musve knowit Orfing ben ready to try it 1 way or a nother.'

He said, 'Yes its funny how youwl do. I dont think I ever beleavit I wer man a nuff for what I wer. For Pry Mincer. Time that yellerboy stoan come in to Fork Stoan being Goodparley wer a hevvyness I wer pernear ready to put down. I dint have my hart in it no mor. I cudnt keap thinking on all them things you have to keap thinking on if youre going to stay on top. Time Id put Orfing on the road to Cambry and Lissener headit the same I musve ben perwel ready to let it happen. After you gone to Cambry this morning I thunk on it and I knowit I bes have a nother look at things in Fork Stoan. Id lef hevvys there to help the qwirys on them other bloaks what ben beckoning that boat only I hadnt stoppit to see to it my self. Wel I shudve knowit them hevvys all ben in it to gether and Orfing ready to take over with them. I had Belnot Phist in my mynd poor littl bloak.'

I said, 'I dont think he knowit nothing of it nor I dont think them Fork Stoan hevvys ben beckoning. Theywdve ben looking a woal lot sharper a long that shoar if they ben waiting on a boat with all the storm there ben that nite. May be that bloak in the boat bint even heading for Inland may be he jus ben blowt here.'

Goodparley said, 'Wel may be. Any how it dont matter now. That yeller boy is luce now and ½ of it with us.'

I said, 'All that what you said about the Punch show wer that jus to get the yellerboy stoan out of there?'

He said, 'No it wernt. I wantit to hol on to it the same as you but what I said about the Punch show wer strait it jus happent youd put the 2 of them to gether.'

I said, 'Theres a Power in it right a nuff look how it made the 2 of us get it a way from them others.'

Goodparley said, 'O wel you cant help trying to shortin the odds longs youre a live but Im so tiret Riddley. Too many Drop Johns on me by now. After a wyl its all jus 1 girt big Littl Shyning Man nor you cant put him to gether. O them dretful Eusa faces. Wel Orfing he ben all ways feeling bad for them now heres his chance to make it right with them. Granser Drop Johning me and all. Wel why not. The old man never dyd nor the boy never be come a man. Every thing is stil where it wer may be when I grow up Iwl be Pry Mincer.'

On we gone roading thru the dark and rain roading for the aulders and the chard coal berning. In your mynd places be come the name of what happent in them. Like Iwd say in my mynd 'befor Cambry' or 'after Cambry' meaning befor or after what happent there. Thinking on the aulders it wer a jumbl of words and picters all mixt up. All kynds of diffrent things in it when I said 'the aulders' in my head. Like what the Ardshipd said about his dead father: 'I can feal him in me when its moving I can feal him in me when its stil.' Why that? May be becaws the aulders put me in mynd of seed of the berning and hart of the chyld. The berning chyld and the dead father may be its all 1 thing. And Goodparley trying all them long years to man for his self that wer part of it the same. With Granser and the bloody meat and boan.

So roading thru that rainy dark my mynd wer saying to its self: Now for the aulders. Saying the name of what wer going to be yet not knowing what itwd be. Jus saying that over and over: Now for the aulders.

We wernt doing no mor talking we sunk in to a sylents. It wer slow going Goodparley wernt up to much by then. Hed had like a hy after they blyndit him. Hy on stil being a live nor not being Pry Mincer no Mor. Hy in some kynd of way on being blyn. 1ce that begun to wear off he be come a plain woondit man slow and herting.

Time we come over the Bundel Downs it wer broad in the day. Stil raining it wer. Looking down from the hy groun in to the aulders you cud see in to the chard coal berners fents. Smoak and steam coming up in the rain from the harts and huts all huddelt they wer crouching in the wood like girt old shaggy wet naminals sleaping. The harts with roun backs and the huts with humps. Beyont them you cud see the rivver you cud hear it running hy in the col grey rainy morning.

I cud see a littl fire going unner a littl humpy roof on poals and a chard coal berner sqwatting by it with his back to us. He stood up and ternt roun it wer Granser. We come down off the hy groun to the fents it wer jus thin poals and flimsy for easy moving made in seckshins and peggit to gether it wernt much mor solid nor a fit up you cud pernearve kickt it down and dogs cud cernlyve got unner it easy a nuff. Coarse that dint make no diffrents to Granser. I wunnert if all them chard coal berners wer dog frendy. I stood at the gate and callt, 'Trubba not.'

Gransers face come up over the top of the fents he had his neck stretcht out and looking at us hard. He said, 'Is that who I think it is? Is that who I ben waiting for so long?'

Goodparley said, 'You know it is you stinking crows meat and glad you are to see me brung down aint you.'

Granser opent to us the dogs dint try to come in they rathert keap on the out side of the fents. Granser throwing his arms roun Goodparley he wer hugging him and kissing him and muching over him he wer saying, 'O my poor boy my poor poor boy my poor old boy.'

Goodparley said, 'Yes you rottin old barset its your poor old boy and youre in joy of it aint you youre getting a hard on from it you filfy old thing why dint I do a parper job of it when I stuck that knife in you.'

Granser said, 'Becaws you never wantit to kil me o no you dint want to do your old Granser dead you dint want to Drop John him you lovit your old Granser too much for that you wantit me to live. Which I knowit that and I knowit youwd come back to me 1 day my poor dear boy.'

Goodparley said, 'Be you going to healf me or you going to stan there wanking?'

Granser said, 'Iwl see you right dear boy you neadnt worry. Whatve they done to you whatve they done to my poor old Abel?'

Goodparley said, 'Theyve put my eyes out Granser I cant see no mor Iwl never see nothing no mor.' He begun to cry then.

Granser said, 'Never you mynd Abel Iwl look out for you youre hoam now you can res easy from now on.' He took him in to a littl hump back hut then I lef them to it and going down by the rivver for the loan of my thots.

I have to keap counting to keap it strait in my mynd what day it wer. Wel I have noats but what I mean is I have to keap counting to beleave how far I come in my life 1 day to the nex. That morning it wer the 9th day from my naming day. That day when it come that las boars tern to dy on my spear in the grey morning girzel on them very same Bundel Downs. 9 days dont soun like a long time yet I stil cudnt take in all whatd happent. Seeing that boars face in my mynd that morning in the aulders and seeing it in my mynd now I have the same thot I had then: If you cud even jus see 1 thing clear the woal of whats in it you cud see every thing clear. But you never wil get to see the woal of any thing youre all ways in the middl of it living it or moving thru it. Never mynd.

We stoppit there then with Granser in the aulders it wer a good place to ly up. Granser he dint have no crowd there he wer oansome like the chard coal berners mosly wer. The forms all ways give them road crowd and hault ther fentsing 1 cutting to a nother then they fentst them in and lef them til they finisht ther berning and ready to move on. This year the chard coal berners ben doing the 6 year cutting in the aulder coppises all up and down the rivver. They had long flat boats for the fentsing and the chard coal there wer 1 tyd up by Gransers cutting with bags of chard coal covert with hard clof. All up and down the rivver you cud see the loppt off aulders when they wer fresh cut they wer red they ternt pink after. Red wood. Red wud. Seed of the red. All ways words in things. 6 year cuttings. Which this wer a Ardship year and a cutting year boath. Every 2nd cutting yearwd all ways be 1 of them 12th years when a Pry Mincer and a Ardship gone the Fools Circel 9wys. Them aulders wer trying to tel me some thing I knowit that much.

It wer on the forms to keap the chard coal berners in meat. Granser had a stoar of pittaters and sweads he had roady and sossage from Good Mercy plus some times they brung fresh meat. Goodparley and me we all ways kep low when any 1 ternt up. I gone foraging with the dogs every day we et good there. I kep myndful of How Fents no moren 3 faggers off I dint want to run in to none of ther foragers jus then. Some times Iwd see them in the farness without them seing me which that took me strange. My crowd what use to be.

Granser wer putting poltises on Goodparleys woons all the time and Goodparley mending steady. We hadnt ben talking on it but I thot wewd parbly start in showing Mr Punch soons Goodparley wer fit to road. Right then he wer sleaping moren he wer doing any thing else. Him and Granser slep in 1 hut and I wer in a nother with a doss bag Granserd give me. I wunnert if the 2 of them talkit over old times and I wunnert if Granser tryd to start any new times.

I wer wunnering when Granser wer going to say some thing of what we ben talking on 1st time I seen him. I dint say nothing to him I jus waitit. Them chard coal harts kep him on the hop he wer all ways hanging over them doing 1 thing and a nother hewd be shovveling earf on them or hewd be shiffing his wind screans a bout. He wer all ways scortching his self and his cloes his red jumper wer bernt ful of hoals and the sleaves of it all blackent. He wer looking at it 1 time and he said, 'Im about due for the new red.' Which then he begun singing $\frac{1}{2}$ unner his breaf:

> Mort your clof with Saul & Peter
> (Dy it red)
> Mort your clof with Saul & Peter
> (Eusa said)

Looking at me sydling wylst he sung it like he wantit me to take noatis. So I said, 'All right then what is that Saul & Peter whats it all about?'

Granser he larft and sung:

> Mort your clof with Saul & Peter
> (Keap the way)
> Mort your clof with Saul & Peter
> (Wait the day)

Goodparley said, 'What day wud that be then?'

Granser said, 'We dont know the day but wewl be ready when it comes Abel. Which Ive give blood for it and got a scar to show for it enn I.'

Goodparley said, 'I aint never heard nothing about no day nor no scar.'

Granser said, 'No you aint and thats how its meant to be. If the Pry Mincer knowit then it wunt be no berners and dyers seakert wud it.'

Goodparley said, 'Berners and dyers is it. Les see that scar then I mean les have a feal of it.'

Granser liffit up his jumper and his vesses and there on his belly wer the same and very scar Goodparley and me had on ours only on the lef in stead of the right. I said, 'Thats a Eusa scar.'

Goodparley run his finger over it he said, 'What do the berners and the dyers call this scar Granser?'

Granser said, 'Abel I swoar when I took this scar dint I. Swoar I wunt never tel no seakerts.'

Goodparley said, 'Granser you know youre dying to tel your seakerts and youwl cernly dy if you dont tel Iwl pul you a part like a chikken sames Eusa done the Littl Shyning Man. Then therewl be a new figger in the show the Littl Smelly Man.'

Granser said, 'Wel you know I never cud say no to you Abel we call that scar the 3 of the 1.'

Goodparley he stil had his head all rapt up and you wud all mos think he wer looking right thru them rappings the way he leant tords Granser. He said, 'What 1 wud that be Granser? That wunt be the 1 Big 1 wud it?'

Granser said, 'There wont never be no 1 Big 1 for us Abel we aint got the clevverness for it but befor there ben the 1 Big 1 there ben the 1 Littl 1 and wil be agen. Which weare waiting for the day and ready.'

Goodparley said, 'Ready with what?'

Granser said, 'Ready with 2 of the 3 aint we and ben ready this long time and keaping ready and til it comes never mynd how long it takes the chard coal berners wil be wearing red and keaping ready.'

Goodparley said, 'Til *what* comes Granser?'

Granser said, 'The yellerboy stoan.'

Goodparley and me we boath let out our breaf at 1ce. Goodparley said, 'The yellerboy stoan.'

Granser said, 'Thats right Abel weve got the other 2 all ready.'

I said, 'Pig shit.'

Granser said, 'Thats right pig shit it is which thats what they make the seed of the red from thats how they make the Saul & Peter.'

I said, 'Hart of the wood is the chard coal.'

Granser said, 'Right you are agen. Hart of the wood and seed of the berning and hart of the chyld which is the chard coal time back and time to come.'

Goodparley he wer leaning tords Granser he wer lissening hard. When he talkit then his voyce soundit like he wer stil Pry Mincer. He said, 'Thats the 3 of the 1 is it? The 3 of the 1 Littl 1 is yellerboy stoan and Saul & Peter and chard coal?'

Granser said, 'Thats it Abel there you have the knowing what ben kep safe right the way from time back way back which it ben the chard coal berners and the dyers done that safe keaping nor no 1 else. Ours the salts and us the savers.'

Goodparley said, 'Wel wel wel here I ben stressing my self and straining and wearying and worrying this long time and all that time this here knowing ben right unner my nose. 1 Littl 1 who wudve thot it.'

Granser said, 'O yes there bint nothing else like that savit ben there. O no that 1 Littl 1 thats the onlyes banger any 1 knows of. I tel you Abel that yeller boys going to come up this here rivver 1 day and wewl make such a noys then yes we wil my good old boys.'

Goodparley said, 'Whatre you going to do then?'

Granser said, 'O therewl be big zanting I can tel you that. Therewl be hy telling and seakert rights in the Ful of the Moon o yes therewl be big doings.'

Goodparley said, 'Then what?'

Granser said, 'Wel then wewl have it wont we. Then wewl have that

> Seed of the littl seed of the wyld
> Seed of the berning is hart of the chyld

Goodparley said, 'Granser dont you take my meaning Im asking what youre going to *do* with that 1 Littl 1 when youve got it.'

Granser said, 'Abel havent I ben telling you that same and very.'

Goodparley said, 'Whos the Big Man of the chard coal berners?'

Granser said, 'O it aint that kynd of thing Abel the chard coal berners aint no fents nor form nor Mincery weare the childer of the woodlings.'

Goodparley said, 'Ah. Childer of the woodlings. Howd you get to be a chyld of the woodlings then?'

Granser said, 'It ben you what done that Abel it ben you what happent that for me when you stuck that knife in me and lef me for dead. You have in memberment where it wer you done that do you?'

Goodparley said, 'Good Mercy Form.'

Granser said, 'Which there it is that same and very place whats jus acrost the rivver from us right this minim. That same and very where you stuck your knife in me nor you dint show me no good mercy at all Abel no you dint. Nor them formers dint nyther whatd they care for a old roader and him mosly dead. Only 1 of the dyers them bloaks what boyl up the pig shit they all ways stink like any thing they mosly keap to ther selfs he seen me lying there and red with my oan blood my oan seed of the red you see what I mean. That dyer he cudnt tern his back on dying me becaws the seed of the red is seed of the berning you see its hart of the chyld which theyve swoar on it and ben swoar to it. That dyer took me down to the rivver which he put me in a boat and he rowit me over to you know where dont you.'

Goodparley said, 'This here wood where we are now.'

190

Granser said, 'This same and very aulder wood. Which the healing and the healf is in the hart of the wood you see. The hart of the wood by the run of the rivver what goes to the dead stoan hart of Inland where the stoan wood lives. Right here in this wood is where the chard coal berners healft me back to life. Abel you know I wer jus only joaking when I said I wer Drop John I never meant to ride your hump for what you done I never hevvit no gilt on to you. What you done to me I brung it on my self with what I done to you when I wunt let you be come your oan man. I wunt let you be come what you wer going to be nex. Thats the woal seakert of the 1 Littl 1 you see.'

Goodparley said, 'Whats that seakert then?'

Granser said, 'It wants to be its nex thing you see its a showing of the Master Chaynjis in littl. Them wite kirstels and that black chard coal and that yeller boy theyre coming to gether to show you the Power in the changingness of things. Which is the hart of the Girt Chyld of the Every Thing and the worl aint nothing only a idear in the mynd of that chyld. Which that chyld wants us to think all the diffrent parts of that idear to keap the worl in good hart and healf.' Granser wer looking at poor old Goodparley with his blyn rapt up head he said, 'Abel be you thinking on how the 1 of the 2 of us come a part and gone 2 diffrent ways?'

Goodparley said, 'Yes Im thinking on that.'

Granser said, 'You gone with the Mincery and I gone with the chard coal berners. What do the chard coal berners do. We bern 1ce to bern agen you see the blip of it. Ben thru the fire in the hart of the chyld and ready to bern agen. The Mincery and all the other mincerys what ever ben they dont know nothing only to bern 1ce and go every thing a way. Go the worl a way. Keap them poor crookit peopl in a hoal and asking roun your Fools Circel for whats long gone and far pas.'

Goodparley said, 'Granser whatwd you do if we put some of that yeller boy in your han wud you know what to do with it?'

Granser said, 'Cernly I wud I tol you that knowing ben kep safe amongst the chard coal berners and waiting on the day.'

Goodparley said, 'Wel old cock this is the day becaws weve got jus a littl of that yellerboy stoan right here.'

Gransers mouf hung open when I showit him the yellerboy stoan. He said, 'Whered it come from?'

Goodparley said, 'From over the water dinnit. There come over jus only 1 littl bag of it which this is ½ of that nor it dont look like a nuff for moren a try out.'

Granser said, 'Les try it out then.' He took the yellerboy and gone in to the hut where he kep his exter gear and jumbling a roun in there.

Goodparley said, 'Watch how he does it Riddley.'

I said, 'I dont want to know.'

He said, 'Eusas sake be you simpl or what? The way thingsre going it looks like every 1 in Inlands after the yellerboy and the knowing of what to do with it. Somewl have 1 and somewl have the other and somewl have the boath. And them what dont have nothing theywl be out of it.'

I said, 'Wel I ben out of it up to now enn I.' I wer thinking of what come to me in Cambry when I wer looking at Greanvine. Keaping in mynd how much that face lookit like Goodparleys face. I said, 'The onlyes Power is no Power.'

He said, 'O Eusa you aint going to weary me with that kynd of boar shit are you. Nex thing youwl be telling me the Littl Shyning Man hes jus what ever cant never be put to gether or some other kynd of Orfing qwickness.'

I said, 'I dont think he *can* be put to gether.'

Goodparley said, 'O yes and whats our frend Erny doing right this minim Iwl give you odds hes trying his hardes to put that same and very Littl Shyning Man to gether jus as fas as he can.'

I said, 'You mean hes trying to make it right with the Eusa folk?'

He said, 'I mean hes trying to do the same what Gransers doing this very minim. Befor Orfing took over he talkit like he wunt never Trubba no 1 he wantit the woal worl to love him. And all the time progamming to sneak me and parbly dealing for yellerboy even if you dont think so. Whatd he do soons he took over? Hung me up and put my eyes out dinnee. Yes it wer the Eusa folk done it but it wer him as let them. You think you can keap out of it thats your fearbelly talking. Running afeart wont help you nothing. 1 day youwl be blowt to peaces with some 1 elses doing then youwl wish youd lissent to your poor blyn old Nunkel Abel youwl wish youd stood forit like a man and took it in han.'

'And wankt with it,' I said. Yet I done like he tol me I gone in to that littl hump back hut with Granser. He wer pounding the yellerboy stoan to a fine powder. Then he done the same with some chard coal. Done it with a boal and pounder. He had the Saul & Peter all ready that wer kirstels like salt. He took littl measurs and measuring out yellerboy and chard coal and Saul & Peter. Mixing them all to gether then and me watching. It wer like the 1st time I seen a woman open for me I wer thinking: This is what its all about then.

Granser singing to his self wylst he mixt the 3 of the 1:

Wewl make such a noys
Such a noys
Such a noys
Wewl make such a noys
My good old boys

Granser said, 'Now comes the las of the mixing which Ive got to say the words.'

I said, 'Wel go on and say them then.'

He said, 'O no I aint saying them words wylst youre lissening thems the fissional seakerts of the act aint they. You bes go off a littl way.'

I said, 'All right then' which I gone out of the rivverside gate and walking by the water I dint want to sit by Goodparley I dint want him to weary me with why wernt I watching Granser.

I jus begun to roal up a smoak when WHAP! there come like a thunner clap it wer like when litening strikes right close it eckowit up and down the rivver. There come up a cloud of smoak from the fents it wernt the regler blue smoak it wer 1 big puff of grey smoak and things wer peltering down out of the trees like when you shake down nuts. The dogs begun to howl.

I gone back inside the fents. That littl hump back hut where Granser ben doing the mixing it wernt there no mor it wer jus only sticks and sods scattert wide. Granser he wer like throwt a way on the groun he lookit emty like when you take your han out of a show figger. His head wernt with the res of him his head wer on a poal. The gate a way from the rivver it had a hy poal on each side of it and Gransers head wer stuck on the poynt of 1 of them poals jus like it ben put there for telling.

Nor that wernt the stranges of it. Goodparley wer stil where Id lef him sitting leaning agenst the other hump back hut. I wer stil looking tords the gate I said, 'Gransers head is on a poal.' Which he dint anser me nothing then I ternt to look at him and he had Gransers pounder sticking out of the front of his head. Clout stil rapt roun his head and that stoan pounder drove right in to his skul.

There hung over the place a kynd of scorchy smel a kynd of stinging scorchy smel and the grey smoak driffing thru the blue smoak of the chard coal harts. Twean lite it wer the 1st dark coming on. Bat lite it wer and dimminy the pink and red stumps glimmering in the coppises like loppt off arms and legs and the rivver hy and hummering. The dogs wer howling nor it wernt like no other howling I ever heard it wer a kynd of wyld hoapless soun it wer a lorn and oansome yoop yaroo it soundit like they wer runnying on ther hynt legs and telling like thin black men and sad. Crying ther yoop yaroo ther sad tel what theyd all ways knowit theywd have to tel agen.

I gone to where Gransers head wer on the poal. His eyes wer closd his mouf wer shut. I said, 'Granser wil you tel?'

Lissening him then words come to me: What if its you whats making all this happen? What if every thing you think of happens?

I said, 'I never thot of my father getting kilt did I.'

Words come: Dint you?

Then I wernt sure. I said, 'I wont think no mor.'

Words come: That dont make no diffrents. If you dont think then some thing else wil think your thots theywl get thunk any how.

I said, 'What can I do then aswl be my oan doing?'

Words come: Whats the diffrents whos doing it?

The dogsd stoppt ther yoop yarooing. They come to the fents I heard them wimpering like los and greaving childer. All roun I heard the twean lite lissening. I took a las look at Goodparley I $\frac{1}{2}$ thot I myt see vines and leaves growing out of his mouf. Then I slung his fit up and my bundel on my back and off I slyd.

17

My feet begun to walk me down rivver tords Cambry. Thats where the senter is. All roun myt be a fools circel but the senter is stil what it is and where it is.

I kep wel in from the rivver side I kep wel wide of the coppises I dint want nothing mor to do with chard coal berners for a wyl. Dark nite it wer Dark of the Moon but where the woodlings littlt off to barrens I cud feal it on my face the open of it and I had a fealing inside me I never had befor. Sour groun and dead the barrens are you cudnt grow nothing on them only the dry dus blowing in the summer and the grey mud in the winter. Even the wind blowing the dus is some thing moving tho it aint jus only dead groun in a stilness. Seeds blow in the wind and what is earf but a deadness with life growing out of it? Rottin leaves and dead branches and naminal shit and that it all makes live earf on the dead groun and if you look at woodlings edge all roun the barrens youwl see the runty coming up where skin of earf growit back on nekkit groun. Nekkit groun what ben the bloody meat and boan of Bad Time covering its self with skin of earf and grass and woodlings. I thot: What ever it is its my groun. Here I stan.

We ben roading like all ways with the black leader josseling nexy but ½ way acrost the barrens he pusht his nose in to my han. He never done nothing like that befor I cudnt beleave it. Him what lookit like Death on 4 legs with his yeller eyes what dint even care if he livet or dyd and he wantit me to pet him. Thats when I cryd for the dead.

After a wyl I cud feal on my face a littl stilness where the wind wer cut off I cud hear the sylents of the stannings of the

Power Ring. Feal the goast of old Power circeling hy over me. Only this time I fealt a Power in me what circelt with it. Membering when that thot come to me: THE ONLYES POWER IS NO POWER. Wel now I sust that wernt qwite it. It aint that its *no* Power. Its the not sturgling for Power thats where the Power is. Its in jus letting your self be where it is. Its tuning in to the worl its leaving your self behynt and letting your self be where it says in *Eusa 5*:

> . . . in tu the hart uv the stoan hart uv the dans. Evere thing blippin & bleapin & movin in the shiftin uv thay Nos. Sum tyms bytin sum tyms bit.

Looking up in to the black where the goast of Power circelt blyn and oansome like a Drop John roun the los hump of Cambry I larft I yelt, 'SPIRIT OF GOD ROAD WITH ME!'

Dark of the Moon it wer. Pas the failing moon of my getting and fulling on tords the moon of my bearthing I gone to the hart of the wud I gone to the stoan wood in the hart of the stoan I gone to the woom of her what has her woom in Cambry.

The black sky dint change colour nor the stoans dint go wite nor the dogs dint runny on ther hynt legs with the shyning colours coming thru them it jus stayd solid black. No lerting from the dogs so I lit a candl. Up jumpt the shadders and shaking on the walls and rubbl. In amongst them stoan trees there wer what you myt call a notness of some 1. Some 1 ben roun there nor not too long befor me. No 1 there now tho. Lookit in the hidey hoal where Greanvine livet. Emty.

Lookit in the out poast. HOAP OF A TREE stil on the wall and the picter of Goodparley with the vines and leaves growing out of his mouf. No 1 there.

I said to the black leader, 'Garn the track and fynd?' We gone scanning here and there til finely on the other side of Cambry some way out from the senter the dogs begun harking like they do when theyve got some thing hoalt up.

I callt in to the dark, 'Who is it?'

There come back Erny Orfings voyce he said, 'Its Erny Orfing Riddley.'

Hed got his self up hys he cud get on a mounding of rubbl and hed like walt his self in he had to move big stoans out of the way befor I cud get to him. I said, 'Whatre you doing all walt up like that?' Taking the murky jus a littl.

He said, 'Overing the nite. Which I come here looking for you and Goodparley.'

Snick snick I wer striking for the fire I can stil hear in the ear of my mynd that snick snick in the dark that nite in Cambry. I lit the candl and there jumpt out of the dark the face of Greanvine and the face of Orfing. It snuck me this time how much Greanvine realy did look like Goodparley even tho Id all ways thot of him with littl eyes and Greanvines eyes they wer so big and so wide open.

Orfing said, 'Looks like him dunnit. Looks like Abel. Befor they put his eyes out I mean.' The candl flame shimmying in the wind and the tears roaling down his face. He said, 'He aint with you now is he. You aint with him no mor youve lef him oansome in the dark youve lef him dead havent you.'

I tol him what happent and he covert his face with his hans. After a littl he took his hans down he said, 'Riddley dyou think theres hoap of any thing?'

I said, 'Theres new earf on the barrens all the time.'

He said, 'Parbly them from Good Mercyve took him a way and bernt him by now. How it pangs my hart to think of him jus ashes and blowing in the wind!'

I said, 'Trubba not and withry speck but aint you the 1 as put him on that windy road when you brung him down?'

He said, 'Riddley you know as wel as I do if you put 1 figger on your right han and a nother on your lef the 1 wil go agenst the other some how some time. It dont matter nothing if you call them Punch & Pooty or Goodparley & Orfing.'

I said, 'Orfing & Ardship?'

He said, 'Yes you may wel say Orfing & Ardship. Which the hardship be come the Orfing dinnit. At leas I come out of it with my life. For a littl wyl any how.'

I said, 'What happent?'

He said, 'Wel we had our littl bag of yellerboy stoan dint we. Same as you. Which thats Power innit. I mean that and the knowing of what to do with it. If 1 comes to you youwl go looking for the other I dont care who you be youwl do it. Becaws theres Power in the 1 sames its in the other nor it dont matter nothing which comes 1st. 1ce that Powers luce itwl fetch itwl work itwl move itwl happen every 1 whats in its road. *Some* 1s got to happen it. If it aint me or you it cud wel be some 1 wersen us cudnt it. So I wer on for letting it happen.

'The Ardship he begun to gether with the Eusa folk they all took off ther cloes and tangelt ther selfs to gether all nekkit and twining like a nes of snakes which they callit that some poasyum. Which they done trantsing with it and hy telling. Doing it in that old Power Station in Fork Stoan where the out poast is. Which that place its so big and eckowing it wer realy some thing to hear them telling of the many cools of Addom and the party cools of stoan and all the diffrent colourt seeds and that. It put you hy your oan self even tho you mytnt know nothing of it yet you cud get jus the fayntes glimmer of what it musve ben to be the Puter Leat. To have them boats in the air which they callit them space craf and them picters on the wind which that wer viddyo and going out beyont the sarvering gallack seas. Not jus singing it you know. Acturely going it acturely roading out thru space. Jus try to get it in your mynd try to happen it in your head o dint they trants hy you cud feal the thrus and the boost of it you know the jynt woosh of them liffing off and to the stations. Which they jumpt 1 station to the nex you see and til they jumpt right out beyont them gallack seas. I tel you Riddley lissening to them trantsing and telling it wer all mos like being in 1 of them space craf o the yoaring and the roaling o the nertial and the navigation of it.'

I said, 'Did they ever get to the knowing of the mixter of the 1 Littl 1?'

He said, 'No they dint you see what it wer they gone so far

beyont any thing that simpl they cudnt qwite track back to it they cudnt littl down to the Nos. of it.'

I said, 'So you never gone bang then?'

He said, 'O yes we did we gone bang right a nuff the same as you. Some of the hevvys they gone to Hoggem Form which they come back with a dyer and they helpt some qwirys on him til he give them the Nos. of the mixter which he knowit them Nos. the sames your chard coal berner done. Which all them years I never knowit nothing of all that with them berners and dyers nor Goodparley dint nyther and us the Pry Mincer and the Wes Mincer.'

I said, 'Yes but what about the bang howd it go?'

He said, 'Wel the hevvys took the yellerboy stoan and the other gready mints and they done that mixter like the dyer tol them which they packt it in a iron pot and they had what they callit a fews which the dyer give them it wer a bit of chemistery roap. The Ardship wernt interstit in that kynd of thing that han mixing he rathert have mor vantsit theary. Him and the Eusa folk they wer carrying on with ther some poasyum wylst the hevvys wer larking a bout with the iron pot of mixter they wer pist and singing songs they wer fummeling them nekkit Eusa women. The Ardship he tol the hevvys to stop ther singing and the res of it which it wer giving him inner fearents with his trantsing. Which them hevvys then they lit the fews and throwit the pot in to the middl of the Eusa folk thats when it gone bang and peaces of iron pot and Eusa folk wizzing all roun. It toar the Ardship all a part and peaces of him raining down on them girt shyning broakin machines plus it kilt 3 mor Eusa folk and woondit others of them which then the res of the Eusa folk gone for the hevvys. Thats when I vackt my wayt I slyd out of there I thot I bes take my chance elser and elsewys. I realy had to voat no kynd of fents in that lot I cudnt see how I wer going to mincer any thing out of them.'

I said, 'Whyd you ever want to take over any how?'

He said, 'I all ready tol you dint I. You put 1 figger on your right han and 1 on your lef and the 1 wil take over from the other plus Iwl tel you any 1 what ben Goodparleys shadder mincer wudve done the same yes youwdve done it jus the same as me. He had that way about him he jus made you want to bring him down. Which that ben what he wantit and all he dint have no res and til he made it happen. I never progammit to do it realy it jus put its self to gether. I dont think them hevvys ben beckoning that boat I think parbly that dead bloak ben a farring seakert tryer from other side which my read of it is he ben coming to try his Luck he ben out to bargam yellerboy for knowing when he got nitefel in a storm and the marse come down on his head. When Good-parley made some of the hevvys help the qwirys on others of them they wer ready for the bringdown which I jus clymt on it and movit with it.'

I said, 'What dyou think wil happen now dyou think the hevvys at Fork Stoan wil sen ther oan farring seakert tryer to bargam some thing with the other siders?'

He said, 'Wel its luce now innit. Its luce and itwl fetch. Every 1 as can get the Nos. of the mixter and them 3 gready mints of it theywl have a go wont they. Somewl go 1 way with it some a nother. You can get jus as dead from a kick in the head as you can from the 1 Littl 1 but its the natur of it gets peopl as cited. I mean your foot is all ways on the end of your leg innit. So if youre going to kick some 1 to death it aint all that thrilling is it. This other tho youve got to have the Nos. of the mixter then youve got to fynd your gready mints then youve got to do the mixing of the mixter and youve got to say the fissional seakerts of the act befor you kil some body its all that chemistery and fizzics of it you see. Its some thing new. Which ever way you look at it I dont think Aunty and her red eyed rat be too far from us. Be that a fit up on your back?'

I said, 'You know it is and you know whose.'

He said, 'Its all ways the littl man as carrys the fit up whynt you let me have it.'

I said, 'Erny you know you aint no littlern me the 2 of us is jus about the same bigness.'

He said, 'Riddley thats as may be but I feal littler all the time I wish youwd let me carry it I wont feal right else. You know its all ways Orfing as carrys the fit up.'

I said, 'And its Goodparley does the show. Be you making me Goodparley now?'

He said, 'I cant make no 1 nothing you know that. Nor I never fealt right when them hevvys wer calling me Goodparley nor I wunt put that name on you nyther les jus call it Walker & Orfing.'

I said, 'Why not Orfing & Walker?'

He said, 'The name as comes 1st is the man as works the figgers and does the voyces. Which I never ben no good at that I never do nothing only strait man for the patter. So Walker & Orfings what itwl have to be.'

Erny slung the fit up then and we gone back to the out poast. Which I fealt like sitting down to a tabel with a candl and putting some words on paper. That ben the beginning of this writing and Im sitting at that same and very tabel now. Longs we had the dogs to keap look out we thot why not hoal up there and til such time as any new hevvys myt be coming in. Its ben a 14nt now tho nor there bint no blip of hevvys nor no 1 else. It looks to me like that Fools Circel is broakin now I dont think therewl be no mor regler hevvys nor Eusa folk in dead towns from now on. Parbly all the hevvys and any Eusa folk whatre stil a live theyre all too binsy running a roun trying to go bang. Plus a woal lot of other peopl as wel by now parbly. Fars we know there bint no mor bangs yet but we dont have the leas idear whats going to happen. Right now there aint even no Pry Mincer its what they call a care maker Mincery with regenneril guvner men from the Ram at all the forms.

How it looks to Erny and me and strapping the lates from what littl datter weve got we pirntow the other siders mus have plenny of yellerboy and theywl be senning out mor farring seakert tryers. Parbly itwl be a littl wyl befor they sen a nother 1 to Inland but the thing is luce now. By nex mooning Iwl bet you can walk from here to other side without

202

getting your feet wet jus stepping from 1 boat to the nex and every 1 of them boats after yellerboy.

Orfing and me we know weare living on burrow time but then who aint. The way things are now it aint jus only you dont know whos going to go bang nex you dont even know where the arrer myt come from with your name on it you cant be too sure whos your frend and whos your nemminy life aint qwite as simpl as it use to be. It use to be if you wer agenst the Ram youwd be agenst the forms becaws you knowit they wer all 1 thing jus like a body and its head. Now the head myt say 1 thing only you dont know what the body wil do. 1 thing Lucky them dogsre stil with us and longs that black leaders on our side I dont worry too much about getting snuck. Orfings getting a littl dog frendy now even tho when he come oansome from Fork Stoan to Cambry he said he ben measuring his life from 1 tree to the nex and when he come to the barrens he said he jus tol his self 1 way or a nother he parbly wunt be a live too much longer. Which 1ce he got use to that idear then every minim he wer stil a live he wer that much a head.

Walker & Orfing. I liket the idear of making up shows only with things how they are now I wernt all that kean to road no show I ratherwd live qwyet and ly low til we seen who come out on top. It wer Orfing as wantit to start showing.

I said, 'Wunt it be bes to wait til things settl down a littl?'

He said, 'The sooner we do whats on us to do the sooner thingswl settl down.'

I said, 'You know Erny theres places where it mytnt be the safes thing in the worl for you to put foot. You what brung down Goodparley and let them crookit peopl put his eyes out.'

He said, 'Wel Riddley if I brung him down for any thing it ben becaws he thot you cud move the out side of things frontways and leave the in side to look after its self. Which I think its the in side has got to do the moving its got to move every thing and its got to move us as wel. If I say diffrent time after this itwl be fearbelly talking I know I aint brave. But thats what Im saying now. Its moving me the way its moving me and Im going with it fars I can.'

So we begun to ready our selfs for the road. When I unbundelt Goodparleys fit up to do a littl prackters work it come to me agen the 2ness of things. Any other fit up I ever seen there ben 1 bag of figgers in it which you hang it inside when youre showing then youve got the figgers ready to han. Only Goodparleys fit up has 2 bags becaws theres 2 sets of figgers. Theres the 1s for the Eusa show then theres the 1s for the Punch show. That show what he never showit to no crowd only odd times done it for his self and that 1ce for me.

You take a figger out of the bag nor it aint nothing only some colourt clof with a paintit wood head and hans. Then you put it on. You put your head finger in the head you put your arm fingers in the arms then that figger looks roun and takes noatis it has things to say. Which they wont all ways be things *youwd* think of saying o no them wood heads the hart of the wood is in them and the hart of the wud and all. They have ther knowing and they have ther saying which you bes lissen for it you bes let it happen. 'I never look for my reveal til its ben.' Thats what my dad said time back. My dad the connexion man. In my woal life Ive only ever done that 1 connexion which Ive wrote down here I begun with trying to put it to gether poal by poal only my reveal dint come that way it snuck me woaly. I wer keaping that in memberment now. Ready to cry ready to dy ready for any thing is how I come to it now. In fear and tremmering only not running a way. In emtyness and ready to be fult. Not to lern no body nothing I cant even lern my oan self all I can do is try not to get in front of whats coming. Jus try to keap out of the way of it.

You myt talk about how youre going to show you myt think about it only on the nite there it is if its the 1st time or the 100th it aint never happent befor it aint nothing you know any thing about. You look out thru the weave of the back cloth and you see the torches shimmying and glimmering you hear a hummering and a mummering from the crowd in front of you. Theres a prickling all over your skin and you feal like therewl be sparkls coming off you in the dark.

Time back is in them Punch figgers. Dead hans and gone carvit them heads and colourt them and follering some idear they dint jus happen random. Its a lot of work to carve a head that wel you have to have it in you to begin with then you have to take the neak of it thru all the diffrent episodes of the work from the rough cut to the finel smooving and the pryming and the painting of it.

I knowit wel them figgers never ben made up jus only for that 1 littl show what Goodparleyd showt me. It aint in the natur of a show to be the same every time it aint like a story what you pas down trying not to change nothing which even then the changes wil creap in. No a figger show its got its oan chemistery and fizzics. What it is its all ways trying to fynd out what it is jus now this same and very minim going thru its chaynjis. Which Ive wrote that in the old spel becaws its them same and very Chaynjis what the Littl Shyning Man tol Eusa of.

Punch says to me, 'What am I?' Says it to me in his oan voyce which now I can speak that voyce the same as Goodparley done. In the figger bag I foun a littl thing its 2 littl curvit peaces of iron with a thin peace of clof rapt roun and in be twean so its like when you hol a blade of grass be twean your thums to shril with it. The iron holding the clof the way your thums wud the grass. This littl thing you put it in your mouf and when its parper wet you can do Punchs voyce with it. Orfing tol me its what they call a swazzl.

And Pooty. I know she aint jus only a plain sow. Ive wrote down early on in this writing that song Lorna Elswint sung me on the nite of my naming day. That Moon Pig song. Iwl give odds Pootys mixt up with that Moon Sow. You look at that sow face of hers and you know you aint looking at some naminal ben fattit for meating youre looking at some 1 ben offert to. And that pig babby that pig chyld. Meat chyld. Theres other figgers Goodparley never showit in that show he done for me. Theres some great grean naminal with long joars and ever so many teef. Theres a black man and other figgers as wel Iwl never know ther story.

Them in the 1 bag and of coarse in the other bag the other lot and the Little Shyning Man with them. Which hes qwite a peace of work that Littl Shyning Man. The way hes made hes all wood hes got a woal varnisht wood body with parper arms and legs and riggit with wires so he comes in 2 or slyds back in to 1. Hes the only figger there is with a cock and balls. Like it says in the *Eusa Story* when he comes in 2 his cock and balls theyre on his lef side his head and neck theyre on his right. Hes hung from a pully you work him with your feet with 2 wires. When hes in 2 and you slyd him to gether the 2 $\frac{1}{2}$s of him come to gether with a clack. I wunner if Goodparley ever thot of a bang when he heard that.

Theres figgers in that bag you never seen in a show. You get to wunnering if you gone down deap a nuff in that bag if you mytnt get right the way down to Bad Time and fynd out all what realy happent. Theres Eusas 2 boys in there I never seen them befor. Cant say for cern its them but I lissen it is. 1 has red eyes 1 has yeller. Them 2 pairs of eyes wide open all them years in the dark inside that bag. Dogs. Folleree and Folleroo with ther toofy joars opening and closing they want to talk like men.

1 figger tho. 1 figger hes the same and very 1 in boath bags of figgers. Mr Clevver. Which hes Mr On The Levvil and hes callit Drop John as wel. There he is the name changes but he dont. In all that 2ness there he comes up hes the 1. Hes your lad for clevver work or Drop Johning which ever myt be neadit there he is the boath of him plus the goast of him. Same red face and littl black beard and the same horns growing out of his head. Same red cloes even. All them diffrent figgers in the 2 bags only he aint diffrent hes the same. You begin to wunner myt he be the 1 Big 1 of it? Or the 1 Littl 1 of it. Or may be there aint no such thing as a Big 1 or a Littl 1 its jus only all 1 and you see what diffrent things you see in the chaynjing lites of the diffrent times of the girt dants of the every thing. Sum tyms bytin sum tyms bit.

If youre a show man then what ever happens is took in to your figgers and your fit up its took in to your show. If you dont know whats happent sooner youwl hear of it later youwl hear your figgers tel of it 1 way or a nother. That boar kicking on the end of my spear hewl be in my shows I dont know how but hewl be there. That crow what callit, 'Fall! Fall! Fall!' and my smasht father that greyling morning at Widders Dump and that old leader with his yeller eyes and woar down teef. Gransers head glimmering in the twean lite and Goodparley sitting qwyet in amongst the black and nekkit aulders loppt off pink and red in the hart of his wud with the stoan in his head and the twean lite holding its breaf and lissening. In amongst it all the thot of may be I wer the aulder kincher. May be the idear of it ben waiting all them years for me to come a long and be it.

Wel of coarse there wer the matter of letshow. We dint know if that care making Mincery wer going to let us run luce with our fit up and our 2 bags of figgers. We pult datter and we pirntowt we wer roading Goodparleys show which he ben give letshow by Orfing in that littl time when Orfing ben Goodparley. So there wer letshow on that fit up which that wer good a nuff for us. If them guvner men thot diffrent wewd parbly fynd out soon a nuff.

So we got our selfs ready and off we gone with our fit up and our figgers and our dog crowd. It wer in boath our mynds to do our 1st show at Weaping Form which that ben Bad Mercy Fents time back it ben Goodparleys hoam fents when he ben littl. Its about the same farness from Cambry as How Fents only its Wes of Cambry and its wel Wes of the Sour its on the A251 2 or 3 faggers Norf of Moal Arse. Its on the track to Fathers Ham which roun there its hard line Eusa country moren some other places are. Some say Mr Clevver use to live in Fathers Ham befor he come to Cambry.

Any how here we come out of Cambry on a grey day with a littl girzel and roading Wes for Weaping on the old iron track. Dogs strung out in parper roading form the nation they all ways had a cuppl in the poynt plus 2 on each wing them dogs are real hevvys. I askit Erny if he dint think we bes proach up to that gate without no dogs and say we forkt off from a trade crowd or some thing. He wernt having none of that he said, 'This here aint Goodshow & Slymouf its Walker & Orfing. We myswel begin how we are and go on the same.'

Coming in to Weaping we blowit the horn from a littl way off we dint blow 'Eusa show' becaws it wernt no Eusa show. We blowit a diffrent call which we meant it to say 'New show'. When we come up to the fents the dogs layd back out of bow shot but there they wer you cud see wed roadit in with them. Come to the gate I fealt like I wer seeing it mor with my stummick nor my eyes you know how it is some times when you come to a thing. You ben coming littl by littl from far to close and littl by littl you seen it growing from littl to big in your eyes then all on a suddn there it is in front of you and this is now and you feal it in your stummick. There we wer and this wer now I lookit up and I said, 'Trubba not its a new show.' Tryd to make it soun like 'Eusa show' but you cant realy.

The bloak on the gate he took a long look without saying nothing then his head dispeart. In a littl his head come back and some others with it. 1 of them hyern the others and some grey in his beard so I said it agen to him, 'Trubba not tsnew show.' Like that.

He come back at me with a girt deap voyce he said, 'When Eusa come back to Cambry he wer blyn and bloody he stood outside the gate and the dogs licking his soars. Them on the gate they larft at him they said, "Why dont you say 'Trubba not' if you want in?" Wel we know Eusa cudnt say "Trubba not" cud he. Becaws wel he knowit he had Trubba roaling off him like sweat in the summer he had Trubba ponging off him you cud smel it from a good farness even up wind of him he dint try no goodshow he jus said strait out, "I cant say that." Now here comes you I know you aint Eusa nor you aint blyn nor bloody yet here I see you roading with dogs and roading with him what ben shadder mincer and Pry Mincer and now hes no mincer. Which youve said "Trubba not" and may be you beleave you aint brung no Trubba with you only I aint too cern of that my self. What about that no mincer can he talk ord they cut his tung out when they throwit him a way after he brung down Abel Goodparley?'

Orfing said, 'I can talk Rightway.' Which that wer the name of the Big Man we wer talking to. Rightway Flinter.

Rightway Flinter said, 'Wel then if you can talk praps youwl be good a nuff and tel me if you can say "Trubba not". You what brung down the bigger man and better you what ternt the crookit luce and now youve got your new boy and your dog crowd. This here partner of yours hes said "Trubba not" hes greasd my surents now I dont have to worry about nothing no mor. Now whatre you going to say be you going to Trubba not me as wel?'

Erny said, 'No Rightway I cant say "Trubba not". Parbly weare Trubba right a nuff.'

Flinter said, 'There you be Erny out of your oan mouf youve said it and I think Iwl yes with that. Poor old blyn Goodparley and a old chard coal berner gone bang the 1st in Inland since time back way back. 1 minim they wer men and the nex they wer peaces of meat nor it wernt done by knife nor spear nor arrer nor sling stoan it wer clevverness done it and the 1 Big 1. That old chard coal berners head took off strait up like a sky lark only parbly not singing. Up it gone and down it come thwock on a poal and ripe for telling. Goodparley sitting there dead with a stoan pounder in his skul. You myt say after all them years of looking for that 1 Big 1 it finely come in to his mynd. Twean lite it wer when it happent. Dark of the moon when the dark come down and the Black Pack yoop yarooing all roun. 1st big bang since Bad Time and who ternt it luce who put that 1 Big 1 on the road to this place and every other place?' He wer looking strait at me.

Erny said, 'It bint the 1 Big 1 it ben the 1 Littl 1. Which youre looking at Riddley Walker but it bint him ternt it luce it wer a farring seakert tryer from other side and looking to goatch the wayt he wer looking to bargam a seakert gready mint for the Nos. of the mixter. Which 1ce his boat gratit on the shingel that 1 Littl 1 wer luce in Inland it wer on the road to blow up some 1 and you cud be sure some 1 wer roading fas to be there when it come.'

Flinter said, 'It dint have to be Abel Goodparley did it?'

Erny said, 'Rightway Iwl tel you what I think Iwl tel you what I pirntow from my unnermos datter. If it hadnt ben the 1 Littl 1 kilt Abel Goodparley it wudve ben some thing else becaws it wer his time and come. That man wer pulling he wer fetching he wer sucking in his Luck he wer wynding in the end of his life like a kid wynding in a kite.'

Flinter looking at Erny hard and he said, 'Wel youwd say that wunt you. You what brung him down.' He wer pulling his beard you cud hear his thots grynding in his head like mil stoans.

Erny said, 'Wel Rightway whats it going to be? Be you going to put on your wig and hold the bailey and pour the ounts of judgd men or you going to let wester day go down and ter morrer come up?'

Flinter said, 'O ter morrerwl come up Erny. Ter morrer all ways comes up the thing is to be 1 of them as comes up with it.'

Us stanning there in front of that gate nor it cudnt get no bigger realy only it kep like biggering in my eyes. Them dark heads and the grey sky behynt them. There come up then 2 mor heads it wer Granser and Goodparley. They ben smoakit like roady ther faces wer dark. Tree faces stoan faces. Wood faces.

I have to stop here for a littl.

18

All them heads looking at us the live 1s on the peopl and the dead 1s on the poals. Rightway Flinter said, 'You know these heads ben telling.'

Erny and me we dint say nothing. I tryd to lissen that black leader I tryd to put my mynd where he cud lissen me. I dont know what I thot he cud do only come in to bow shot and get his self kilt. He lissent me tho. He begun to yoop yaroo and all them other dogs the same. The woal pack yoop yarooing.

The hevvys on the gate uppit bow at us with arrer on string. Rightway Flinter said, 'You know these heads ben telling.'

I thot: Whyd we come here? Id knowit some kynd of thing like this myt happen. Whynt we stay hoalt up? Whynt we go somers far a way? Becaws you cant stay hoalt up. Becaws there aint no far a way. Becaws where you happen is where you happen.

Rightway Flinter said, 'You know these heads ben telling. And you know *what* they ben telling. They ben telling of Eusa how he gone that circel of the towns after Bad Time. Him what done the clevver work for Bad Time.'

Erny said, 'You know Rightway we aint Eusa. Youwl go a head and youwl do what youre progammit to do only dont tel your self weare Eusa becaws we aint.'

Flinter said, 'Wel Erny you myt terpit your way but Iwl terpit my way and parbly my waywl be the Rightway wunt you say.'

Erny kep shut then he dint say nothing.

Flinter said, 'Theres all ways some kynd of clevverness waiting somers near or far its all ways waiting to happen its all ways waiting for some 1 to pul it some 1 to fetch it some 1 to bring it down on the res of us. And them what fetches it who ever they myt be theyre Eusa. If its 1 or if its many dont make no odds. Its Eusa. Which time back way back every place as seen Eusa helt the bailey dint they. Every 1 as seen him pourt the ounts of judgd men dint they. Howd Eusa come back to Cambry he come back blyn and bloody he come back cut off he wernt a man no mor he wer what wer lef. You see what it wer hed had his chylding when he ben littl hed had his manning when he ben big. And whatd he do with his manning? He done clevverness and fetching the same. So he had to pay for it dint he. All them what dyd when the wite shadders come they payd dint they. All them what ther seed gone crookit when the groun gone sour they payd dint they. You see what it is Erny youve got to pay for 1 thing befor you go on to the nex. You and your yung partner here youre Eusa which of coarse youve got your chaynjis to go thru youve got things youwd like to do nex only befor you get to them youwl have to pay for the las things what you done.'

I had all of Goodparleys figgers in the fit up only Punch which he wer in my pockit. Not the old blackent 1 it wer Goodparleys Punch I had. Which I had the swazzl in my pockit as wel and when wed come up to Weaping gate Id put it in my mouf and wetting it I thot Mr Punch myt have some thing to say.

I ternt my back to the gate and Mr Punch come up looking at them over my sholder. He wer waving his stick he made his cock fessin noys. Rrrrrrrrrrrrrr. He said, '*Ah putcha putcha putcha.*' Which he begun to beat me with his stick. Them on the gate begun to larf. I cud feal ther eyes on Punch and I wer hoaping hewd say some thing funny. He dint tho. He stoppit beating me and he wer looking up at them. He wer staring at them and waving his stick. Dint say a word. Dogs ben yoop yarooing the woal time til then. Now they stoppt suddn and in jumpt the sylents. Them on the gate looking at Punch and Punch staring back and waving his stick. Not saying a word. Dead men in my mynd.

Nex there come Rightway Flinters voyce he said, 'You myswel come in and do your show. Whats on you is on you. I wont bring nothing down on this crowd.'

So we dint dy at Weaping Form nor we dint get cut off nor blyndit. We livet and we kep our eyes and our cocks and balls that time any how. What the nex time wil bring no 1 cant never say.

We tol them it wernt no Eusa show nor we dint think we shud do no wotcher only ther connexion man Deaper Flinter he wer Rightways brother he said they wunt let us show without we wotchert 1st. So we got our hash and rizlas only diffrents wer he said if it wernt no Eusa show we shunt get the woal wotcher. He give us 1 cut hash and 25 rizlas each in stead of 2 cuts hash and 50 then he said ther meat our meat and the res of it.

There we wer then. Hard to beleave it. Stil a live and the torches shimmying for us. Shimmering and glimmering. All fittit up and the crowd waiting for what wer coming. All the seanyer members of the form in front plus the regenneril guvner man from the Ram his name wer Riser Partman. Erny out in front for the patter and me looking out thru the back clof.

They wer mummering in the front row it wer about the show talk. Deaper Flinter said it wernt right doing the Eusa show talk if it wernt no Eusa show. Which Rightway Flinter said there wernt going to be no show without no show talk not wylst he wer Big Man any how. Then Deaper said wel what shud he say when he done the show talk shud he say 'Down that road with Eusa'? Which Rightway said he shud jus say what he all ways said and les get on with it. Which Deaper said Rightway cud do what he liket only he wernt going to say the name of Eusa if it wernt no Eusa show. Then Rightway said he dint care what Deaper said only les get on with the show befor the torches bernt out.

Deaper stanning up then he said to the crowd, 'Now this here show what weare going to see it aint no Eusa show its some kynd of a new show.'

Then there come some mummering.

Deaper said, 'So les keap in mynd now wylst weare doing this show talk weare leaving Eusa out of it.'

213

There come a hevvy mans voyce from the crowd it said, 'You bes go careful Deaper.'

Deaper said, 'I *am* going careful nor I dont nead no 1 to tel me do I.'

The same voyce said, 'Wel if you think you can leave Eusa out of any thing you aint going careful youre going foolish.'

Rightway Flinter then he ternt roun he said to that bloak, 'Easyer you neadnt to worry over our connexion man going foolish wylst Im Big Man. What you need to worry over is if your joars as hard as my fis.'

Easyer gone qwyet then only you cud hear some shiffing roun and some breaving and sying.

Deaper finely begun his show talk then he said to the crowd, 'Weare going aint we.'

They said, 'Yes weare going.'

He said, 'Down that road.'

They waitit for them other 2 words which them words dint come.

Then there come Easyers voyce loud and clear he said, 'With Eusa.'

Then the res of them said, 'With Eusa time and reqwyrt.'

Deaper said, 'Where them Chaynjis take us.'

They said, 'He done his time wewl do our time.'

Deaper said, 'Showing for us.' In stead of 'Hes doing it for us.'

They said, 'Hes doing it for us weare doing it for him.'

Deaper said, 'Keap it going. Chances this time.'

They said, 'Chances nex time.'

Deaper said, 'New chance every time.'

They said, 'New chance every time.'

Easyer said, 'With Eusa.'

Rightway Flinter clincht his fis only he dint tern roun nor say nothing. He noddit to Erny and me.

Erny come over to the fit up he said, 'Wel whos coming up to show then?'

It seamt like I had too much breaf in me I musve ben holding it. I had to breave out a littl befor Punch cud say any thing. Then he said, '*Ah putcha putcha putcha. Ah putcha putcha way.*' He dint come up he jus stayd down and said that.

Erny said, 'Whos that talking is that Mr Salty from Salt Town or who is it?'

Punch said, '*Thats me Im Old Man Salty from Salt Town which Ive got the stick to prove it.*'

Erny said, 'Salt aint sticky.'

Punch said, '*May be Im honey then whynt you lick my stick and fynd out?*'

Erny said, 'This aint that kynd of a show. Wud you tel me Mr Salty whatd you mean with all that putcha putcha putcha?'

Punch said, '*I aint Mr Salty realy that aint my name.*'

Erny said, 'Whats your name then?'

Punch comes up then hes swanking hes zanting a bout hes waving his stick. Soons he comes in site you cud hear some breaf took in sharp you cud hear a littl sylents then Easyers voyce come strong he said, 'That figgers crookit.' Funny. Them bloaks on the gate when we 1st come to Weaping they hadnt said nothing. Wel stranger hevvyswl do that some times. Jus not give you no word nor syn what ever. This crowd tho they wer giving words a nuff and syns in plenny. A womans voyce said, 'You know theres women here and carrying.' Which there come some shuffling and that musve ben them carrying women carrying ther selfs out.

Easyer ups his voice agen he says, 'If that aint sucking in your Luck I dont know what is. Bringing a crookit show like that in to your hoam form.'

Rightway Flinter he says, 'You know Easyer theres moren 1 kynd of crookit. Theres crookit on the out side and theres crookit on the in side. Which Im beginning to think may be this here humpy figger is some kynd of a nindicater.' He says, 'Walker & Orfing you carry on with this here show.'

Erny says to Punch, 'Wel Mr Salty if your name aint Salty what is it then?'

Punch says, '*Come closer and Iwl tel you what it rimes with.*'

Erny comes closer and Punch gives him a smart whack with

his stick. Whack! Erny jumps a way he says, 'Ow! Youve give me a whack.'

Punch says, *'Thats right thats what I rime with.'*

Erny says, 'O I see your names Jack then.'

Punch says, *'No stupid my names Punch.'*

Erny says, 'Wel whack dont rime with Punch.'

Punch says, *'Thats becaws you jumpt a way too soon. Come close agen.'*

Erny comes close and qwick Punch gives him a woal lot of whacks. Punch says, *'Now Ive give you a bunch hows that for riming.'*

Erny says, 'Wel I think Ive had a nuff of riming Mr Punch. I wunner wud you please be good a nuff and tel me what that putcha putcha means?'

Punch says, *'You mean that putcha putcha putcha?'*

Erny says, 'Thats it.'

Punch says, *'You mean that putcha putcha way?'*

Erny says, 'Thats it thats the same and very. Whats it mean?'

Punch says, *'Putcha self closer and Iwl tel you.'*

Erny puts his self closer. Punch whacks him on the ear with his stick. Whack! Erny says, 'Ow! Thats 1 mor whack youve give me. What wer that 1 for?'

Punch says, *'Thats what putcha way means. If you putcha close Iwl whack you but if you putcha way I cant.'*

Erny says, 'Wel Mr Punch Im thanking you for that lessing and that lerning only that aint what I putcha my self here for.'

Punch says, *'Why did you putcha self here then? Why did you putcha putcha putcha?'*

Erny says, 'I wer hoaping for a look at Pooty. Jus a littl glimpo you know.'

Punch says, *'No I dont know. You dont nead no look nor you dont nead no glimpo you can see her by her pongo. All you nead to do is breave deap and youwl get the woal picter of Pooty right a nuff. Youwl see the 3s and the Ds of her so sharp youwl think you can grab a hanful.'*

Erny says, 'Stil and all Iwd like to how dyou do her.'

Punch says, '*You what?*'

Erny says, 'Iwd like to how dyou do her.'

Punch says, '*O youre a clynt then?*'

Erny says, 'Which Iwd like to be a frend.'

Punch says, '*O wunt we all tho wunt we jus. Pooty she dont have no frends tho. She dont give no 1 sumfing for nuffing.*'

Pooty comes up then with the pig babby she gives it to Punch she says, 'Whats this then if it aint some thing for nuffing?'

Punch says, '*Nuffing! You calling my part nuffing?*'

Pooty says, 'You said it I dint.'

Punch terns to the crowd he says, '*Now you see why I've got the hump.*'

Pooty says, 'This aint no time for humping Im frying now.'

Punch takes a littl tase of Pooty he says, '*You aint done yet.*'

Pooty says, 'I know that wel a nuff thats why Im going down to get on with it now wil you mynd the babby?'

Punch says, '*Not a bit. Mmmmm. Yum yum yum.*'

Pooty says, 'Whyd you say "Yum yum yum"?'

Punch says, '*I wer jus clearing my froat.*'

Pooty says, 'For what?'

Punch says, '*So I can sing to the babby.*'

Pooty says, 'What kynd of song you going to sing?'

Punch says, '*Yummy py.*'

Pooty says, 'Whatd you say?'

Punch says, '*Lulling by. I wl sing the babby lulling bys.*'

Pooty terns to the crowd she says, 'Wud you please keap a eye on him wylst Im frying my swossages. Give us a shout wil you if he dont mynd that babby right.'

Theres plenny of voyces in the crowd then speaking up theyre saying, 'Dont you worry Pooty wewl keap a eye on him.' Easyers voyce says, 'Wewl see your babby right Pooty that littl crookit barset he bes not try nothing here.'

Punch he dont anser nothing to that. When Pooty goes down hes zanting a littl with the babby its a littl jerky kynd of dants. Hes singing:

'*There wer a littl babby*

A piglet fat and juicy
Who ever got ther hans on him
They cudnt tern him lucey
Ah yummy yummy yummy
Ah slubber slubber sloo
Ah tummy tummy tummy
Ah piggy piggy poo'

Which when they hear that some of the crowd begin to yel, 'Pooty! Pooty! Come up qwick!'

Punch he terns on them he says, '*What kynd of peopl are you as wont let a father sing to his oan littl chyld?*'

Pooty shes up then she says to the crowd, 'Whats he ben doing then has he droppt the babby or any thing like that?'

Some 1 says, 'Hewl do wersen that you bes take that babby a way from him.'

Pooty says to Punch, 'Now you wont let no harm come to him wil you. Our oan sweet littl babby.'

Punch says, '*Harm is where the hert is.*'

Pooty says, 'Wel there you are who wud have the hart to hert a babby.'

Punch says, '*Hart is where the wud is.*'

Pooty says, 'What wood wud that be?'

Punch says, '*Its all ways the same wud innit. That 1 jus over there. Wewl do a littl walky walky there.*'

Pooty says, 'Thats it a littl walky walky wil do the babby good. I wont be a minim Iwl jus get on with that frying.'

Pootys down agen and Punch hes got the loan of the babby. He puts the babby down he backs off a littl way he hols out his arms he says, '*Walky walky.*'

That littl pig babby it goes slyding tords him like its on a string. Punch hes smyling tho his wood joars they cant realy open can they. He says, '*O wot a good babby!*' He puts the babby back where it startit from he says, '*Walky walky.*'

The babby says, 'Wah!'

Punch says, '*O no dont cry you musnt cry.*'

The babby yels, 'Wah!'

Punch says, '*O so juicy o so terbel juicy!*' He grabs the babby.

No sooner does Punch get his hans on that babby nor in comes a big hairy han which it grabs Punch and my han inside Punch.

Its Easyer he yels, 'You littl crookit barset I tol you not to try nothing here!'

Over goes the fit up and me and Punch and the babby and Easyer with it. 1 minim Easyers on top of me and the nex he dispears theres a han grabbit him sames his han grabbit Punch. Its Rightway Flinter which when I get my self untangelt from the fit up and on my feet its him and Easyer pulling datter to see which 1 wil walk a way when theyre finisht.

Its Rightway walks a way. Easyer is laid out flat. Rightway says to Riser Partman the regenneril guvner man from the Ram, 'When he comes roun you myswel let him be Big Man here hewl work hard at it.'

Riser Partman he aint a bad looking kynd of man hes got inky fingers he says to Rightway, 'What about you?'

Rightway says, 'Ive got elser to be.'

We dint over the nite there we roadit out in to the dark which Rightway had it on him he wantit to be on the move right then. Him and his brother Deaper they boath come with us they dint want to stop at Weaping no mor. They boath of them have wives and childer the woal lot roadit out with us they jus slung ther bundels and a way.

When we gone out thru the gate there wer a kid up on the hy walk sames I use to be up there all times of nite when I wer a kid. 7 or 8 he wer may be. Sharp littl face liting and shaddering in the shimmying of the gate house torches. Sharp littl face and he begun to sing:

    'Riddley Walkers ben to show
    Riddley Walkers on the go
    Dont go Riddley Walkers track
    Drop Johns ryding on his back'

Now whered that kid ever hear of Drop John and what put it in his mynd to sing that of me? Why dint I ask him? I dont know. May be I dint want to know.

Why is Punch crookit? Why wil he all ways kil the babby if he can? Parbly I wont never know its jus on me to think on it.

Riddley Walkers ben to show
Riddley Walkers on the go
Dont go Riddley Walkers track
Drop Johns ryding on his back

Stil I wunt have no other track.

Afterword

Only faint earth-green outlines remain of the fifteenth century wall painting, *The Legend of St Eustace*, in the north choir aisle of Canterbury Cathedral. Across the aisle from it is Dr Tristram's reconstruction, in sections, with the printed legend. The story of Eustace moves from the bottom to the top of the vertical composition, the scale of the figures and other elements varying according to their importance and chronology. The central figure and the largest, the one to which the eye is immediately drawn, is that of Eustace standing in a river, praying. His wife has been carried off by pirates and now his two little sons are taken away, one by a lion on the right bank and the other by a wolf on the left bank. Eustace is all alone in the middle of the river, hoping for better times. Seeing him for the first time that day in 1974 I had a strong fellow-feeling.

People ask me how I got from St Eustace to *Riddley Walker* and all I can say is that it's a matter of being friends with your head. Things come into the mind and wait to hook up with other things; there are places that can heighten your responses, and if you let your head go its own way it might, with luck, make interesting connections. On March 14th, 1974 I got lucky.

It was my first visit to Canterbury; I'd given a talk at the Teachers' Centre the evening before, and next morning my

---

On the facing page: "The Legend of St Eustace." Reconstruction by Professor Tristram of wall painting (c. 1480) in the north choir aisle of Canterbury Cathedral. Reproduced with the permission of the Dean and Chapter of Canterbury.

host, Dennis Saunders, County Inspector for English, showed me around the cathedral. I'm writing this in 1998, in the Oprah Winfrey era when millions are bursting to share their most private experiences with other millions; but I find that the Canterbury in me, having worded its way into *Riddley Walker*, wants to stay mostly unworded now. The cathedral is what it is; as soon as we came into the nave I could feel the action of the place, and by the time we reached *The Legend of St Eustace* I was ready for something to happen.

As I stood before the picture there came to me the idea of a desolate England thousands of years after the destruction of civilisation in a nuclear war; people would be living at an Iron Age level of technology and such government as there was would make its policies known through itinerant puppeteers. I know it sounds strange but that's how it was.

Why puppets? Punch and Judy had been in my thoughts ever since reading, some time before coming to England, two *New Yorker* articles by Edmund Wilson about English puppeteers. I hadn't yet seen a show but soon after my Canterbury visit I saw Percy Press and Percy Press Jr do one in Richmond; after that it was inevitable that Mr Punch would find his way into *Riddley Walker* sooner or later.

In my first Page One on May 14th there was a Eusa man with puppets but the writing was in standard English. Here are my first paragraphs:

The Eusa man stood outside in the rain and sent his partner in first. The partner was well over six feet tall, had a bow and a quiver of arrows on his back, a big knife, and four rabbits hanging from his belt. He had hands that looked as if they could break anything or squeeze it to death. He poked about with his spear, looked here and there behind things. He seemed to take the place in with all his senses at once, took in the feel of it as an animal would.

The Eusa man stood with his bundle on his back and leant on his stick while the steam came up from his sweating back and the dogs sniffed him. He didn't seem to mind the rain that came down on his little old hat or the mud he stood in.

'Okay,' said the partner.

The Eusa man bent down so his bundle would clear the opening and came inside.

'Wotcher?' he said.

That first Page One had domesticated dogs in it but soon these disappeared and in later drafts the only dogs were the killers that Riddley became friendly with. I like those dogs; there needed to be danger outside the fences and they were it—forlorn and murderous, full of lost innocence and the 1st knowing. Activated by the ancient blackened Punch he finds in the mud at Widders Dump, Riddley goes over the fence and joins up with the danger that's waiting for him.

In that first Chapter One the Littl Shynin Man hasn't yet become the Addom—he's Lilla Jesu. From the start the story had a life of its own; the metamorphosis of Lilla Jesu into the Addom showed that it was finding its way.

Early on the language began to slide towards Riddleyspeak; I like to play with sounds, and when alone in the house I often talk in strange accents and nonsense words. The grammatical decline began with the dropping of the auxiliary verb in the present perfect tense; many of the children I went to school with in Pennsylvania spoke that way: 'I been there' and 'I done that.' One thing led to another, and the vernacular I ended up with seems entirely plausible to me; language doesn't stand still, and words often carry long-forgotten meanings. Riddleyspeak is only a breaking down and twisting of standard English, so the reader who sounds out the words and uses a little imagination ought to be able to understand it. Technically it works well with the story because it slows the reader down to Riddley's rate of comprehension.

I did a fair amount of research in Kent while working on the book and the place names came to me without much trouble. In a camper van with my wife and our small sons I explored the Wye valley and the Crundale (Bundel) Downs and visited the towns in Fools Circel 9wys. Horny Boy is Herne Bay; Widders Bel is Whitstable; Father's Ham is Faversham; Bernt Arse is Ashford; Fork Stoan is Folkestone; Do It Over is Dover; Good Shoar is Deal, where I paid a boatman to take me out to the Goodwin Sands; Sams Itch is Sandwich; and of course Cambry is Canterbury. Sometimes special trips were required, as when I rode on the pillion seat of Richard Holt's motorbike to a forest near Canterbury to ascertain whether I could see my hand in front of my face on a moonless night. I couldn't. Frank Streich flew me over the South Downs in his Cessna. I drove to Reculver (Reakys Over) where I saw the Roman wall and the ruin of the Victorian church and listened to the lapping of the sea. Ordnance Survey 1:25,000 maps were my constant companions; nautical charts also. Drop John the Foller Man got his name after I found the part of the Thames Estuary called Knock John.

I had a lot of fun letting words wear themselves down into new words and new meanings. I did this with people's names also; apart from the obvious ones there are Belnot Phist (Nobel physicist) and his father 1stoan (Einstein) Phist; Straiter Empy would in our time be a morally upright M.P.; Erny Orfing, unlike Pry Mincer Abel Goodparley, who is a capable smoothtalker, is an earnest political orphan. If words aren't working for you they're working against you, so I tried to get as much story action into my words as possible: 'I had to voat no kynd of fents' for example, as an expression of no confidence.

After two years I had five hundred pages in which too many people were running around over too much geography; the story wanted to be lean and spare, very concentrated; so I went back to Page One, started over, soldiered on for three and a half more years, and in 1979 on Guy Fawkes Day (auspicious, I thought) *Riddley Walker* declared itself done and began to let go of me. I was a good speller before I wrote that book; I no longer am but I can live with that.

A final word about my friend with the hooked nose and the hunch: Mr Punch has appeared at my house twice in shows performed by the great Percy Press, now dead, and Percy

Press Jr. The look of Punch and the sound of his swazzle*
voice, the whole rampant idea of him stayed with me through
five and a half years of revisions and rewrites; it is with me
still. 'He's so old he can't die,' Percy told me. 'He's a law unto
himself.' He's certainly a reliable performer, and *Riddley
Walker* would be a poor show without him.

---

*A device held on the puppeteer's tongue.

Notes

I found that I needed to write a lot of notes in order to get my head around Riddley's world. Here are a few of them. I did some drawings of Punch too, for the same reason. I've reprinted the one that worked best for me.

28 May 1974
[Riddley when he was still thinking and speaking in standard English.]

> No rumpa,
> No dums,
> No zanting
> When Eusa comes.

Street Rhyme

They sing it now the same as I did when I was a child, hopping slowly and chalking the pavement: the stag and the cross and the ship, the river, the wolf and the lion and the rest of it. The Garble Time is long past, everything goes by its straight name now but the children still sing it the old way. The straight rhyme is:

> No trumpets,
> No drums,
> No dancing
> When Eustace comes.

Rumpa by now has come to mean any kind of vigorous noise-making. Zanting is not only dancing but running, jumping, fooling and larking about in general. Children are sifters and shapers, the words they keep are mostly useful ones.

30 May 1974

Eusa wants to make and he wants to unmake. He wants to live and he wants to die. He wants to "win" and he wants to "lose." He wants to stay and he wants to go.

Innana's descent

A long time after the devastation the Eustace pictures and the sparse text of the legends are found. In time the name of Jesus stops being used. He is just a man with outstretched arms. The idea of a man being pulled apart develops, and with it the idea of the coming together of what has been pulled apart, the dynamic blending of opposing forces.

Eusa as a space voyager. At the same time of the book people are living at a primitive level. There is in them a collective memory of a time when man could do anything, go to the stars even. Collectively they are like the individual who blots out what is too painful in his memory. Their minds turn away in fear from man's past accomplishments and the disaster that came from them.

The race of man haunted by the thought of what it used to be, ashamed of what they are, afraid of what they were.

The myth:

Eusa works for Mr Devvil. He destroys the world, looks for a new one with his wife and sons. Sees little man pulled apart. He tries to get away on an airship. The Captain says money is no good any more, takes Eusa's wife and leaves Eusa behind.

Eusa wanders with his two sons.

The action of the play:

Eusa with Mr Devvil. War and bursting fire.

Eusa leaves Mr Devvil, looks for new place, sees little man pulled apart by dogs, doesn't help him. Little man says, "My turn now, your turn later."

3 June 1974

The Connexion Man

Sometimes I just sit and bang my head with my fist. My head is harder than my fist. I *know* there's more to being human than what we have. I know there was a time when people could think better. I'm a stronger thinker than most of them here. I think in pictures that change faster and I think in words as well, often for long stretches without pictures. A lot of my thoughts are on things that there aren't any pictures for. Most of the people here, most of their thoughts you could draw a picture of. Most of mine you couldn't. I have that. Sometimes that's what I have to do, think of what I *do* have. Another thing I have more than others, I can think how things would be that haven't been that way yet. Like the overwater thing. The river was too wide, we didn't have anything we could put across it that was long enough. There wasn't any tree that we could cut down that would be long enough. It came into my mind how you could do it with ropes. Two ropes across the river and other short ropes slung between them, hanging down in a belly. Then we laid short pieces of wood tied together all the way across the river in those belly-ropes. Everybody laughed when they saw it, nobody had ever thought of *hanging* an overwater thing. Everybody said, "How did it come into your mind?" Well, it just did. I've never looked at any pictures of what was before. Maybe I will sometime.

There was more, there was more, I know there was more. Sometimes you find bits and pieces of things, mostly you throw them away. Bad luck. Pieces of paper with words and pictures that crumble into ash and blow away. Paper, what about that? There's a paper mill in Cambry. I haven't seen it but that's where the rizlas come from. Well, they say you have to have something for trading, you can't always carry everything with you. So they have rizlas and matches and tobacco as the trading things mostly. But how come they know how to make paper and matches? All that kind of thing is bad luck. What was I thinking, yes, the *more*. Starboats, you hear about that. Sometimes someone will draw a picture in the dirt to show what they looked like. The boats we use on the river are made of skins stretched on bent wood frames. People say what if there *were* starboats, that doesn't mean they were more or better long ago. They were just different. But if you look up at the sky, look at the stars, what a load of cobblers that is. Just different! To think out a boat to go to the stars! To make one, to actually *go* in it!

There's a *shame* I feel. Draw a picture of that, hey? We live in huts and holes in the ground and our minds are slow. People know there was more but they're ashamed and they say we're just *different* from the people long ago. The gulls on the beach, I think a long time ago those were *flying* birds, not just walking ones like now. I'm sure of it although I don't know how I'm sure. They must feel something like the way I do.

VIEWS OF PUNCH

Glossary

A Short Guide to Riddleyspeak

As much as possible I tried for more than one meaning in the words. For example, when Riddley says, on page 8, 'I wer the loan of my name' he means that he is the lone carrier of his name, living on borrowed time. Life among his people is usually hard and short.

Some words that look strange will explain themselves when sounded out; others may require a little more work. This is a sampling to help the reader.

arga warga: Onomatopoeia suggestive of gobbling-up.

axel: 'Axel rate' means accelerate.

batcherd: Badger.

Berstin Fyr: Explosives. Note that the Eusa Story is written in an archaic form of the demotic current in Riddley's time. This is because language went through a near-total breakdown in a dark age after the destruction of civilisation.

Blobs: 'Blobs your nunkel.' This comes from 'Bob's your uncle,' old slang meaning 'Everything is perfect' or 'That wraps it up.' 'Blob' in this case is suggestive of the mutations of the Eusa folk.

catwl twis: Catalyst.

divvyt: Divided. The divvy roof at How Fents is a roof on poles, open on all sides, where meat from the hunt or anything that has been gathered or gained is divided.

[Master] Chaynjis: The big transformations; also means infinity and the mysterious origins of everything. When Brooder Walker dies he goes 'into the dark, into the 1st knowing and the Master Chaynjis.'

nebyul: Used only with 'eye' to mean nebulae; the flaming nebyul eye sees everything.

nexter: One who is next in authority or command.

No rumpa no dum / No zantigen Eusa cum: No trumpets, no drums / No dancing when Eusa comes. (See also Notes for May 28, 1974)

oansome: That thing 'whats in us lorn and loan and oansome' is forlorn, alone, and all on its lonesome own.

Parments: Parliament's, as in 'Parments in the mud you know.'

pirntowt: Printout.

Plomercy: Diplomacy; looking for mutual accommodation. In some cases Plomercy is a plea for mercy. When the old dog makes his Plomercy he isn't negotiating—he's been crowded out of his pack and he's favouring Riddley with his death.

poasyum: 'Some poasyum' means symposium.

reqwyrt: Required, but has a little more weight depending on the context. Also resonates with 'helping the qwirys,' which derives from the current formula 'helping the police with their enquiries.' Helping the qwirys on someone in Riddley's time usually leaves bruises. 'Time and reqwyrt' in the Eusa show talk means that the crowd will go down that road with Eusa as many times as necessary. Helping him (bruiselessly) with his enquiries.

revver newit: '[T]hey all ready ben Shorsday Week which they revver newit the fraction for the Ram. . . . ' Translation: '[T]hey [Goodparley and Orfing] had already been here in the week of the shortest day of the year when they raised the tax to be paid to the Ram. . . . ' The word 'revenue' has been broken down into 'revver new' and is used here as a transitive verb. The Ram has *revved up* the tax engine to demand a *new* tax.

rizlas: Cigarette papers (made at the local paper mill). In 1974 the widely used brand in England was Rizla.

Sarvering Gallack Seas: Sovereign Galaxies. Gallack Seas would suggest to Riddley's people sky-seas that might be crossed by boats in the air. Readers might think of galleons, carracks. 'Sarvering' is the participle of 'sarver,' which hints at severing, cutting off something for oneself, saving it for one's people, claiming a territory.

sess men: Assessment men, assessors.

sharna pax: Sharpen the axe. There is some irony in this for the U.K. reader because 'Pax!' ('Peace!') has for generations been a schoolboy expression (in public-school circles) of surrender that ends a fight. The sound here is important—'Sharna pax and get the poal when the Ardship of Cambry comes out of the hoal!' falls naturally into a chant.

suching waytion: Situation; such is the way things are.

thinet: Pronounced *thigh-net*, means twined. 'We thinet hans roun the fire'; harks back to 'thine' in hymns.

wotcher: A cockney greeting; derives from 'What cheer?' Here it means 'Wotcher [What have you] got for me?' This part of the pre-show ritual is called the wotcher.

wud: Means wood as in forest; also 'would,' intention, volition or desire. The hart of the wud is where Eusa saw the stag who was the hart of the wud. The heart of the would is also the essence of one's wanting, the heart of one's deepest desire. The crypt in Canterbury Cathedral with its stone trees is the spiritual hart of the wud.

A NOTE ON THE AUTHOR

Russell Hoban is the author of many extraordinary novels including *The Lion of Boaz-Jachin and Jachin-Boaz*, *Turtle Diary*, *Kleinzeit*, *Pilgermann*, *The Medusa Frequency*, *Angelica's Grotto* and *Amaryllis Night and Day*, all available from Bloomsbury. He has also written some classic books for children. He lives in London.